KING OF THE HILL

KING OF THE HILL

George Vercessi

authorHOUSE®

AuthorHouse™
1663 Liberty Drive, Suite 200
Bloomington, IN 47403
www.authorhouse.com
Phone: 1-800-839-8640

First published by AuthorHouse 3/31/2009

ISBN: 978-1-4389-7517-7 (e)
ISBN: 978-1-4389-7085-1 (sc)

Printed in the United States of America
Bloomington, Indiana

This book is printed on acid-free paper.

Also by George Vercessi

We the People

SEAL ~ Test

Alma's World

For Jessica Leigh Skelnik

December 10, 1990 – February 12, 2008

Organized crime will put a man in the White House some day, and he won't know it until they hand him the bill.

Donald R. Cressey, "Theft of a Nation: The Structure and Organization of Organized Crime in America" (1969) (Harper & Row)

Look like the innocent flower, but be the serpent under it. - Macbeth

Author's note.

To accommodate the story I have on a few occasions altered locations as well as the time and sequence of historical events. These changes are not meant to deceive or mislead the reader, but rather to advance the plot, which is a work of fiction. References to real people, events, establishments, organizations, or locales are intended only to provide a sense of authenticity, and are used fictitiously. All other characters, incidents and dialogue are drawn from the author's imagination and are not to be construed as real.

GV

Prologue

Nikki stood in the shadows watching her husband. The routine was always the same, like a ritual. He'd hold the ring, and study the fiery stone for a long moment before returning it to its place. For Julius Caesar Vittorio, it was the last tangible link to his father. Memories of the man always percolated in his mind, but they were especially vivid tonight, when the routine would change.

CHAPTER ONE (APRIL, 1958)

It was eight a.m., far too early to be so warm. Washington's torturous summer had arrived early, but neither of the two law students waiting in brooding silence against the backdrop of a campus idled for Easter recess seemed to notice. Certainly not Julius Caesar Vittorio, who was pacing the curb and scanning the quiet street for the cab that would take them to Union Station.

"Where the hell is he?" he said. His companion simply shrugged, a gesture that went largely unnoticed. Disconnected from the world around him, Vittorio was still struggling to understand the previous night's phone call.

"Julie, this is Uncle Nunzio," the older man had said, his voice unduly somber. "I got bad news."

Immediately, Julie's thoughts had flown to his mother, and he braced himself. "What is it?"

"He's dead."

"What?!" Had he heard wrong?

"Your father."

"My father's dead?" His chest constricted, breaths coming short, as he tried deciphering the message. Reason

1

told him it was his aging mother, not his robust father. "I don't understand. How's that possible?"

The rest of the brief conversation had been a blur, with the detached voice recounting something about a shooting, and Julie numbly agreeing to catch the morning train back to New York.

Now, waiting for his ride, he knew little more than what he'd read in that morning's *Washington Post*, now folded and tucked firmly under his arm in a useless attempt to conceal the screaming headline, *Mafia War Heats Up In NY*. And beneath it, the jarring story.

> *New York (AP) - Police report another victim in the rash of mob shootings plaguing the city during the past month. In a bold daylight assault, Anthony 'The Gent' Vittorio, a prominent Bronx businessman and reputed boss in the secret Mafia organization, was fatally shot yesterday in his Hunts Point office, the victim of an apparent gangland slaying.*

> *Lacking signs of a break-in or struggle, the police believe the assailants were known to Vittorio, whose body was discovered by employees late yesterday afternoon. While information is sketchy, sources wishing to remain anonymous indicate Vittorio was shot several times at pointblank range.*

> *"Incredible!" declared New York Police Chief Thomas Nolan, at his Manhattan office. "The man's gunned down in the middle of the day and no one remembers hearing shots or seeing the gunmen." Pressed for his assessment, Nolan responded, "I don't expect we'll find the killers. These guys are pros. Vittorio was a big man in the organization, so I don't imagine anyone wants to get tagged for this one."*

Adding to Julie's distress was a sidebar story tying the murder to an internal Mafia shakeup prompted by a police raid the preceding year at crime boss Joe Barbara's rural 58-acre estate outside Binghampton that netted sixty top bosses and sent chieftains scurrying across upstate Apalachin farms. But more disturbing was the gut-wrenching photo of his father's bloodied corpse juxtaposed with two other overplayed news photos; those of Albert Anastasia's bullet-riddled body on the floor of Manhattan's Park Sheraton barbershop, and a heavily bandaged Frank Costello, grazed in the head during a botched attack in front of his Park Avenue apartment.

"I'm sorry," Julie said once they'd boarded the train, "don't expect much conversation. I just don't have it in me."

His companion replied, "I wasn't expecting it."

Sanford (Scott) Remmington III and Julie had been friends since entering Georgetown University Law School together nearly three years earlier. During that time there'd never been any mention of links to the ultra-secret Mafia. But now, with the story on everyone's lips, Remmington was anxious to learn what he could. Rather than probe, he opted to wait; certain a few details would slip out during their journey north, tidbits he could share with his family at the dinner table in Connecticut that evening.

To his disappointment, Julie remained silent for the first hour, directing his attention to the passing countryside instead. It wasn't until they'd left Baltimore that he opened up.

"Look what they've done to the family name," he lamented, tapping the newspaper beside him.

"Not everyone believes that drivel," Remmington replied. "Certainly no one who knows your father."

"You think so?" he said wanting to believe him.

"Absolutely."

Julie merely shrugged and fell silent again, as he watched a man and boy waving at the passing train from their backyard. The scene reminded him of earlier times, when he and his father had strolled together through the old neighborhood, and it left him wondering what life would like without him.

"They did a helluva job on him," he said without turning from the window.

Remmington folded his magazine. It was the opening he'd been waiting for. "Looks like they didn't give him a chance."

Julie looked at him. "Not the killers. I mean these bastards," he said indicating the newspaper.

"Yeah, terrible," he agreed.

"Don't patronize me."

"No I'm not," he protested."

"Cut the crap. You're thinking he's one of them."

The man who bore the name of one of Connecticut's leading families reddened. "You say he's innocent and that's good enough for me." Adding, "But it is a compelling story."

"Is that so?"

Remmington moistened his lips. "Well, I don't imagine those fellows go around shooting law-abiding citizens." And when Julie stiffened, he said, "I'm sorry if I offended you, but one reads these stories and naturally assumes there has to be some connection."

"You folks in Greenwich don't have a clue about life in the city, where if you own a business, particularly a successful one, like my father, you don't have a choice. You're forced to deal with these people."

"Deal with them how?"

"In ways you don't want to."

"What about the police?"

Julie laughed. "You have a lot to learn about extortion."

"Are you saying they killed your father because he refused to yield to them?"

"I'm saying he had no choice but to pay." And when Remmington mentioned the police again, Julie put him off. "They can't help. You protect yourself by dealing with them."

"Who are they?" asked Remmington.

Julie studied him. "I don't know. But they weren't any associates, as the papers would have you believe."

"How does it work?"

"Any number of ways. They might start by forcing you into a trash hauling contract. It doesn't matter how, the point is they squeeze and you pay."

"How do you know this?"

"Like I said, that's the way it is in the city. You needn't be one of them to know. More importantly, just because a man's killed doesn't make him one of them."

"I was just trying to understand, that's all."

"Then understand this," he said before turning away again, "my father was an honest businessman who worked hard for his family. Everything else they're saying about him is bullshit."

It was nearly one-thirty when they rolled into Pennsylvania Station and parted, Remmington continuing on to Connecticut, and Julie heading for the uptown subway.

CHAPTER TWO

Julie was exhausted, and he was soon asleep after dropping into the first available seat. It seemed he'd only just dozed off, when the train climbed the el and shards of sunlight reflecting off Bronx tenements filled the car, jarring him awake. Soon the grimy buildings fell away and the land flattened, allowing a clear view of Long Island Sound and LaGuardia Airport. He was back in familiar territory and feeling desolate and desperately sad. When the train stopped at Hunts Point, not far from where his father had been murdered, and where as a youngster he'd often spent Saturday mornings keeping the old man company in the office, his despair worsened and he wished he could slow the train, better still, reverse time.

At one point, wishing to delay his arrival home, he considered getting off at Middletown Road and walking the rest of the way, but he couldn't muster the energy. Nor was he able to at Pelham Bay Park, the final stop. Instead, he sat in the empty car watching the few remaining passengers move down the platform, the street sounds below rising up to meet him.

Only when the motorman came through changing the signs to Battery Park for the return trip, the man glancing at him without comment, did he force himself up. It was nearly three o'clock; he could be home in twenty minutes if he hurried, but that wasn't likely.

His legs moving mechanically, he descended the stairs to Westchester Avenue, pausing mid-way to take in the familiar scene. The neighborhood looked the same. Life didn't change much in this section of the Bronx. Yet, for him it had changed dramatically. His father's killers were out there somewhere, and that frightened him. In that instant, he glimpsed a knot of men lingering beside a newsstand across the street, and immediately he knew they were there for him. Sure enough, they were off the curb the moment their eyes locked, and without a second thought he was sprinting back to the platform.

"Hey, Vittorio!" someone shouted, which made him run faster.

At the top, he paused to glimpse back and immediately regretted doing so. One of them had reached the steps, the others, heavier and older, were close behind. He saw the train doors still open, and vaulted the turnstile, catching his suitcase on the bar and dropping it.

"Hey, come back, you punk!" the lone figure in the booth shouted when he bent to retrieve it.

He didn't need to look back now to know they were gaining; he could hear the rush of footsteps clearing the landing. He also heard the rising pitch of the engine, and knew the train was about to leave. With several feet to go, he saw the car doors closing and, in one swift movement, tossed the suitcase and lunged between them, catching his foot between the rubber caskets and falling hard. He'd made it. Lying there on the floor of the last car, his knee throbbing, he heard an angry fist pounding the door and turned to see its owner running alongside shouting.

Once certain the train wasn't going to stop, he jumped up and, pressing his face to the window, saw his pursuers racing back to the street and knew he wasn't free of them yet.

At Buhre Avenue, the next station, he watched the doors open and struggled with the notion of getting off and working his way home through the neighborhood, or staying on. He had no idea of how many men were out there looking for him. He might round a corner and walk right into them. Yet, the ones who'd chased him might be waiting at one of the other stations. What to do? The choice was made for him when the doors closed.

Thereafter, he scanned every platform expecting to see them, and only stopped when the train dropped below ground again and crossed back into Manhattan. It wasn't until reaching Grand Central Terminal that he felt secure enough to leave. Gathering his courage, he rose and followed the crowd to the street, where he walked aimlessly through midtown Manhattan until finding himself standing before the Biltmore Hotel.

His sister Anna Marie answered on the second ring, her voice was less vibrant than usual.

"Sis, it's me," he said from the bank of phones in the lobby.

"Julie! Where are you?"

"Nothing to worry about. Just got delayed is all," he said, crafting his excuse as he went on.

"But we expected you hours ago," she said as if pleading with him.

"Just listen," he said. "We had a problem outside Philadelphia. Been sitting on the tracks for two hours. We just got in and they're saying we can't continue because of a leak in the lines. They aren't being very helpful."

He waited as the girl hurriedly relayed the story to the others. He could hear his mother in the background, asking, "When will he be home?"

"Tell her, first thing in the morning," he said instantly regretting the lie.

Again, she passed on the message, and this time he heard her say, "Tell him to come as soon as possible."

"You hear that," she said. "She needs you." Then, tearfully, "We all need you."

Now, wondering if he'd misread the events at the station, he said, "I'll be there, Sis."

"We're due at the funeral home before ten. Mamma wants to be there before it opens. It's going to be a long day, Julie. We need your strength."

He ached to hold and comfort her. "I'll be there, sweetheart," he promised, before asking, "Is Uncle Nunzio there?"

"Yes."

"Put him on."

"Hey, kid, what're you doing in Philly? Yer mom's a wreck and this ain't helping."

"*Zio*," he said, "listen but don't say anything till I'm finished. Okay?"

"Whatever you say."

Julie thought his tone was light, lighter than it should've been. "I'm not in Philly," he said. "I'm in Manhattan, at the Biltmore. I got to the Bronx but something happened at the station." Quickly, he related the story of the men and his retreat.

"Well, I guess trains break down. Do the best you can. I'll look after everybody till you're here."

"What's going on? Is it safe to come home?"

"Absolutely," he said in that same easy tone.

"Then why were those men after me?"

"We'll talk tomorrow."

"That's it?! That's all you're going to say?"

"Yep, for now."

Julie heaved a sigh. "If you say so."

"I say so."

"All right, I'll see you in the morning then."

"It's easier to meet at Riccio's," his uncle said, referring to the funeral home. "Say, nine-thirty, in the back where they park the limos. Got it?"

"Rather than the house?" he asked, thinking it strange.

"Yeah. And get some rest."

Wanting to believe his uncle, but unable to dislodge the intensity of the chase, he went to the desk and took a room using Scott Remmington's name. Once upstairs, he wedged a chair against the door and fell across the bed.

CHAPTER THREE

R iccio's Mortuary, set beside the el in the shadows of surrounding apartment buildings, was a short walk from the Westchester Square station, but Julie didn't get off there. Still wary of yesterday's encounter, he exited the train a stop before the Square, at Zerega Avenue, and, circling the neighborhood, approached the mortuary from the rear. Arriving thirty minutes before he was to meet his uncle, he slipped into a nearby alley and waited. At precisely nine-thirty, after seeing no one either enter or depart Riccio's, he took up his suitcase and walked cautiously to the fenced parking lot. There, he found Nunzio's Buick Roadmaster, all eighteen feet of gleaming black steel and chrome, parked in the far corner between two hearses. Regretting his doubts, he strolled over and peered inside expecting to find his uncle inside. From behind, a hand gripped his shoulder.

"Aaagh!" he yelled, spinning around and swinging out blindly. "What the...! Where'd you come from?!"

"Easy does it, Kemo Sabe," his uncle said, catching his arm. "Everything's fine."

"Fine?! You scared the shit out of me! What the hell's going on?" he demanded in a shaky voice.

13

"You've been under a lot of stress, kid," he said in an even tone. "I don't blame you for being uptight. It's natural. Probably I'd do the same thing. But you gotta relax now. You listening?" he said, tightening his grip and drawing Julie's attention away from the two men behind him.

"I'm listening," Julie said pulling himself free, but he couldn't keep from eyeing the weapons beneath their unbuttoned jackets.

"Look, a lot's been happening," his uncle said. "Complicated stuff. So you gotta trust me on this. These guys are friends of your father, and the boys from yesterday work for 'em. Out of respect for your father, they want to talk to you, which is what yesterday was all about."

My father! he thought, a wave of guilt washing over him. Concerned for his own safety, he'd allowed the dead man's memory to slip from his thoughts.

"A lot of people are coming to pay their respects today, including these guys and the ones from yesterday," his uncle was saying. "So I don't want you getting spooked when you see them. Like I said, they're all friends, but there'll be others who aren't. But you got nothing to worry about with them," he added quickly. "Today, all you gotta do is support your mother and sister. After, when your father's put to rest, we'll talk. *Capisce?*"

Julie shook his head. "No, I don't understand, not one bit."

Nunzio heaved a sigh. "I don't have time to explain. For now," he said, taking Julie's arm and leading him across the lot, "you need to look out for your family." When they reached the side entrance, he clapped Julie's shoulder and, eyeing him squarely, cautioned, "Stay alert today."

Alarmed, Julie replied, "To what?"

"Just watch what happens," he said, before turning and joining the others.

"Where're you going?" Julie called. "Aren't you staying?"

"I'll be back later," he said over his shoulder.

Confused and apprehensive, Julie stood in the warm sunlight for several minutes after they'd departed, trying vainly to draw comfort from his uncle's assurances that all was well and he had nothing to fear. When he stepped inside, he found the corpulent mortician waiting.

"*Caro!*" Riccio said, coming over and embracing him. "My heart aches," he said, his Old Spice cologne doing little to mask the sickly sweet fragrance of formaldehyde that clung to his clothes.

"Mine too," Julie said before asking what had been troubling him most. "Did he die quickly?"

Riccio gave an emphatic nod. "I'm sure of it. He didn't suffer."

"How does he look?"

"Good, now. He looks at rest," he said with the pained smile of a man who'd known his father since boyhood. Then leading Julie to the foyer, he said, "I remember when you were just a boy. Now look at you. Your father was very proud of you."

Just as they reached the large entryway the front door opened and Julie saw his mother, who, despite a hasty touch of makeup, looked shockingly frail.

"My son," she cried. Her embrace was strong, suggesting they'd endure this tragedy together.

Standing in the doorway behind her, clinging to Nunzio's wife and looking fearful of entering, and pathetically older than her thirteen years, was little Anna Marie. Seeing her brother, she ran to him and fell into his arms, sobbing, "What a horrible thing." And when she caught her breath, she looked up and, trembling, asked, "Why would anyone want to kill daddy? I don't understand."

"I wish I knew, princess," he whispered while stroking her head.

"He wanted so much to see you graduate," she said. "That's all he talked about. Now he'll never see it."

Julie held her tight. All he could say was, "Be strong. It's what he'd want."

Noting the time, Riccio came over and led them to the viewing room, while telling them that since there were no other funerals he'd been able to combine two adjoining rooms into a single large one to accommodate the mourners. But even that wouldn't be adequate, he acknowledged, indicating the crush of flowers in an adjacent room.

Standing with his mother and sister before the casket, Julie thought his father looked as he remembered him, and for that he'd thank Riccio. Now, though, leaning down and touching his cold, lifeless hand, he tried lifting his mind to God, but couldn't get beyond cursing his father's killers.

The doors opened at ten, and by ten-fifteen the place was filled, mostly by neighbors. Regardless, all were greeted by Riccio, who stood in the burgundy carpeted lobby directing mourners to one of two guest books, a recent precaution at funerals and weddings after the feds began seizing them to expand their database of rank-and-file mobsters. Later, he would deliver both books to the house, but until then, the second one, the one the feds would've liked to have had they known of it, remained with him.

Throughout the morning Julie periodically assessed the crowd as his uncle had advised, but he detected nothing unusual. Then, shortly past noon, two distinct groups began gathering in the rear of the room in opposite corners. And while they kept to themselves, it was evident each was scrutinizing the other. Shortly after they'd formed up, two elegantly tailored men joined them within minutes of each other, causing heads to turn and conversations to stall. Approaching the casket together, they stood before it for a silent moment, before turning and offering Julie and his family their condolences.

Intrigued by the cold gaze of the one with the lazy right eye, Julie whispered to his mother, "Who are they?"

"The first one's Paolo Gava, a friend of your father."

"He looks vicious," he said, wondering why he'd never seen him before.

"He has *l'occhio da spadaccino*."

"The swordsman's eye?"

"Assassin's eye," she corrected.

That he understood. The man looked evil. "And the other? Who's he?"

She shrugged. "I don't know, but if he's with Gava, I'm sure it's business."

Business? What business could they be conducting here? Determining this was what his uncle had hinted at, he excused himself and, following them, watched as they headed down the hall to Riccio's office. Upon drawing closer, he found the door ajar and the conversation within heated. Curious, he paused, and peering in met the twisted face of the one not known to his mother. The instant their eyes locked he felt a paralyzing rush of fear. Unable to retreat, he watched the man step forward and kick the heavy door shut, the sound reverberating down the hall to where Nunzio and Riccio shot him a look connoting this was not the place to be.

The remainder of the day proceeded without further incident, and that night, tired and emotionally drained, Julie and his family dined in relative silence. In his grief, Julie forgot Nunzio's promise that all would be explained.

Chapter Four

He knew the purpose of inviting mourners to the house after the funeral was to ease the grieving process, but it did little for him. Finding the ritual intrusive, he soon slipped outside, where he found Riccio coming up the driveway, a large carton under his arm.

"Julie," the mortician called, "how you holding up?" And then nodding at the long line of cars and the house, he said, "You don't need all this."

Julie shrugged. "They'll be gone soon."

"It was a fine service, eh?" he said more brightly. "The priest, he did a good job."

"Yeah. Which reminds me, I appreciate what you did."

The comment made the man teary. "I'd do anything for your father," he said swallowing. "You know, we went to school together, played together," and smiling, "even dated the same girls. He was the best." And when Julie didn't reply, he said, "I understand." Then squaring his shoulders, he extended the box. "This belongs to you. I'll have the death certificate and other papers in a few days."

Taking it and holding it tightly, he thought, ah, yes, the business of death.

After showing Riccio inside, he slipped into the library, where he could be alone among his father's prized possessions—his fine books, artwork and music—and where he might feel closer to the dead man. Hadn't the priest said at the grave site, that when someone dies, they're no longer where they were, but now they're wherever you are? Closing his eyes, he tried sensing the dead man's presence but drew a blank. It was a touching notion, he mused bitterly, but it wasn't working, not for him. His father was lost forever.

Placing the box squarely on the desk, he opened it and, peering inside, drew out a small envelope containing his father's two rings; his wedding band, and his gold ruby ring. Knowing his mother would want the band he set it aside and slipped the other one on. It fit loosely—his father was taller and heavier than he was—and he shifted it to his middle finger. And while it didn't muster any images of his father, wearing it felt right.

Next, stepping to the record player, he raised the polished lid and flipped the switch. The arm swung over and dropped gently on a recording of Puccini's *La Boheme,* one of his father's favorite operas. Now the tears came; at first large slow ones that rolled down his cheek and which he brushed away. But having started, he was unable to stop them, and soon they came with a force that left him breathless. It was the first time he'd cried for the dead man, and standing before the window, the music filling the room, he made no attempt to stop. When he'd cried himself out, he lifted the arm and carefully lowered the lid. Then, removing the ring, he slipped it in his pocket.

"There you are," his sister called as he stepped into the hall. "I've been looking for you."

"Just putting some things away," he said turning. "How're you holding up?" He was pleased to see color in her cheeks again.

"Numb," she said, with a tired smile. "I didn't think I'd make it at the cemetery, but I'm better now."

He squeezed her shoulder. "Dad would've been proud of you. I know I am. Here," he said, reaching for the tray of pastries, "I'll give you a hand."

She shook her head. "I got it. Besides, Uncle Nunzio's looking for you. He's in the garden."

The garden extended away from the house toward Long Island Sound. A sizeable plot, with thick hedges separating it from its only neighbor, it was once part of a large estate that had been subdivided and acquired at a Depression era auction. And like the library, it saw few visitors. So it was with some distress he saw the two men from Riccio's parking lot sitting with his uncle on the two benches beneath the cherry tree, the special place he had shared with his father since childhood.

As he walked toward them he breathed in the familiar sweet aroma of freshly turned soil, a sign his father had recently been working there. He noticed, too, the protective winter tarps folded and stacked beside the two bare fig trees. Removing them after the last frost had been his job prior to heading off to Georgetown. Now, for the past three years, the task had fallen back to his father, whose next chore would've been transplanting the young tomato plants from the adjacent hothouse. Those

21

and similar preparations were part of the season's rhythm that had provided both father and son a sense of quiet pleasure over the years.

All three men stood as he neared.

"Julie," his uncle said, "I want you to meet two friends. They worked for your father, but you probably never saw them around. Nino Testa and Pippo Bustamente," he said as each man stepped forward and offered his hand.

"What we have to say is difficult for a lot of reasons," his uncle said when they were seated. "Here your father's in the ground a couple of hours and we're having this meeting. Not the best way to do business. But life goes on and the living have to do what they have to do."

Julie's face grew warm. *Business! What business could be so important now?*

"I know how your father felt about shielding you from this part of his life, but things change and, well…, You're not a kid anymore."

Feeling his resentment swelling, he thought it best to remain silent.

"You know he dealt with the organization," his uncle continued.

He nodded, recalling the men who came at odd hours and met with his father behind closed doors, or walked the grounds with him, their heads close together. And while it was rarely discussed, he'd reasoned at the time that if his father wanted him to know his business he'd have told him.

"Well, he was a very important man in the Bronx. What we call a *capo*."

He'd not heard the word in that context and he listened with interest to his uncle's description of a *caporegime's* role within the organization—the high-ranking boss of a crew of soldiers—and how his father had arrived at that honored position.

"Now, I have to tell you the hardest part," he said, leaning forward and clasping his hands. "Why he was killed."

The words exploded in his head, and suddenly his heart was pounding. *What the hell's happening? Is this real?* Were these somber-faced men somehow responsible for his father's death? Things were happening much too quickly for him, and he struggled to catch his breath.

"The organization's been experiencing a lotta changes," his uncle droned on, "and in our business changes don't come easy. You remember reading about the bust upstate in Apalachin last year?"

"What?" he said, laboring to follow his uncle's words.

"The raid that made all the papers," Nunzio said.

"Yeah, I remember," he said in a disconnected voice.

"Well, till then, they were like shadows on the wall. Nobody outside the organization knew the bosses or that most of 'em even existed. But things changed after they were picked up.

"You know," he continued, "every business has overhead, and ours is no different. The grease still has to be spread no matter what. So, with the feds onto them, the bosses lost a lot of opportunities and, as a result, there wasn't as much cash coming in. You follow me?"

"I'm with you," he said with no sense of where this was heading.

"Good. Then came the McClellan hearings, and soon punks were shooting off their mouths. That's when some bosses figured it was time to go underground and let the lieutenants run the show till things cooled down. Well, it didn't take long for the new guys to figure they were entitled to more of the action, and before long they were cutting deals with others in the organization."

Now it was Bustamante's turn. "That's when it got messy," he said. "Kidnappings. Shootings. World War III. Anyone who might've been a threat to the bosses was a target, even the big guys. You read about Anastasia?"

Julie nodded, recalling vividly the news photos augmenting the story of his father's slaying.

"Well the feds couldn't have planned it better if they tried," Bustamante said. "It was like somebody waved a magic wand. Just like that, nobody trusted anybody."

"Including my father?"

All three nodded. But it was Testa who said, "Your father's loyalty was two hundred percent, but when people feel threatened everybody's a suspect. And in our business that's all it takes."

Nunzio leaned forward. "A big part of the problem came from the Sicilians."

Stories of clashes between the transplanted Sicilian Black Hand Society and their Neapolitan Camorra rivals were common, including how the city had been divided between them, with much of the Bronx falling to the Neapolitans, and most of the rest to the more powerful Sicilians. This wasn't news to Julie.

"So, with things messed up like they were," his uncle said, "the Sicilians decided it was time to make a move. Which meant, now we had the feds *and* the Sicilians to worry about."

Julie said nothing, his anger rising.

"The Sicilians were cutting deals with some of our lieutenants, and sure enough we had defections," Nunzio said. "And in all that confusion your father was killed. But it wasn't because he crossed over. He was strictly a victim. It shouldn't have happened," he said, shaking his head, "but every war has casualties." He looked at the others, and they nodded.

"Yeah," Testa said, "it shouldn't have happened."

The story sounded fanciful, but rather than challenge them, he said, "Get to the bottom line. Who killed him?"

"It could've been anybody. A lot of guys were moving back and forth," his uncle replied. "And I ain't sure we'll ever know. But what's important," he said, straightening up, "is getting on with life."

"That's right," Testa said. "We hafta look ahead."

"The meet you saw at Riccio's yesterday happened because the bosses want a truce," Nunzio said. "Which means no more double-dealing and no more turf grabs."

"Why are you telling me this?" he said bitterly. "You think I give a shit?"

"I know how you feel," his uncle said. "We feel the same. The truce should've happened sooner. Nobody wanted your father to die, especially me. He wasn't just my brother-in-law, he was my friend. But it happened, and now we have to move on. I know it sounds cold, but we can't let it stop us from getting back to doing what we do best. Which is making money. Money's the name of the game. It keeps the powerful powerful. Your father knew that better than most and if he was here, he'd tell you the same thing."

25

"But he isn't here!" he said, his voice rising. "You think I care about the bosses and their power? My father's dead because their convoluted scheme went haywire."

"You got every right to be pissed. We're all pissed," his uncle said. "This whole mix-up shouldn't have happened. But don't get out ahead of me, okay?"

Julie looked past him, to the house, and thought of his mother and sister, and how they were going to get through this. "Go on," he said.

"Like I said, your old man didn't want you in the business, but now that he's gone you have a right to know who he was in the organization and what he did. He made the organization a lot of money, and for that he was respected. And no matter how it looks to you, we believe in loyalty and justice. It ain't the justice you're studying, but it is justice."

"I'm sure."

Nunzio ignored the barb. "These men are here to make you an offer. Now you have to know these offers don't come around often, so all I'm saying is that you should at least hear 'em out. You okay with that?"

"I'm listening," he said, anxious to conclude this insanity.

"They sent the men to the station. But things got out of hand and you did what you had to. That's history. We're here now and that's what counts."

Julie wanted desperately to be alone, away from these madmen and their self-destructive feuds.

"First, I want to say I'm sorry for the screw up," Testa began. "We were trying to reach you before you got home and got wrapped up with all this other business," he said, gesturing to the house. "It was stupid. We should've waited. For that, I apologize."

"Like my uncle said, it's history."

"Good. So what I have to tell you is simple. If you want, you can come in. And if you don't, then we never talked. Okay?"

Jesus, they want me to join them!

"First," Testa cautioned, "you should realize that if you accept, you're not taking over for your father. But you won't be starting at the bottom either. The upside is that the money's good and membership has its benefits."

He was tempted to ask about the downside—like the inevitable bullet in the head—but said nothing.

"We offer this out of respect for your father," Testa went on. "If you come in, you come as a soldier, but not here in New York. Instead, you get a new territory in Washington."

As he listened, he wondered why they would welcome an amateur like him in their ranks. Of what possible use could he be?

"All that's happening in Washington now is a little street action—numbers and some loan sharking," Testa continued. "And it all comes under Baltimore. But that changes if you accept, because you'll be working for us. And, if you're half as sharp as your old man," he said, "you'll do good. So," he said, as if there could be only one response, "whatsitgonnabe?"

They're expecting an answer now! he thought shooting a glance at Nunzio, whose blank expression gave no hint of what he should do. "Let me get this straight,' he said. "You want an answer today?"

27

The question surprised them. "That's right," his uncle said. "They do."

The notion that he would even consider joining them was absurd, and he was about to tell them so. But he held back instead. "This is all happening very quickly," he said. "You're going to have to give me some time."

"Yeah, sure," Testa said with a shrug.

Taking a long breath, he rose and, with a hundred disconnected thoughts whirling through his head, walked slowly to the far end of the garden, where, reaching the hedge line, he looked back at the three dark figures hunkered like vultures beneath the tree and silently cursed them for being part of the world that claimed his father. Pacing the narrow path, he watched them talking confidently among themselves, and thought, what right had they to invade his life with this insane offer? And how could they possibly think he would survive, when veterans like his father couldn't? Mostly, he condemned them for violating his father's wishes—for pulling him into their violent world—and he determined to have nothing to do with them.

His decision made, he swelled his chest and walked purposely back to them. He would thank them for the offer and then decline it. But something strange happened. As he neared them, he slipped his hands into his pockets and feeling the ring, knew instantly he shouldn't shut himself off from their world, not if he wished to know who killed his father.

"I accept," he told them.

CHAPTER FIVE (1959)

Julie spent the summer preparing for the August bar exam, and, afterward, in September, he, Testa and Bustamente met with Sonny Bruno, the powerful head of the Philadelphia family, whose territory extended far beyond Washington. The meeting was a formality, simply an opportunity for Julie to establish contact with the mobster.

Later, he asked his uncle about the new arrangement.

"The price for getting Bruno to let us take over Washington is to back him in getting a five-year labor contract for the Baltimore dockworkers," he told him. "Which right now they don't have, and which Bruno needs." And when Julie asked why he needed the contract, Nunzio said, "Once he gets it he'll control every port between Philly and Savannah. Add that to the truckers union and nothing moves without him getting a piece of it."

"And Gava has that kind of sway?"

"He ain't that big. But the New York families are."

Julie considered it. "And what do they get out of it?"

Nunzio smiled. "Now you're catching on. They get a piece of Bruno's operation."

* * *

By October, Julie was overseeing the mob's street action while legitimately employed by the influential National Maritime Shipping Association.

As Nunzio explained when sending him off, "You just go down there and make sure everything runs smooth for the family, and use your job with the association to make contacts with the feds. There ain't nothing to it."

But like most plans, there were unanticipated issues.

"I wish you'd told me what to expect," Julie complained when back home for Christmas. "Between the action and working the federal maze, I don't have two minutes to rub together."

They were alone in his father's library, everyone else in bed. Outside, gusts off the Sound kept the windows rattling. Inside, Julie was taking little comfort from his uncle's easy manner.

"Give it time, things'll smooth out," he assured him. "It ain't no different than any other job. You're the new guy, so you run a little faster and play little harder till you catch up. That's life."

Julie shook his head. "Is that so? Well I don't know too many guys starting out who're responsible for a million dollar bank?"

"Business is business. Get used to it."

"It's not the same," Julie insisted.

They were seated across from each other, a low table with an ivory and onyx chessboard and matching pieces between them.

30

"If you knew last spring what you know now, would it have made a difference?" his uncle asked.

"I suppose not," he said rubbing his father's ring.

"So quit bellyaching."

"Still, you have to admit," Julie insisted, "you throw a million dollars into the equation and it isn't the same as your normal nine to five job."

"Can't take the pressure? That what you're saying?"

Julie stared across the table. He'd been expecting support, not censure. "I haven't had a decent night's sleep for three months worrying about that damn money."

"Stop thinking like that," Nunzio snapped. "And more important, don't ever talk like that outside this room. People hear you and you're finished before you start. Anybody thinks you can't handle the zeros'll clean your clock."

"But..."

"Listen! There are guys out there who ain't finished high school pushing around bigger bankrolls. A million's no big deal. The bosses spread that much around in a month."

"I'm not a boss," he reminded him.

"And you ain't ever gonna be one if you don't wise up. Now look," he said drawing a breath, "it don't matter how many zeros are behind the number. Your job is to keep it flowing—just like you've been doing. It ain't that hard. You got your bettors and you got the guys who can't make it from one payday to the next. They're all losers. All you gotta do is keep hooking up with them and you'll do okay."

"You think so?"

"We wouldn't be having this talk if I didn't. But there's one thing you gotta remember."

"What's that?" he said glumly.

"Protect the dough like it's yours. And that goes for the money that comes from that money, every penny of it. 'Cause if you don't…" He let the thought hang there a moment.

"That's what I've been saying. Maybe I'm not cut out for this."

"Do me a favor and stop feeling sorry for yourself. You think it's different out there in the business world? Like they got different rules? Forget it. It's all the same, been that way a thousand years.

"I thought you'd figured that out by now. It ain't about money. It's about power, the power that comes from spreading the money around. And to keep it we need a steady flow of cash. That's why the bosses never leave a penny on the table, and why they don't take excuses—just like those Wall Street big shots. It's the same no matter who you hook up with. They all do whatever it takes to keep folks in line.

"Look," he said less harshly, "don't sell yourself short. All you gotta do is learn the rules. The rest is easy. It's no different than chess," he said, motioning to the board. "You still play?"

"When would I have time?"

"It don't matter. Just be sure to keep ahead of everybody and you're a winner."

Julie studied the board and thought of his father who'd taught him the game, and wondered how he'd erred.

"Now let's take care of some business," his uncle said. "Before you started whining I was going to give you some good news. Starting next month you'll be making more dough."

Julie looked puzzled. He was already earning fifty thousand at the association, far more than any of his classmates. "You mean from the association?"

"No, meathead."

"The street action?"

"Bingo!"

"I don't get it."

"It's your share of the action."

"Share?"

"Ferchrissake," his uncle groaned. "We're not running a charity here. The money from the association is salary. It's what you report to the feds as income. It's got nothing to do with the other stuff. Whatsamatter? You don't think you're entitled to something from that, too?

"I thought the fifty covered it."

Nunzio threw up his hands. "You know what I think? I think sometimes you think too much. The association dough is for you to look after your mother and sister and set yourself up in Washington. That's your legitimate income. No matter where you are in the organization you need that cover—we all do. That's what your father's business was about, giving him a cover. Now that you've shown you can handle the action, you get a piece of it. Trust me, you'll need it later. He'll tell you about that."

"He? Who's *he*?"

"Gava. Starting the first of the year, he takes seventy percent and you and Bruno split the difference."

"Bruno? I thought he was out after the union deal. What's he got to do with it?"

"It don't work that way. Nobody gives up anything in this business. Once you own something, you got a permanent claim. Only suckers walk away from an operation. The way it works is you always hold back something when you negotiate. Sometimes you might have to give up more than you want, but unless somebody's holding a gun to your head you never give it all away. That way you got an interest in it if things get bigger later. Remember that," he said.

Julie nodded, thinking, another rule. "We need to have more of these talks."

"Sure, don'tworryaboutit," he said, crushing out his cigarette. "Now, when your share comes in, you put it back on the street along with the other dough. And the profit from *that money* is also yours. You don't share that with nobody."

"What about Gava? Doesn't he mind the competition?"

"Don't be stupid. Everybody looks out for number one. It's expected. He don't care what you do so long as he gets his. What he does expect is for you to hustle. It's when jerks think they're smarter than the bosses and cross the line that they get in trouble."

Again his father came to mind, as he wondered what the margin of error was between hustling and crossing the line. He hoped it wasn't too narrow.

"So," Nunzio said, "all you have to do is keep your share of the profits floating and in no time you'll be matching your legitimate salary. A hundred big ones, not bad for a college kid, uh? Now," he asked, of the former Baltimore crew, "how you getting along with your people?"

The question surprised him. "All right, I guess. I mean, no problems, if that's what you're asking."

Nunzio rubbed his chin. "That ain't what I'm hearing."

Julie flinched. "What're you hearing?"

"Some bitching."

"Bitching?"

"Nothing serious, not yet anyway."

"If you mean they were happier under the old regime, that's natural. Nobody likes change."

"What I'm hearing is resentment."

"*Resentment!*"

"Look. Nobody's gonna complain outright, not with New York behind you, and Bruno onboard."

"What have they got to complain about?" he said, suddenly feeling betrayed.

"In case you haven't figured it out, guys without experience don't get a territory like yours handed to them."

"Those idiots are pissed off because I got this through my father?"

Nunzio pushed up from the chair and crossed to the desk. "Yeah," he said, absently toying with a sterling silver letter opener. "But you can't let it bother you."

"Then why're you telling me?"

"I'm telling you because you need to know so you can stay ahead of them," he said pointing the opener at the chessboard. "At least two steps ahead. *Always.*"

Julie snorted. "Christ. Keep ahead of Gava, but don't screw with his money. Keep the money flowing, and stay ahead of the crew. I'm beginning to feel like I'm on a friggin' merry-go-round."

"What do you want me to say, get out and go do what your father wanted? Well I'm not. This life is a good one. It was good for him and it's good for you. Look around and what do you see? People busting their humps, and for what? For peanuts. But take a guy like your father. You saw the respect he got. There wasn't nobody who didn't tip his hat to him. He walked in a room, men stood."

Julie shook his head. "I don't know. This isn't what I expected."

"I'm telling you, it ain't hard. The key is don't spread yourself too thin. Your crew has to see you paying attention to the small stuff. And, most important, you hafta help 'em make money. It's that simple."

Julie laughed. "That simple," he said mockingly.

Nunzio tossed the letter opener down and came over. "Don't sweat it, kid," he said clapping his nephew's shoulder. "You'll get the hang of it." Then, returning to his chair, he said, "As long as we're at it, there's something else you need to remember."

Julie groaned. "I can't wait."

"Everybody in the business is a con artist. Some are better than others, but we're all scammers. It's what we do. Before we get out of bed we're thinking, somebody's going to screw me today, so I have to do my part first. That's the way it is, and that's why you gotta keep alert."

"Terrific! So, in addition to everything else, I can't trust my own people? You know, you could've told me this before I signed on."

"What'd you expect, the Boy Scouts? It's all part of the game."

Julie looked incredulous. "*The game?* You call walking into someone's office and emptying a gun into him a game?"

"Forget it. That ain't gonna to happen to you. I already told you why your old man got it. That's behind us now, the war and the rest. It's history. These are different times."

"For how long?" he wondered aloud.

"What you need is somebody to help you. You got somebody in your crew you trust more than the others?"

"How the hell do I know?" he said, rubbing his temples.

"Think about it."

After a moment he said, "There is a guy who seems straighter than the others. But now I wouldn't bet on it."

"Isn't that what life's about, taking chances? Make him your number two, your go-between."

"Like a lieutenant?"

"Exactly. Somebody to look after things when you're doing your other stuff." Then, standing and rolling his shoulders, he said, "That's enough for tonight. Go to bed. You look like shit."

* * *

Sleep didn't come easily that night, or the following night. Two days later, when he next saw his uncle, Julie was prepared to quit. The day was wet and cold, with lingering patches of dirty snow from the previous week's storm piled curbside. Nunzio had phoned earlier to say he'd pick him up around noon without saying why or where they'd be going. It wasn't how he'd wanted to

37

spend the day, trapped in his uncle's smoke-filled car, looking for an opportunity to tell him of his decision.

"When do I get to meet Gava?" he asked, as they left City Island and entered the traffic circle that splintered off to Orchard Beach in one direction and the police shooting range at Rodmans Neck in another.

"Soon," his uncle replied.

"That's it? Soon?"

Nunzio turned to him. "What's the rush, you thinking of quitting?" Then with a harsh look, "You are. You wanna walk away, don't you?"

Julie blanched. "I'm working for the guy since September and, other than seeing him at my father's wake, have yet to meet him. I know nothing about him or, for that matter, what he thinks of me."

"Not a helluva lot," Nunzio replied. And when Julie stiffened, he said, "Relax, ferchrissake, I'm kidding."

They drove in silence to Pelham Bay, where Nunzio followed the el west toward the Square.

"What're you worried about?" he teased.

"I don't like this waiting around."

"Better learn to loosen up. You're too edgy."

They'd been in the car for over an hour, circling the area, beginning in nearby Throgs Neck and then out beyond the boat yards on City Island, with Nunzio making frequent stops and leaving Julie behind while he darted into an office or storefront, and then emerging with a satisfied grin.

"Be right back," he said, double-parking and forcing traffic around them. "I need some smokes."

Several minutes later he appeared in the doorway surveying the neighborhood while casually hammering a fresh pack of Camels against his palm.

His uncle had several annoying idiosyncrasies, one being the unvarying way he pounded each unopened pack of cigarettes before carefully removing the Cellophane wrapper from the bottom, so as to leave the blue tax stamp on top intact. The procedure could be especially irritating to watch, particularly after driving around for an hour without any meaningful conversation.

"Noon tomorrow," he announced through a cloud of smoke as he slid in behind the wheel. "That okay with you?"

"Is what okay with me?" Julie replied, finding little pleasure in the game.

"When you meet with Gava."

Julie looked at him. "How long have you known?"

"Just called him. Told him he'd better get off the dime if he wants to see you, 'cause you're heading back to Washington soon."

"Very funny."

Nunzio squeezed his nephew's knee harder than necessary. "When're you going to lighten up? It's been set up for a week, but you've been so uptight I figured why say anything. By the time the meeting comes around you won't be worth a sack of shit."

"Thanks," he said, prying his hand away. "You're a real prince."

"Ain't I though?" he said, easing back into traffic.

* * *

39

The following day the weather was no better, nor was Julie's mood. He'd had a restless night and now, gazing at his uncle sitting on the bed watching him dress, he wanted to tell him he had no interest in the meeting, that he'd just as soon forego it and return to Washington.

"Whatsamatter," Nunzio finally asked, "you nervous? Ain't this what you wanted, a sit-down with the man?"

Julie drew a breath. "Yes, that's exactly what I want."

"So what're you nervous about?"

"What makes you think I'm nervous?"

He grinned. "You're nervous."

"You win, I am."

"Don't be. It makes people think they can't trust you. Just remember, you got a lot going for you. Be yourself and don't try bullshitting him. Gava and your father was this close," he said, holding up two fingers. "He ain't interested in scamming you. All you have to do is show him respect. And that goes for when he ain't around, too. During the war they had a saying," he said, leaning back on his elbows. "Loose lips sink ships. It's the same now. The less you say the better."

Julie rubbed his palms together. "Who's going to be there besides Nino?" he asked, referring to Testa.

"What's the difference? A couple of guys. There always is."

"What about them?" he asked, choosing a tie. "What do I need to know?"

"Just that they'll be watching you. Nice tie."

Julie looked over. "You sure know how to put a guy at ease."

Nunzio laughed. "Attaboy. Don't lose that sense of humor."

Twenty minutes later Julie was beneath the el waiting behind a bus for the light to change, a cold hard rain drumming the roof of his car. Outside, Westchester Square was nearly deserted. The light turned and when the bus pulled away he saw a rare parking space and quickly pulled in. He was less than a block from Jack's Diner, where he was to meet Gava. A good omen, he thought.

Water puddled around his feet as he stood in the narrow entryway searching the noontime crowd for Testa. The old place looked tired, more so than he remembered it. Its once white tile walls and long counter had yellowed over the years. The chrome stools were now dull and pitted, and their torn plastic seat covers were crisscrossed with tape. Even the staff looked spent; particularly the wiry and once-feisty short-order cook, Slim, who'd been flipping eggs as long as Julie could remember, and his bubbly longtime counterpart at the register, Roxy, who now seemed to be applying her makeup with a spatula, and teasing her lacquered strawberry hair to new heights. Still, the smell of coffee and the buzz of friendly conversations gave the place an inviting air on this wintry day.

Roxy's greeting hadn't changed much, the rush of words still coming out in a long stream of cigarette smoke. "Hiyadarlin'. Coldenuffawya?"

She was perched on a stool by the door, behind a tiny J-shaped counter cluttered with food checks speared to a set of wire spindles, a crumpled pack of Winstons, and a lipstick-smeared coffee cup, its saucer overflowing with crushed cigarette butts. She and Slim were fixtures, always there, no matter the day or season, leading Julie to wonder if either had a life outside the place.

"Hi, Roxy," he replied, without interrupting his search. But he'd already lost her attention to the person edging in behind him.

Shrugging out of his coat, he sidestepped his way past the counter to his left and the rows of booths to his right, toward Testa, who was waving at him from the rear.

"Hiya doin', kid!" Slim called, offering a gapped-toothed smile. "Long time no see," he said without breaking stride.

"Doing good, Slim," he replied, slowing a bit. "Thought you'd be retired in Florida by now."

The comment drew a tired laugh. "Onea these days, kid. Onea these days. Happy New Year." And as Julie moved along, "Nice seein' ya."

Testa's ashtray suggested he'd been there a while. "Happy New Year," he said, extending a beefy hand. "Coldern shit out there. Bet you wish you were down south." Then, summoning the waitress, "'Nother coffee over here, gorgeous."

Julie slid in opposite him, facing the mirrored wall that gave a view of the entrance. "Good seeing you again," he said, noting the bulge beneath Testa's jacket.

The man's creased prizefighter's face made him appear much older than Julie, when, in fact, he was only a few years older. Like many neighborhood kids without direction, he'd been lured from school to high-paying construction work soon after turning sixteen. But rather than staying with the trade, he found more rewarding work as a mob collector in the south Bronx.

While they waited, Julie asked how long he'd worked for his father.

"Off and on, about four years. I liked your old man," he said earnestly. "He was tough, but fair. Didn't take crap from nobody."

The comment made Julie realize how little he knew of this aspect of his father's life. Certainly, he recognized those same qualities—tough and fair—but not in the context of applying them to men like Testa. And he wondered if being tough but fair in the organization meant ordering someone's legs broken rather than their skull. But before he could probe further, Testa cut him off.

"*Basta!*" he said, looking past him. "Here's the boss."

Julie looked up to see Gava and two escorts marching toward them. Whereas he'd had to weave through the crowd, those in the aisle were now pressing against each other to make room. A few, he noted, even bowed slightly, but more significantly no one looked directly at him, not even the two uniformed cops he brushed past. Like at the funeral home, there were momentary lulls in conversations as he passed. Even Slim held his tongue. Watching Gava approach was like watching a cresting wave heading uninterrupted toward shore.

In his charcoal gray topcoat, matching homburg and silk maroon scarf, he looked oddly out of place in this working class establishment.

As the trio drew near, Jack the owner wordlessly yielded his seat at the end of the counter to one of Gava's men and disappeared into the kitchen.

Following Testa's lead, Julie rose as far as he could within the small booth and smiled.

"Happy New Year, boys," Gava said passing his hat to the man at the counter. His raspy voice was as Julie remembered it from Riccio's, so too the steely gaze of the dominant left eye. "You guys recovered from the parties?" he said sliding in beside Testa.

"The head's fine, boss," Testa said, patting his flat stomach. "It's the waist that took a beating. Mom goes crazy for the holidays."

"Don't they all," Gava replied with a smile. "How about you? How you feeling?" he asked Julie.

"Fine. Can't get enough home cooking. But as far as the parties go..., Well, we're still mourning," he said, unable to ignore the man pressing against him as if he wanted the entire bench.

"Naturally," Gava said, angling his head to favor his good eye, a gesture which only Julie seemed to notice. "But it's good being back in the Bronx, eh?"

"Coming home's always good," Julie agreed.

The waitress approached and was immediately waved away by Gava's sidekick.

Meanwhile, Gava folded his hands, allowing an inch of gleaming French cuff to creep forward. "So, how's it goin' down there?"

It appeared the conversation was to be between them, and Julie answered, "I guess you heard I passed the bar."

"Yeah, your uncle told me. Your father would be proud. It's good having a lawyer in the family, but I hope I never need your services. You know, in Italy the best lawyers are Neapolitans. No matter where you are, you're in trouble you get a Neapolitan. Even the Sicilians hire them," he added with a laugh.

Heeding his uncle's advice, Julie said of the job and generous salary, "I want to thank you for your assistance."

"I loved your father like a brother. You and your family, you need anything, you let me know. I want your mother and sister to be comfortable, just like your father would've done for them. Understand?"

"Yes, perfectly."

"Nunzio told you about the new arrangement?"

"He mentioned it."

"You okay with that?"

Julie nodded. "I appreciate it."

"Good. Now tell me about Washington. I hear there's a chance this Senator Kennedy's going to make a run for the White House."

"That's the rumor," Julie confirmed.

"I'm interested in knowing what he's all about. We know he don't like Italians, but he takes our money while his punk brother busts our chops on that McClellan Committee. If you can find out, I'd like to know what's their game." And when Julie didn't reply, he said, "Like they say in the Army, we need some good intelligence. Naturally," he stressed, "everything has to be *sotto la tavola*."

"From what I hear most folks don't give it much credence, his running, that is."

"Why, 'cause he's Catholic?"

"Mostly."

45

"Forget that. It don't mean nothing with the right people behind him. That's why we need to know his game plan. See if we want to back him or not."

Again, that word game. "His game?" Julie asked.

"Yeah. Who he's hooked up with. How he wants to spend those federal bucks if he's elected. What he plans to do with that prick brother of his."

"I see," Julie replied, wishing he knew more of Gava's game plan, but not confident enough to ask.

"Good." In the next instant Gava was on his feet. "We'll be talking. It's good seeing you. *Buon anno,*" he said before putting on his hat and checking it in the mirror.

The meeting Julie had been so anxious for was over. "Jesus," he said watching Gava and his men advance down the aisle. "What was that all about? We're just starting to talk and he's gone. Was it something I said?"

Testa looked at him. "Don't worry about it. It's how he does business—one, two, three. He don't like being in one place too long."

Julie shook his head. "I just wish somebody'd warned me, is all."

Testa laughed. "You'll catch on."

Julie doubted it. Still, he asked, "What about the other guy, the one beside me?"

"What about him?"

"Who is he and what's his problem?"

"Sometimes," Testa said, pulling on his coat, "it's better not to know too much too soon. He's a fella, is all."

CHAPTER SIX (1959)

Julie sped south on the turnpike, past the frozen Jersey marshlands. By the time he reached Trenton he'd stopped brooding over Gava's silent muscleman, who'd done a fairly good job of intimidating him back at Jack's the previous day. He was focusing instead on Washington and the Kennedys, and feeling less unsure about his role in the organization. With this new tasking from Gava, it was all going to be fine, he told himself.

Immediately upon returning to Washington, he followed Nunzio's advice and appointed Vinnie Monte his lieutenant, reasoning, Monte, the oldest and smartest of the crew, seemed also to be the most trustworthy. With that done, he turned his attention to using his Maritime Association position and his line of ready cash, to court and befriend ranking government officials which, in turn, quickly gained him entry to Washington's social network. As the months passed, invitations led to more invitations, and soon his days as an affluent bachelor were filled with receptions and dinner parties. It was a heady environment for one so young and inexperienced, and it didn't take long before it consumed most, if not all, of his time.

It wasn't until early June, while taking advantage of the lull during a Congressional recess, that he learned the consequences of his inattention. It was Friday; the day Monte turned over the weekly collections. But rather than meeting in Washington, he had Monte come to Annapolis, where he was negotiating a summer rental.

As they walked down Main Street toward the city dock, Monte said, "There's something you oughta know."

What is it?" Julie asked.

Monte took a final drag of his cigarette, flipped it, and said, "It's about that two grand in vig Charlie held back two weeks ago."

Charlie was Charlie Fazio, a matchstick-chewing reed of a man, known variously as Charlie Sticks, or, as he preferred, Charlie Matches, because, as he often asserted, he was the man to see for an arson job.

He'd asked for an extension, and Julie had willingly consented. "I remember. He needed it to cover a string of lucky bets."

"Then you gave him another week."

"What about it?"

They were approaching Captain Ed's Raw Bar, a narrow store-front restaurant off the traffic circle, popular among the townies.

Monte hesitated. "Boss," he said after an awkward moment, "don't buy his bullshit."

Julie stopped, forcing tourists to walk around them. "What do you mean?"

"There's no lucky streak with the bettors. Charlie's got the dough."

Julie didn't understand. "So why hasn't he paid up?"

"He's holding back to see what you'll do."

"See what I'll do?" he said, his stomach tightening.

Monte sighed. "When you bought the story the first time he wanted to see how far he could push it. Next time he tries it, he'll hit you with a different excuse and hold back more."

"To what end? He still owes the money."

It was clear Monte wasn't enjoying this, his expression suggesting anyone else would've caught on immediately. Drawing a breath, he explained, "He gets to put the money back on the street as a short-term loan. There's no shortage of guys who'll pay a premium for some fast dough. What he makes on the difference is gravy."

Julie felt his face warm. He'd been scammed by one of his own, just as Nunzio had predicted. What made it worse; he was clueless about what to do about it.

"Don't take it personally," Monte said. "He saw you were wrapped up with other things and made his move. You didn't see it coming."

Julie shook his head. There was no excuse. He'd been warned. "How bad's it look?" he asked, not sure he wanted to know.

The other man clicked his tongue. "It ain't the end of the world," he said, carefully, "if he don't get away with it."

Julie wished he could ask how to handle it, but Monte had already done all he could. Knowing that how he dealt with Charlie would determine his future in the organization, he said, "I appreciate this. No one's going to know, I promise."

Monte nodded. "Thanks. One more thing. Charlie and me go way back. He's a hustler but he ain't stupid.

In all my time with the organization I never seen anybody pull this on a boss. These scams we do between ourselves or to outsiders, but never to a boss. Of course," he hesitated, "the bosses are always…,"

"Yeah, I know," Julie said, not wanting to hear the rest.

"It's no secret you're here because New York wants it that way. Which is good enough for us. We don't ask questions. But like I said, Charlie's been around. So I don't understand why he's doing this. Unless…,"

"Unless what?"

"Unless somebody's messing with you."

The midday sun was warm on their backs, a perfect counterpoint to the cool breeze off the Chesapeake, but it went largely unnoticed as Julie thought of Gava's nameless companion at Jack's. After a moment, he said, "Let's pass on lunch."

"Sure. No problem."

When they reached Julie's car, he said, "Next week have the boys bring their payments here. I want to see them, especially Charlie. I'll let you know where and when."

Confused and angry, he climbed in and drove south along a little-used ribbon of highway that cut through long stretches of tobacco farms. He drove with the windows open, trying, without success, to clear his head. He'd gone about twenty miles when he spotted a faded *Guns and Bait* sign above a roadside store and made a hasty U-turn.

"I want to buy a gun," he told the owner.

"Sure enough," the fellow replied with an easy smile. "Got a pretty good collection," he said, as he led Julie to the rear. "What'd you have in mind?"

"Let's see what you got," he said, not having thought that far ahead.

"Hunting or target?" the man asked.

There were a dozen or so rifles in a wall cabinet, and an assortment of handguns in the display case.

"Protection," he said. "Something'll make the wife feel safe when I'm away."

The man nodded knowingly while sliding the door open. "Get a lot of that these days. This here's a popular one with the ladies," he said, placing a snub-nosed 38-caliber Smith & Wesson on the dull wooden counter.

"This a good one?" Julie asked, taking it and pointing it at the man.

"Mind pointing in another direction?" he said calmly enough.

"Sorry," Julie said, putting it down.

"No harm done."

"So, is this a good one?"

The man offered a crooked grin. "This baby'll stop a gorilla if you hit him right."

"Wrap it up."

Driving back, he could think only of the gun on the seat beside him. He'd never owned much less fired one. By the time he reached Galesville, a tiny enclave on the West River, he was anxious to hold it again. With no one around, he slowed and pulled onto the shoulder, where he picked up the box and read that he'd just purchased a five-shot, double action Smith & Wesson Chief Special, along with a box of .38-caliber ammo. The lid opened easily,

51

and he carefully removed the oily wrapper and hefted the unloaded weapon. It was heavy, heavier than he'd remembered back at the store, and nothing like the sleek cap pistols he'd known as a boy. Nor was it balanced as they'd been. Finger twirling this one would be difficult. Still, fascinated, he gripped the checkered walnut handle and whipped it in a broad arc at waist level. Its size didn't make it look menacing, but its solid mass made it feel that way, causing him to think perhaps he should toss it into the woods before inadvertently injuring himself. What held him back was the notion of Charlie and the others ridiculing him, and suddenly he was taking aim at a nearby tree. Squeezing the trigger slowly, he watched the hammer rear back and fall against the empty barrel with a solid metallic click. "Take that, you bastard."

* * *

He spent that weekend moving into his rental, a modest green and white shuttered bungalow in the semi-private beachfront community of Round Bay, on the Severn River. Built during the twenties for working-class Baltimoreans seeking relief from oppressive summers, the homes were now converted year-round residences. And while he liked the privacy afforded by the single road in, he'd chosen the house for its waterfront location and the dock that came with it.

Owning a boat had been a childhood dream nurtured along the craggy shores of Pelham Bay and the adjoining expanse of Long Island Sound, a dream that was never fulfilled because of his mother's irrational fear of water. And while his father sympathized with him, there was little he could do to persuade her to allow them even the smallest runabout. Now, having decided to spend his weekends in Annapolis, he would not be denied.

From what the seller had said Julie was the first to answer *The Evening Capital* ad for the 1940 Chriscraft, a masterfully built twenty-three-footer with a powerful inboard engine and expansive rear deck. In every detail, it was the type of boat he'd coveted as a boy, the top-of-the-line model he'd seen in boating magazines. The owner, a retired admiral who'd obviously given it the same meticulous attention he'd reserved for the ships he'd commanded, was parting with it reluctantly, as a concession to his arthritic wife. And because the decision had been a difficult one, he'd purposely set the price high. But the ploy failed to discourage Julie, who, sensing the admiral's mood didn't negotiate. As a result, the old sailor threw in the use of his boathouse during the off-season. "She's too pretty to be stored like some knockabout in one of those damn boatyards," he'd said at the time.

* * *

That following Friday, Julie rounded the Naval Academy seawall and smiled at the sight of Charlie and the others waiting on the dock in their city clothes, all of them looking out of place among the tourists and boaters.

"Shoes off," he called before they climbed aboard. "This mahogany doesn't do well under leather. "Sit anywhere," he told them. "Beer's in the cooler." And when they'd cleared the dock, he said, "This'll take about twenty minutes."

The day was warm and the men quickly removed their jackets. Once they were on the Severn, Julie throttled the engine, allowing the bow to briefly rise before settling down ahead of its wide V wake. Then turning to meet Charlie's gaze, he grinned and asked, "Enjoying it?"

Charlie smiled back. "Beautiful."

They took care of business quickly at the house, each man delivering his money with little comment, except for Charlie, who acknowledged the favor extended him. "Thanks for the extra time," he said away from the others, the match bobbing between his teeth.

"What good is it if we don't support each other?" Julie replied. "But don't let it happen too often."

The thick marinated steaks came from Rookies Supermarket in the center of town, known for its quality cuts. The crusty bread, wine and pastry had been delivered earlier from Baltimore's Little Italy.

Around seven-thirty, when the wine was nearly gone and the sun began dipping toward the tree line, Julie walked among them announcing, "I hate breaking up the party, boys, but it's time to head back."

Moments later, as they walked down the dock, he called to Charlie, "Untie the lines before jumping in, will you?"

"Sure thing, skipper," the little man said, the issue of the money forgotten.

And when they reached the center of the river, he turned to Charlie again. "I hear you were in the Navy," he called over his shoulder.

"Three years on a tin can in the Med," Charlie said.

"Then you should be able to get us back to town without running aground. Care to show us what they taught you?"

"You serious?" he asked screwing his mouth around a new match.

"Only if you know what you're doing," Julie said. And when the others laughed, he said, "Don't mind them, come on up."

"Why not," he said with a shrug, while Julie held the boat steady. Then, weaving his way forward, he looked around, and said, "You assholes wouldn't know the bow from the stern."

They were still ribbing him when Julie shoved the throttle forward and spun the wheel to starboard, sending Charlie overboard. And when two men rose to help him, he shouted, "Keep your seats! This is between me and Charlie."

They and the others froze, not so much at what he'd said, but because of the gun in his hand. "Don't anyone get in the way," he told them as he began steering a tight circle around Charlie, who was treading water and trying to figure out what happened.

"Think you can screw me and get away with it, you little bastard!" Julie shouted.

"Don't let me drown," Charlie called as the waves buffeted him.

"Whatsamatter, Charlie, didn't they teach you to swim in the Navy?"

"It was a mistake," he cried while struggling to keep from swallowing water. "Honest."

"You bet it was!" Julie said, before breaking the circle and heading away.

"Boss! Don't!" Monte shouted.

"Shut up!" Julie barked.

Behind them, Charlie screamed, "DON'T LEAVE!!"

"Don't worry, Charlie, I wouldn't think of it," Julie called as he turned the boat around.

It took Charlie and the others a moment to realize he wasn't coming for him, but aiming at him. And in the next instant Charlie was diving to avoid being hit, his feet kicking wildly on the surface, as the boat swept past him. When he popped up Julie repeated the maneuver, revving the engine and coming at him again, this time the boat crossing several feet ahead of him. It went on like that two more times, Julie crisscrossing dangerously close, and Charlie diving to keep from being hit, until it was apparent he wouldn't survive much longer.

Slowing the boat, Julie finally came alongside and, reaching down, grabbed Charlie's arm and hauled him partially out of the water. "One of us doesn't belong in this boat," he said, their faces inches apart.

"Please," he gasped, "no more."

"Don't ever hold back on me. Don't even think about it."

"Never. I swear," he said coughing the words, his hands wrapped tightly around Julie's wrist.

When Julie didn't respond, there was a tense moment when all aboard, including Charlie, thought he might toss him back. Then, turning to the others, he said, "All right, bring him aboard."

No one spoke after that. And when they reached the city dock and climbed ashore, their farewells were brief and barely audible.

They hadn't gone far when Julie called out. "Hey, Charlie!" And when the man turned, "You owe me three weeks vig on the money you held back."

CHAPTER SEVEN (1959)

The following Sunday, Julie rose early and set about washing and polishing the boat. As he worked, his thoughts were on the afternoon cocktail party, where, according to Rear Admiral *Blackjack* VanDoren, the man who'd sold him the boat, he'd be meeting some of the town's prominent citizens, including several legendary naval aviators.

"It'll be a great experience," he'd promised when extending the invitation. "You'll meet men who led us through battles at Saipan, Coral Sea, Guam, Midway. All of them real heroes," he stressed.

When the phone rang at noon, Julie was sipping coffee by the window and enjoying the river, the incident with Charlie largely forgotten.

"Hey, kid," his uncle said in an upbeat tone.

"What's up?"

"I just heard from Gava about your little boat trip."

"That was fast. It only happened Friday." Then more tentatively, "What'd you hear?"

"Probably a lot more'n you know about."

"Really?" he said, thinking perhaps he'd gone too far with Charlie. "I'm listening."

"Well, you did good. His holding back was way out of line. But more important, it was a setup."

"Oh, yeah?" he said, expecting Nunzio to fill in the blanks.

Instead, his uncle said, "I have to tell you, kid, I wasn't in on it. I only just found out."

"You think Gava had something to do with it?"

"Nah. What I do know is guys are going to screw with you."

"What about Sonny Bruno?"

"Ain't his style."

"So what're you saying?"

"I'm saying you can't take it personally, these things happen." Then he explained, "It goes back before you were born, to the Castellamarese war, when the feds put the heat on and the bosses decided only blood relatives were allowed in. It stayed that way till a couple years ago, when they relaxed the rules, and they've been having problems since.

"What problems?"

"Some capos were selling memberships to guys who didn't belong. Of course they're history, but it still makes people nervous about newcomers. From what I hear, the bit with Charlie was to see how you'd handle yourself."

"It was a test?!" he asked, his anger rising.

"Yeah. To be sure you're not some jamoke who lets guys walk over him. I gotta hand it to you," he said with a smoker's laugh. "You couldn't have played it better."

"You think so? And do you and those clowns realize I could've killed him?!"

"But you didn't. Instead you took it to the limit. Sure, you could've slapped him around, and that would've been good, too. But settling it like you did, in front of the others, sent the right message. It was perfect."

Julie was about to tell his uncle what he thought of their little test when Nunzio suddenly cut him off. "Gotta go, kid. Keep up the good work."

Holding the dead phone, he gazed at the point in the river where he'd dumped Charlie and wondered how many more idiotic hoops he'd have to jump through before they were satisfied.

That afternoon, while approaching the admiral's pier, he realized VanDoren or his neighbors might've witnessed Friday's drama. Well, he thought, he'd hear about it soon enough if they did. A clumsy rescue is what he'd say, if asked.

"Ahoy," VanDoren called, waving. "How's she running?"

"Like a greyhound," he said, referring to the Navy's sleek destroyers.

"Let's save that kind of sea talk for another day, boys," VanDoren's wife said with a warm smile. Her voice, unlike her thin body, was healthy and robust. Adding just as firmly, "I expect to arrive looking very much as I do now."

"You may be skipper, Julie, but prepare to turn the con over to Miriam," the admiral said as they helped her aboard.

"Pay him no mind, Julius. He gets petulant when he doesn't have at least five fathoms of water beneath his keel."

"Now you know why the Navy doesn't allow women at sea," her husband said, stepping in after her.

Before getting underway, Julie asked, "Mind taking the helm, Jack? It'll give me and Miriam a chance to talk."

"A pleasure," he said without hesitating. Then moving forward and taking the wheel, he patted the gleaming console and asked, "Did you miss me, darling?"

"Wait a sec," Julie called while unfurling a blue Navy pennant with two white stars, thereby indicating the helmsman's service and rank. "Now we're ready."

The glint in Miriam's eyes told him the gesture was appreciated.

The ride was both leisurely and smooth, and they made it to the academy without disrupting her hair, or of any mention of Friday's incident with Charlie.

"That's Worden Field," VanDoren said pointing to the stretch of grass bordering College Creek. "The parade ground, where we... Where the mids hold dress parades. You should visit in the fall when the brigade returns. It's quite a sight," he boasted.

"They're a sight, all right," his wife countered. "If only the little dears would learn to march."

VanDoren cleared his throat. "Did I mention Miriam's father was a West Pointer?" Then, shrugging, he conceded, "She's right, of course, sailors can't march."

Music and conversation spilled from the second floor of the boathouse.

Soon after reaching the large hall Miriam peeled away, allowing VanDoren to introduce Julie to his comrades, a colorful group of square-jawed veterans who could easily have been typecast alongside John Wayne or Robert Ryan. To his amusement they quickly fell into calling each other by old squadron nicknames like Dusty, Boomer, Maverick and Cag, while recounting captivating tales of sea battles, and aerial attacks, and close encounter dogfights with Jap Zeros.

"Are you finding all this a little overwhelming?" Miriam asked when she came up to him later.

Julie laughed. "Does it show?"

"No. But I sense you might enjoy some fresh air," she said, allowing him to escort her onto the balcony. "It's just that I've been part of this family long enough to know how we must appear to strangers. I see it with the midshipmen's girlfriends who stay in our homes, especially the new ones. These masters of the sea have a language that can leave a civilian's head spinning. Of course, between us, the little darlings prefer it that way."

"I suppose that's true of most professions," he said in their defense.

They were standing by the railing, Miriam identifying the different buildings in the distance. As the balcony began filling he failed to notice the woman who'd come up beside them.

"Hello, Nicola," Miriam said. "So nice seeing you. Julius, I'd like you to meet a dear friend."

He turned and met her sparkling gaze. She was fair and tall, nearly his height, with strong swimmer's shoulders.

"Nicola Wainwright, this is Julius Vittorio, a new friend."

"A pleasure, Miss Wainwright," he said, catching his breath.

She smiled with her eyes. "The pleasure's mine. Please call me Nikki. Practically everyone does."

Her voice was strong and her accent crisp and distinctly British. He guessed she was about his age.

After a few minutes, Miriam said, "I hope you'll excuse me while I search for Jack." And they were alone.

He quickly learned she was widowed. That her husband of two years had been an American Navy ASW pilot on exchange duty at England's Mendenhall Air Base, where they'd met and married six months later. And that after completing his tour he'd been transferred to the academy. Four months into his new job, while returning home from coaching the wrestling team, his motorcycle had been sideswiped. She'd been told he died instantly.

"That was over a year ago. April twenty-fifth to be precise," she said, flatly.

"Why have you stayed in America?" he asked, no longer aware of the other guests.

"At first, I thought of returning home," she confessed. "But I couldn't leave him. He's buried over there, on Hospital Point," she said, indicating the hillside cemetery across the creek. "His memory is more vivid here. Though we knew each other longer back home, we had more time together here."

Julie was surprised at her unflinching manner. It was, he thought, as if she'd closed a door on that portion of her life.

"Our friends were marvelous—so supportive and understanding. And before I knew it, a year had slipped by. Now I don't care to leave. I fear if I go back it will be too much to deal with alone. I'm able to handle the loss here because it happened here. Does that sound odd?"

"Not at all."

A gentle smile crossed her face. "Now, please tell me about you, Julius."

"I prefer Julie."

She nodded. "So do I."

Her eyes were magnets, drawing him deeper into her.

"There isn't much to tell, really. After completing law school last year I joined the National Maritime Shipping Association. In Washington," he added.

"Is that all?" She laughed and he did too.

"Boring, isn't it?"

"I'm sure there's more you're not telling me. Perhaps," she said, pursing her lips, "you're shy." And when he didn't reply, she asked, "Have you toured the academy yet?"

He shook his head. "I've only been in Annapolis a short while. This is my first visit to the campus. I thought about it, but those walls are imposing."

She edged closer, whispering, "I'll let you in on a little secret. They're meant to keep the midshipmen from going out, not visitors from entering."

"Why, are they dangerous?"

She smiled. "The local women may not think so."

"Ah, yes, the old testosterone problem," he said with a laugh that turned a few heads.

"Easy does it," she said, touching his arm. "You'll have us both ejected."

His face reddened, more from her touch than embarrassment. "Pardon me."

"You're pardoned," she said in an appealing way. "Now, how about that tour? I'm one of the official guides."

"I'm not really one for groups. More of a loner."

"I suspected as much. Well, you needn't worry. This is a personal tour, just us two."

His face brightened. "How can I refuse?"

She hadn't removed her hand, and he hoped she'd keep it there.

"Would you be available next Thursday? Say two o'clock? We can meet in front of the chapel," she said with a nod at the large dome.

He'd have agreed had she said *midnight, on top of the chapel.* "Sounds just fine."

More guests were moving outside now. A gentle breeze pushed her hair against her cheek, carrying with it a hint of perfume, and suddenly he was wishing it were Thursday. Over her shoulder he spied VanDoren by the door scanning the crowd, and he hoped he wasn't coming for him.

"There you are," the admiral called, as he reached them. "Sorry to interrupt you two, but I'd like to introduce Julie to some friends in the shipping business. These are people you need to know, Julie," he said, coming between them. "You'll forgive me won't you, Nikki?" he asked caringly.

"Of course," she replied.

"Atta girl," he said, shepherding them back inside.

"Well, see you Thursday," Julie said.

"Until then," she replied before moving to a group of younger guests he hadn't noticed earlier.

"They're active duty officers," VanDoren offered. "Naval aviators assigned to the academy. Some are faculty, like her husband, others are company officers. We include them in all our socials. They've been very helpful to

Nikki this past year." Then, frowning, he said, "Did she mention that her husband was killed?"

"Yes," he replied stealing a look back.

"Once you get to know us you'll find we're a close family. We look after our own," he boasted.

Despite his disappointment, he quickly realized VanDoren was right. These were men he should meet. At one point, he glanced across the room and happily caught Nikki doing the same. Later, when the discussion moved beyond maritime issues, he considered excusing himself, but held back when someone mentioned being courted by a local bank seeking state government business.

"They're aiming to get in on those federal-revenue sharing projects," he told them. And when someone pointed out it seemed like a waste of time since the state passed the money on to the contractors, he replied, "That was my reaction, too, but they set me straight."

For the next few minutes Julie forgot Nikki.

"It's called a float," he told them. "Banks use it routinely. In a nutshell, the feds give the states funds for federal projects and then they dole it out in increments, allowing them to retain and earn interest on the balance. They even do overnight floats for large sums. It gives a whole new meaning to the expression, 'time is money'".

"And that's worth pursuing?" the same man asked.

"You bet. It can be a significant source of income for the state, and the bank as well."

"What about the contractors?"

He shrugged. "It's the golden rule. He who has the gold, rules."

"So, do you plan on helping this bank?" VanDoren asked.

"Don't see why not."

Julie thought of Sonny Bruno in Philadelphia, and wondered what this fellow's cut would be for brokering the deal. When next he looked around, the party was breaking up and Nikki was gone.

"She said to say goodbye and that she'll see you Thursday," Miriam said, coming alongside him. Then with a smile, "She's a lovely lady."

"Yes.   Charming," he said, concealing his disappointment.

The VanDorens sat together on the return, looking like the young lovers Julie imagined they were a half century earlier. It had been an extraordinary day, he mused, as they cruised the river.

* * *

Thursday was one of those rare summer days, when the sky was scrubbed clean by a northerly breeze that hinted of autumn. The clock atop Mahan Hall chimed the hour just as Nikki stepped from Bancroft Hall, the massive dormitory across the sprawling campus. She walked with a confident bounce, wearing what Julie guessed was her tour guide's uniform; a pleated tan skirt, plain white short-sleeve blouse, walking shoes, and a blue and gold scarf she used to tie her hair off into a ponytail. She saw him and waved, and he immediately moved toward her.

They met at the raised bandstand beneath the towering oaks and yellow buckeyes.

"Good afternoon, Mr. Vittorio," she said, extending her hand. Her face was radiant and her voice strong, like her handshake.

He liked his name pronounced with a British accent. "And good day to you, Lady Nicola," he replied with a spirited bow.

"Shall we dispense with the titles?" she said jokingly. "They don't ring true here in the colonies."

"Too bad. I practiced all week."

She smiled as if she believed him. "Perhaps there'll be another opportunity. Are you ready for the grand tour?" she asked, taking his arm and leading him back to the chapel.

"I was ready last Sunday," he said, eliciting another smile. "It's a beautiful campus," he noted. "French Renaissance, isn't it?"

She raised an eyebrow. "How perceptive. Do you have any other observations before we start?"

"A few. I recall reading these two hundred or so acres had once been the site of Fort Severn."

"Correct again," she said, enjoying the game.

"And these buildings were constructed in 1913 on partially reclaimed land at a cost of eight million dollars."

"I'm impressed."

"Also, that John Paul Jones is entombed nearby."

"You've been quite busy. Will you be conducting the tour?" she said, when they reached the chapel's heavy bronze doors.

"No. It's all yours."

"Are you sure?"

"Well, I did learn that the man responsible for establishing the school was Secretary of the Navy George Bancroft, who convinced Congress to pay twenty-eight thousand dollars in salaries to the instructors. The rest, as they say, is history."

"Finished?"

"Yep. For now."

"You almost earned yourself a gold star."

"Almost? Where'd I go wrong?"

"For the record, Congress neither paid the instructors' salaries nor approved the concept. It was Bancroft's manipulation of funds through a bureaucratic sleight of hand along with some astute politicking within the Navy that got things going. Congress deserves none of the credit."

"I must've missed that part."

"May we commence?"

"Lead on."

The tour lasted three hours, twice as long as usual, concluding in front of Bancroft Hall, where the new class of plebes was assembling for evening meal.

"Great timing. You've got this down pat," he said as they joined the gathering spectators. "And a delightful ending to a wonderful afternoon."

"Shhhh," she whispered, squeezing his arm. "You mustn't speak."

After the ceremony, when the plebes had completed muster and had marched inside, he leaned in and asked, "May I speak now?" And when she nodded, he said, "I was about to ask if you would let me repay your kindness with dinner this evening?"

"Oh, I'd truly love to," she said with a frown. "But I can't tonight. I'm expected at the Superintendent's quarters. It's the kick-off dinner for next month's Parents Open House Weekend, and I'm chairing one of the committees. I simply can't miss it. After you've been here a while you'll find life centers on the care and feeding of the midshipmen."

"I thought this was the state capital."

"Technically. And we're reminded of that when the legislature convenes in January, but you'd never know it the rest of the year." Then, perking up, she said, "But if you're serious about dinner, how about Saturday? Friends are having a cookout in Cape St. Claire. I know you're not a group person but I'm sure you'll enjoy meeting them. Say yes," she implored.

"I'm not sure I can wait two days."

She smiled and pressed his hand. "Try."

"Where do we meet, the chapel again?"

"That's probably safer," she said, mischievously, "but not convenient. I live close by, just over the bridge in Eastport. Creek Drive. Nine fifty-two. I'm listed. Ring me and I'll provide directions. Okay?" she asked, her eyes dancing.

"Got it." Then, moving closer, he said, "Thanks for a wonderful afternoon. The tour was interesting, but you were the main event."

To his delight, she leaned in and kissed his cheek. "Until Saturday," she whispered.

"Ciao, bella," he said, and watched her walk away, her ponytail swinging with each stride.

* * *

Cape St. Clair was a large pine-forested community fronting the Chesapeake. Like Round Bay, many of its homes were converted summer cottages, most set atop cinderblock stilts sunk deep into sandy soil.

71

Dinner Saturday took the form of a backyard cookout. To Julie's surprise, everyone but the hosts was a civilian, including Francis Xavier Kelly, an agreeable, soft-spoken Villanova grad from Philadelphia, whom he found sitting apart from the others. Julie couldn't say what drew him to the man, nor could he explain why he hadn't moved on after introducing himself. For whatever reason, he slid into a chair and, beer in hand, asked, "So how'd you wind up here?"

"The government recruited me for a position with Social Security in Baltimore," Kelly said, after explaining that he worked with computers. Adding modestly, "They only interviewed those of us with top grades."

"Social Security?"

Kelly's laugh indicated it wasn't the first time he'd gotten that reaction. "I know what you're thinking. Why not something with more pizzazz, like the space program?"

Julie flushed. "I wasn't being critical. I'm sure it's every bit as challenging," he said, thinking it was time to find Nikki.

"No offense taken."

More carefully, he said, "I'da thought the government would hire folks who make computers."

The question drew a thin smile. "This is a new field. There aren't many in corporate America with the requisite skills. The core of knowledge is actually in the federal laboratories where it all originated, and where most of the research is conducted via grants at the university level. So, when the government made the decision to expand its computer applications, it was logical that they recruit from academia."

"Makes sense, I suppose," Julie said, thinking it was time to move on. "So how do you like it? Is it what you expected?" he asked, seeing Nikki moving into the house and wishing he'd caught her eye before she had.

"Oh, absolutely!" he replied, happy to continue. "I couldn't have made a better decision. We work with state-of-the-art equipment, and every day we're pushing the envelope to where our demands are forging the next generation of computers."

"Really?" *Come on Nikki, get out here.*

"The average citizen hasn't a clue of where we're heading. This technology's poised to take off like a rocket. And when it does, you'll see computers everywhere."

Julie finished his beer. "That seems like a bit of stretch," he said, edging off his chair.

"Trust me. In the very near future computers'll be running our lives. And anyone who sees it coming stands to make a fortune."

Julie slid back. "Is that so? I get around. Why aren't I hearing this?"

"That's not surprising. Most folks in government don't understand computers or their applications. So you won't hear it from them. Those who do are in the labs, and they don't say much."

"Why's that?"

"Simple. Scientists tend to be paranoid."

"You're kidding."

"Not at all. In their highly specialized world knowledge translates to money, and those with the knowledge get the federal bucks. So you won't hear it from them." Noting Julie's confusion, he said, "It's every scientist's dream to head a federal project, and the only way to do that is to stay ahead of one's peers."

"I didn't realize it was so competitive. But what about technicians like you? Why aren't you guys out there beating the drum?"

"We're too wrapped up in our work," he said with a shrug.

What strange people.

"Besides, it's been my experience folks aren't interested. Look at you. A moment ago you were ready to walk away, right?"

"Was it that obvious?" he said with a laugh.

"We mention computers and immediately eyes glaze over. Then it's, 'Nice meeting you,' and their off," he said without rancor.

Again, Julie laughed. He was warming to the guy. "Well my eyes are still clear."

"You're a rare breed," Kelly said, buttoning his cardigan against the evening chill.

"So tell me. What's slowing the process? Why aren't the folks in Washington knocking at your door?"

"Human nature. They either avoid that which they don't understand, or dismiss it as irrelevant. The few politicians I've met have told me... Now get this! ... *'This technology's too impersonal. It's anti-democratic!'*" He shook his head, "No wonder the Russians are beating us in space."

Leaning forward, he said, "Trust me on this. Anyone who doesn't take this technology seriously is in for a jolt. We're straddling two extremely different worlds, one foot in the past, the other in the future. And from where I'm sitting the future doesn't look anything like the past. But more important, these changes are inevitable, and those smart enough to anticipate them will leave everyone else in the dust."

Julie suspected he'd just met the man he'd been looking for.

Afterwards, as he and Nikki walked to his car, she asked, "Well, how was it?"

"Very pleasant," he said. "You have interesting friends."

She laughed. "You mean Mr. Pedantic? I saw you two by the tree. I hope Frank didn't bore you. He really means well."

"Not at all. I enjoyed it. Until tonight I assumed everyone around here either wore a uniform or had one hanging in the attic. It was nice getting a different slant on things." Then, catching himself, he said, "Whoops. Don't misunderstand. I'm not complaining."

"I didn't think you were," she said, moving closer.

They were beside the road, moonlight filtering through the pines.

"You're the most electrifying woman I've..." he paused, unable to attach words to his thoughts. "What? Seen? Met? Known? You realize I don't I don't know what I'm saying." And throwing up his hands, "Let try again. It's wonderful being with you. Well, there! I finally completed a simple declarative sentence. Some lawyer."

She smiled. "I know how you feel. I felt it Sunday, too."

They came together and kissed, softly at first, then forcefully.

75

CHAPTER EIGHT (1960)

It was Wednesday, during a mid-afternoon lull at Jack's Diner. The four men were gathered in the rear as they had at that first meeting two years earlier—Gava and Testa, their backs to the wall, Julie and Renato Crotone, or Reni, as he preferred, opposite them. And while Reni was no longer flexing his muscles and intimidating Julie, he still tended to brood. Since that first day, Julie had learned the thirty-five year old henchman was Gava's driver, bodyguard and confidant. His lifestyle, like his attire, was Spartan, and when not tending to Gava he could be found shooting pool at the Playdrome, off Unionport Road, or hefting weights at the local gym. Drafted at eighteen, he'd served five months of a two-year Army hitch before getting bounced with a less-than-honorable discharge, which, according Nunzio, rightly should've been a long stretch in Leavenworth had his victim—his company NCO—survived to ID him. Under the circumstances, the best the Army could do was to declare Corporal Crotone unsuitable for military service and rid itself of him. Free again, the high school dropout returned home and signed on with the Sanitation Department, where he was recruited by a local shylock to

77

perform odd jobs. Preferring money to garbage, he soon became a persuasive collector, which is how Gava found him.

"I want a couple minutes with Julie," Gava announced. And when they were alone, he asked, "You think it matters who wins the election next year?"

Repeating Kelly's mantra, he said, "We're going to see changes regardless of who's elected."

Gava nodded, his weak eye fluttering. "We're going to need money, lots of it," he said.

Julie had since discovered the term for Gava's affliction was amblyopia; a condition the medical journals claimed was caused by the eyes not being aligned. He'd read that in some instances the eyelid simply drooped rather than wander as Gava's did, and if properly diagnosed in childhood it was treatable, which clearly hadn't occurred with him.

"You ain't like the rest. You got the education but you also got vision, which is why I'm counting on you to tell me when you see an opening. No matter how small, you tell me and we'll grab it. Whatever it takes—muscle, money—we're going for it. You follow me?"

Julie wanted to say, *No, I haven't a clue.* Instead he nodded dutifully, certain he'd glean more as they went on.

"Another thing," Gava said hunching forward. "What you find out down there is strictly between us, unless I say otherwise. And when you need to reach me, go through Reni or Nunzio, nobody else. The point is, nobody can know or even think we're expanding, or we lose our edge. Another thing. You can't be coming to New York so much. It'll be tough on your family, but you gotta cut back. That's the way it has to be."

"Whatever you say, Don Paolo." He was wondering where this was leading when a loud clatter had all heads turning toward the front, where a stack of empty saucepans had fallen off the counter.

"Sorryboutthat!" Slim shouted as he bent to retrieve them.

"Better be more careful," Testa warned, as he and Reni holstered their revolvers, Slim gazing up and nodding.

His right eye flickering wildly now, Gava chomped on his nearly-consumed Davidoff Cuban cigar, its distinctive white and brown band still attached, and said, "I've had it with this fucking joint! From now on no more public meets." Then, calming himself, he lowered his voice and said, "Besides, it's better people don't see us together. As you probably already figured out, there ain't many people we can trust. One day somebody's on the team, the next he's crossed over. What it comes down to is, you don't want to wind up like your old man."

"Is that what this is about, the other families?" he said with an uneasy feeling.

"It's always about the other families," Gava told him. "Our Sicilian cousins don't think like us. They're like an octopus," he said, setting his cigar aside and splaying his manicured fingers across the table. "They ain't happy unless they got their arms around all the action. This business we're in, it's like being in the middle of the ocean with those fucking whirlpools. You ever see whirlpools?"

Julie nodded, not sure if he had, but knowing what they were.

"They pop up anywhere, anytime. And whatever's around gets sucked down. Just like that!" he said, snapping his fingers. "It's the same with us. Today, the water's calm. Tomorrow, who knows? But one thing's for sure. If you ain't alert…, Well you get the idea."

In his own way, Gava was affirming Kelly's notion about being ready for change.

"In Italy," he went on, pursuing his nautical theme, "when somebody asks, 'How's it going?' they answer, 'The big fish eats the little fish.' In other words, everything's normal, because that's how life is. Out there," he said grabbing his cigar and stabbing it at the street, "is a load of big fish doing business and figuring they're safe because they got everything tied up nice and neat. Then along comes a bigger fish," he said thumping his chest, "and everything changes."

So much for the truce between the families, Julie mused.

In the next instant Gava was signaling the others. "Don't get up," he said, rising. "We'll talk soon." Then, dropping his cigar on the tile floor and crushing it beneath his heel, he added, "Someplace quiet."

* * *

Soon after returning to Washington, Julie fell in with Bob Jeffries, a young ambitious Florida Democrat on the powerful Merchant Marine and Fisheries Committee, who, like several other freshmen colleagues forced to live on a tight budget, had opted for geographical bachelorhood. Together, they began hitting various nightspots, with Julie always reaching for the tab.

It was Friday, shortly before six, when they strolled into Mr. Smith's, a Georgetown bistro popular with the young professional set. Working their way through the crowd, they elbowed a place at the bar, and called out their order. By seven, getting the bartender's attention required stamina. With his back to the door, Jeffries hadn't noticed the two secretaries who'd come up beside him.

Leaning into him, Julie said, "Don't look now, but we have a couple of damsels in distress. What do you say we come to their rescue?"

Jeffries glanced over, and the one closest to him, a fresh scrubbed, raven-haired gal in a snug cardigan, offered him an encouraging smile. "It sure would be the proper thing to do," he said with an impish grin.

By the time they'd finished their second round, he was entertaining them with backroom tales of Congress. Later, when the crowd thinned, and Julie suggested heading across the bridge to his place in Arlington for a nightcap, the girl who'd attached herself to Jeffries demurred, saying it was late and she had early plans the following morning.

"Don't be a pill," Jeffries coaxed her. "We're honorable men." And when she raised an eyebrow, he pointed to Julie and said, "He'll vouch for me. Won't you?" he asked him.

"But who'll vouch for him?" she said grinning.

"He will," Jeffries said, indicating the bartender. "Right, pal?"

"Sure. I'd trust him with my daughter, if I had one."

"There you go," Jeffries said. "What better endorsement can you ask for than an upright citizen of Georgetown."

She was laughing now. "Okay, but just one drink."

The charade over, they left and quickly hailed a cab. With room for three, Jeffries offered his lap, and she willingly took it.

"We're here, you two," Julie said paying the driver when they pulled up to the curved entrance of the River House, "time to take it inside."

Bleary-eyed and lipstick-smeared, Jeffries emerged on wobbly legs and, looking around, immediately caught Julie's sleeve, exclaiming, "What the hell are we doing *here*?!"

"My place for a drink, remember?"

"*Your* place? *I* live here!"

"What a coincidence. I'm on sixteen."

"Jesus, I'm on twelve," he said, his expression suggesting maybe this wasn't such a good idea.

"Then you won't have far to drive," Julie said, leading them up the steps and across the spacious lobby.

At the bank of elevators, Jeffries stood stiffly with his back to the front desk, trying vainly to distance himself from his partner, who seemed anxious to continue where they'd left off in the cab. Nor did he relax on the ride up. It wasn't until they were safely in Julie's apartment that he loosened up again.

"Say, this is some view," his companion said gazing out at the Pentagon and the brightly lit Capitol in the distance.

"What'll you have?" Julie asked, opening the liquor cabinet.

"The bed," she said, and in the next instant she was leading Jeffries in the direction Julie had pointed.

"I guess that takes care of that," Julie told her friend when the door had shut behind them. "You two did fine tonight."

"What about you?" she said cozying up to him. "Don't you want a little something? You paid for it."

"Don't be stupid," he told her. "There's only one John, and he's in there." Then, pressing several bills in her hand, he steered her to the door. "The desk clerk'll call you a cab."

Should Jeffries ask about her in the morning, Julie would tell him he'd struck out. But Jeffries never asked. Instead, he emerged from the guest room and headed directly for the coffee pot.

"God, she was fantastic," he said after she'd left. "We need to get together more often, neighbor."

* * *

That was February. The following July, while Nixon was nailing down his party's presidential endorsement in Chicago, and Kennedy and Johnson were battling it out in Los Angeles, gang warfare erupted again in New York. To the uninitiated it appeared to be another turf grab, with the usual mid-day shootings and kidnappings. But as Julie quickly learned from Nunzio, it was more complicated than the Gallo brothers making a move against Profaci, as reported in the news.

"Where you calling from?" Nunzio demanded.

"Don't worry, it's clean. I haven't used it before," he said from a pay phone in Union Station. "What's going on up there?"

"It's got nothing to do with us. The commission's forcing Profaci to come to them for help," he explained.

Thinking of the headlines, Julie said, "Are they nuts?"

"That's how it's done," his uncle said. "They give the Gallos the nod to expand into Profaci's territory and then refuse to step in to settle it. The big guy," he said, referring to the top boss, "told the others to stay out of it. Up to now, most of the dead are Gallo soldiers but that'll turn around soon."

"How do you figure?"

"Profaci's laying low in Florida and his men ain't getting the leadership they need, and that'll cost him before it's over."

"And when will that be?" Julie asked, certain he'd never understand how these people conducted their internal affairs.

"That's the sixty-four dollar question. Not right away, that's for sure."

"You realize this is insane, encouraging open warfare like this. We don't need this publicity."

Nunzio gave a short laugh. "Now you sound like Gava. He don't like it either, but the Sicilians, they got their own ways. They use the hungry ones like the Gallos to keep guys like Profaci from getting too big. In the end, the Gallos'll get a bone and Profaci'll lose some power. It all evens out."

"Getting and keeping power."

"Exactly. Now, be smart and don't talk about it. And forget about coming up for a while. There's a lot of bad blood, you could get hurt."

Once again, the old anger boiled within him. "Like my father?"

"Yeah."

Before hanging up, he said, "Tell Gava there's talk of Hoover cutting the number of agents assigned to mob activities and reassigning them to hunt Commies."

"The boss'll like that."

"It's one of those arrangements where he voices concern about the Communist threat, and Congress responds by boosting defense spending in key districts, which, in turn, gains him support on the Hill. It's a sweet deal for everybody."

"Even us."

"Not if we don't keep a low profile, and avoid face-offs like this blowup between Gallo and Profaci."

"You're gonna do better than yer old man," Nunzio assured him.

Julie prayed he was right.

CHAPTER NINE

Another Washington scorcher made worse by oppressive humidity, led Julie to accept Vinnie Monte's invitation to catch the late races at Laurel Race Course.

"Look," he told Julie, indicating a string of bettors at the window. "That guy's one of my cousin's regulars."

"Your cousin?"

"Yeah, runs a small book in Baltimore."

Julie turned and saw Kelly. "Which one?" he asked, wanting to be certain.

"The tall, skinny jamoke at the twenty dollar window with his nose in the program. Looks like a schoolteacher."

"You sure?"

"Sure I'm sure. I seen him around plenty. Nice guy, but he can't stay away from the ponies."

"How's he do?"

Monte shook his head. "Can't pick his nose. Kinda guy'd fall in a barrel of tits and come out sucking his thumb."

Julie laughed. "I know him," he said, turning away. "Let's head over to the clubhouse."

Later, in the parking lot, he told Monte, "Do me a favor and have your cousin call me."

Several days later, Julie invited Kelly boating, telling him to bring a date.

* * *

"Frank doesn't look at all well," Nikki observed as they approached the city dock.

"Probably afraid of getting seasick. He'll perk up once we're underway."

Kelly helped his companion aboard and made the necessary introductions. They learned she worked at Social Security, which was where Nikki said he found most of his dates.

"You okay?" Julie asked once Kelly had settled in beside him.

"I'm fine," he replied with little enthusiasm. "Where're we headed?"

"Kent Island. Been there?"

Kelly shook his head, and the conversation ended there.

As they rounded the Naval Station, Julie leaned over and said, "I know about your problem."

Kelly turned sharply. "What're you talking about?!"

"Take it easy. I just want you to know I'm available if you need help, is all."

"I don't have a problem," he said, squaring his shoulders. "At least none that concerns you."

"Okay. Forget I mentioned it."

Several minutes later, Kelly asked, "What'd you hear?"

"That you're in deep with a bookie, and now it's pay-up time."

"How'd you...?"

"Find out? At a dockworkers meeting in Baltimore a few days ago. One of the guys mentioned booking white-collar bettors around town, and when he said he does business with your organization I asked if he knew you. He said he not only knows you, but that you're a deadbeat. I said he must be thinking of somebody else, but he insisted, saying you're into him and won't pay. I looked at this palooka and thought, Frank's in trouble."

"That isn't true!" Kelly said with a quick glance aft. Then lowering his voice, he said, "I didn't say I *wouldn't* pay. I said I couldn't pay the whole thing at once."

Julie shook his head. "I'm guessing that wasn't what he wanted to hear."

Kelly didn't respond. He didn't have to.

"Sounds bad, my friend." Adding, when Kelly let out a humorless laugh, "Look. I wouldn't do this for anybody, but Nikki thinks highly of you, and so do I."

His eyes widened. "She knows?!"

"Of course not. What do you take me for?"

"You don't understand. This gets around I could lose my job."

"What I heard stays with me. I only mention it because I want to help." And when Kelly didn't reply, "I'm not offering to give you the money. I'll lend it to you. I'm sure you're good for it."

His shoulders sagged. "It's been a hell of a week. First I got this call out of the blue telling me I'm over the limit. I said, 'I didn't know I had a limit.' And he says, 'It's a flexible thing.' Then he goes on about me having done it before, but because things were better then he carried me. This time, he says he's in a bind and needs the whole nut—principal and interest by next Wednesday." He was talking fast, a man unburdening himself.

"When I said I didn't have that kind of money, he said I'd better come up with it or I could expect a visit at the office. And if I still didn't pay up things would get messy." He looked as if he might cry. "He said he didn't like squeezing me—wouldn't do it if he didn't have to—but he had obligations, too, and wasn't getting his head busted to save mine. I'm screwed," he concluded with a sigh.

"How deep are you into him?"

"Twenty-six hundred."

Julie uttered a low whistle. "And how short are you?"

"I can put my hands on five, six hundred, maybe another three with luck." Then shaking his head, "If only I had more time."

"What about your family?"

He stiffened. "Impossible! I can't go to them."

"I guess not," Julie said. Then, after a moment, "I can get my hands on it for you."

"You can?" he said hopefully. "The whole thing?"

Julie nodded.

Kelly considered the offer then shook his head. "That's very kind of you, but I can't let you do it. It's not your problem."

"Don't be foolish. You don't want to mess around with these guys."

"It's a lot of money."

"You'll have it Tuesday, I promise. You can pay me back at five percent."

"But…" Kelly protested weakly.

"If it makes you feel better, the banks are paying four and a half, so it's a good deal for me. Now," he said, clapping his shoulder, "let's show the gals a good time."

* * *

He'd been right about Kelly. Given an easy solution to his problem, it didn't take him long to fall back into debt again, which meant it was time to see Gava.

Following Nunzio's directions, he arrived in New York, changed trains and headed north into Putnam County, and the town of Brewster, where the local taxi ferried him ten more miles to Lake Carmel. As the cab crested the last hill, he looked out over the sparsely populated valley and smiled. Gava had chosen well. It was a place where strangers would surely stand out. The finger-shaped lake looked to be about two miles long and barely a few hundred feet wide. On the main road paralleling the lake they passed several gin mills, a combination hardware-appliance store, a drive-in theater bordered by a Dairy Queen and miniature golf course, a general market, and not much else. Clearly, this wasn't a tourist destination.

After crossing a narrow bridge at the south end of the lake and following the shoreline past several mailboxes, Julie leaned across the seat and pointed to a hedgerow. "In there," he said, indicating the unpaved driveway.

The small cabin sat away from its neighbors on a spit of land that sloped gently to the water's edge.

Julie paid the driver and sent him away with a generous tip. Tired and stiff from the journey, he stood in the long shadows and stretched, enjoying the cool breeze off the lake. A column of smoke and the accompanying aroma of barbeque led him to the backyard, where Gava was busy shuffling a pile of thick steaks along an enormous stone grill.

"*Benvenuto*," he called without pausing or turning.

"Nice place," Julie said, thinking it odd to see him without his retinue.

"Beats the hell outta that volcano down there," he said, waving a pair of steel tongs south toward the city. "It's gotta be worse in Washington. What is it, about two hundred miles?" he said, while testing the wellness of the meat with his fingers.

"From here, more like two-fifty," Julie said, his stomach rumbling. "It isn't the Deep South, but it sure feels like it sometimes. They say it was swampland before some genius decided to make it the capital."

"Hungry?" Gava asked, pulling off his apron and wiping his hands with it.

"I could eat," he said, noticing the holstered revolver looped through his belt.

"Good. C'mon, I'll show you your room."

As they passed through the kitchen Julie was tempted to snatch a hunk of bread from the counter and plunge it into the simmering tomato sauce, and would have had he been alone.

"This is yours any time you want it," Gava said, pushing open the door to a small, but tidy bedroom, which judging from the floor plan, likely mirrored Gava's across the hall. "Come outside when you're ready. The others are on the way." From the kitchen, he called, "Try the sauce."

Julie was in the bathroom toweling his face when he heard the crunch of tires. The others, he was about to learn, were twenty or so relatives and friends from the Bronx who'd settled in the area, and were now seated at three long tables. Like the meal, the conversation was casual and unhurried and proceeded without reference to the organization—as if it didn't exist—which Julie found odd, since everyone knew of Gava's position in it. As soon as the tables were cleared and the food put away, everyone said their farewells, leaving as abruptly as they'd arrived.

"Grab one of those," Gava said when they were alone, taking a chair and dragging it to the water's edge, where he stretched his legs. Once comfortable, he pulled out a cigar, lit it, and said, "This is the life. When I retire, this is where I'm coming."

A pleasant thought, Julie mused, but he didn't believe him—not that he didn't wish to settle here, rather that he'd never retire. Still, he went along. "You couldn't pick a nicer place."

Pointing to the lights at the north end of the lake, Gava said, "That's Lakeview, my cousin Sal's joint. Best pizza around. 'Course, like most businesses around here, I own a piece of it."

"I should've guessed."

"A man's gotta protect himself."

Alone under the stars, and aware voices carried across the still water, they fell into a hushed conversation, with Julie telling Gava of Kelly, and what he planned for him. And when he concluded and sought Gava's consent to proceed, it was given without qualification.

"Go for it," he said. Adding, "It'll be nice when we finally get out from under the Sicilians." And when Julie asked what he had in mind, he replied, "First, let's see where this Kelly thing leads."

* * *

Julie fumbled for the phone, managing a sleepy, "Hullo."

"You still in bed?" the youthful voice teased.

"Sis? What time is it?" he said, certain he'd only just fallen asleep. And when she told him eight o'clock, he groaned.

The night before, he'd found Jeffries's note beneath his door. *Call me*, he'd scrawled, signaling he was ready for another trip to Georgetown. After the fifth or sixth outing, in which they always managed to encounter two accommodating secretaries, Julie decided Jeffries was either incredibly naïve, or he understood the game fully and was content to allow Julie to be his de facto pimp. At least now Jeffries was comfortable enough using his own apartment; still, these late nights were consuming valuable sleep time.

"Shit. You'd sleep your life away," she said.

"Hey!" he said, sitting up. "Watch your mouth, young lady." Then, swinging his feet to the floor, he thought of his mother and asked, "Is anything wrong?"

"Everything's fine. I was just wondering when you're coming home, is all."

All she knew of his life was that he worked with and not for the government.

"I was thinking of Thanksgiving. If you can wait that long."

"Terrific!" Then, with a touch of mischief, "You coming alone?" She'd been needling him about Nikki since he'd first mentioned her.

"You're as subtle as a sledge hammer. As a matter of fact, I'm planning to invite her. That is, if it's okay with you."

"Coool," she said with youthful exuberance.

He looked at the clock when he hung up. In a few hours he'd be meeting with Monte's cousin again.

* * *

When Kelly called several weeks later he was ecstatic. "Great news! Starting next month I'll be an assistant deputy commissioner."

"Congratulations!" Julie said. "When do we celebrate?"

"Actually, that's why I'm calling. How's the week after next, the Wednesday before Thanksgiving? I want you and Nikki to be my guests for dinner. Can you make it?" He sounded like a schoolboy.

"Are you kidding? We wouldn't miss it."

There was a slight pause. "Even though it's in Philadelphia?"

"Philly?"

"It'd mean a lot, you two being there."

"Then count us in."

Kelly wasn't the only one celebrating. When Julie strode into Jeffries' office several days later he was greeted by a sea of smiles.

"Happy days are here again!" the receptionist cried.

Julie laughed. "Only if you're a Democrat."

"Mister Vittorio, who did you vote for?" she asked with a wink.

"That's for me to know." Then, "Is his lordship in?"

She winked again. "For you, always."

He found Jeffries brooding at the window. "Why so glum?"

Jeffries waved him in. "I was thinking how badly this country needs new leadership, and how we almost missed the opportunity."

"That's history," Julie said, knowing what Jeffries didn't about the organization's role in the election. "Kennedy won. What does it matter by how much?"

"You're right, of course. A win's a win. I suppose I should be grateful."

"Exactly. Take it anyway you can. So how's it feel having a Democrat in the White House?"

"Terrific." Then, thoughtfully, "The country needs someone with his energy. Once he's in office there'll be big changes." He was speaking with the confidence of one whose power was about to increase tenfold. "It's been a helluva ride," he said, moving to his desk.

Julie nodded. "Delivering those Southern Baptist votes wasn't easy."

Jeffries frowned. "And those goddamn Brahmans better remember it come January."

"They'd be fools not to," Julie assured him.

"It's a strange town. Anything can happen."

"Don't worry. You'll get what's coming to you." Then, smiling, "How about dinner? You're probably ready for a little fun."

Jefferies grinned. "You must've read my mind, pardner. How about Georgetown? I'm feeling lucky."

* * *

September and October were busy months for Julie and Nikki. Each was occupied with their own affairs;

he expanding both the legal and illegal aspects of the Washington operation, and she attending to the new class of plebes. But that was about to change with the long Thanksgiving holiday. She hadn't seen him for three weeks, and she missed him terribly. If as recently as six months ago anyone suggested she'd be romantically involved again she'd have thought them crazy, but here she was standing anxiously by the front door, her suitcase packed, stealing glances down the street.

The trip north held the promise of new adventures, beginning with Kelly's dinner in Philadelphia, followed by her first visit to New York. They took the scenic route rather than the interstate, and in Philadelphia visited Independence Hall. That evening they met Kelly at Bookbinder's, one of the city's oldest and finest restaurants. Of the other dinner guests, all were family except Father Barone, Villanova's Dean of Students. To everyone's amusement, each of them celebrated Kelly's promotion by sharing stories of his boyhood.

Toward the end of the evening, Julie raised his glass and, addressing Kelly, said, "Nikki and I thank you for including us in this special celebration, Frank. A man's success has its roots in his family, and yours clearly has made the difference. Please accept our best wishes for continued success, and may good fortune continue to smile upon you."

With that, Nikki presented Kelly their gift. "From both of us," she said, "with sincere congratulations."

Kelly blushed. "You shouldn't have. You've done so much already."

"You've been a good friend," she said, not understanding his last comment.

He opened it and gasped. "It's beautiful," he said of the hand-tooled cordovan leather attaché case. "I'm speechless."

"That's a first," Julie said, drawing laughs.

Now it was the priest's turn. Smiling, he set his glass down and spoke of Kelly's academic achievements at Villanova, including his four years on the Dean's List. It was a touching tribute and, Julie thought, an appropriate way to conclude the evening.

As they were leaving, Kelly again thanked them for the expensive gift, while also telling Julie how much he appreciated his help.

"Anytime," he said. "And I mean anytime."

As they walked away Nikki wondered aloud what Frank meant about Julie helping him.

"I guess he's grateful for our friendship," he said with a shrug.

The following morning, as they crossed the George Washington Bridge into New York, he asked, "You nervous?"

"A little," she admitted without shifting her gaze from the city.

"Don't be. They're going to love you, just as I do."

Moments later they crossed Harlem River and she saw the grimier side of the city.

"Welcome to the Bronx," he said. "Named for Jonas Bronck, a Swedish sea captain who sailed for the Dutch and settled here in 1639. Also home to Fiorello LaGuardia, Tony Curtis, June Allyson, Sal Mineo, Bobby Darin, and the Piccirilli brothers."

"Okay," she said grinning, "I'll bite. Who are the Piccirilli brothers?"

"They were sculptors. Born in Pisa and emigrated here."

"And why would I know them?"

"You've seen their work, I'm sure."

"I have?"

"The statue of Abraham Lincoln in Washington."

"What's their connection?"

"They carved it."

"How interesting. Any other Bronx celebrities I should know of?"

"Too many to name. But there's one I particularly admire. Collis P. Huntington."

"And he is?" she asked, keeping the game going.

"Was," he corrected. "He's long dead. Ol' C. P. made a fortune selling groceries to miners during the California gold rush, and later bought up railroads, enough of them that he could literally cross the country without ever leaving his own property."

"And that appeals to you?"

"Yep," he said, holding his grin.

The road had dropped below street level, with rows of tenements blocking out the skyline.

"This is the Cross Bronx Expressway," he said as they passed skeletal remains of abandoned cars.

"Looks like a war zone."

"It's not a place you want to get stuck after midnight."

"Somehow I thought you lived in a less urban area."

"I do," he assured her. "It gets better once we reach Parkchester," he said, pointing to a line of buildings in the distance.

When she could bear it no longer, she said, "I don't mean to sound critical, but would you mind slowing a bit?"

"I've never had an accident," he said easing off the pedal.

She nodded, but kept still.

As promised, the landscape improved as the tenements gave way to single-family homes. Even the highway widened and brightened, but the traffic remained steady.

"Country Club Road," she read once they exited the expressway. "Not quite country unless one compares it to what we just drove through."

"It's changed since I was a kid," he said of the tree-lined street. "There were fewer houses and room in the street to play stickball."

She laughed. "Stick ball? That conjures up all kinds of images. Just where is it that you stick the ball?"

"You know," he said with a grin, "there're expressions you assume have universal meaning until someone like you comes along, and suddenly they sound silly. That's one of them. We've got a lot to learn about each other."

"I hope the experience won't be too traumatic," she joked.

He rounded the corner where the sign on the post read *No Thru Street*. They passed a line of tall hedges and soon turned onto a curving driveway. "Welcome to Villa Vittorio," he announced, nodding at the graceful Victorian, and the sparkling Sound beyond it.

Her eyes widened. "It's so unlike the Bronx we just left. I'm impressed."

"Good. I'd hoped you'd be. It's much nicer when everything's in bloom. It was my father's joy."

She followed his gaze and sensed he was retreating to some special time.

Pointing to the cars parked beside the barn-like structure, he said, "Show time."

"I promise to be on my best behavior," she said.

His sister was out the front door and bouncing down the steps before he'd shut off the engine. "Finally!" she shouted, ignoring him and running for Nikki. "Hi, I'm Anna Marie. Welcome to the Bronx. I understand it's your first visit."

Nikki grinned and, taking the girl's hand, said, "So nice to meet you. I've heard a great deal about you."

"Oh, I love your accent."

"Hey, sport, what about me?" Julie called, as she led Nikki away.

"Welcome home," she shouted over her shoulder.

They were in the living room, encircled by family by the time he joined them, Anna standing as close to Nikki as possible, a post she maintained throughout supper.

"Well," he whispered to his mother, "what do you think?"

"She's charming."

"You're going to love her," he told her.

Later, after dinner, when they were finally alone, Julie suggested taking a walk.

"It would be terribly rude to just leave."

"Nonsense," he said. "It'll give them a chance to talk about you."

The sun had set and the temperature was colder now, causing them to walk against the chill wind with their collars up and hands stuffed inside their pockets.

"Here's where we played," he said standing in the center of the Y intersection, the street lamp casting shadows from the leafless branches above them. "We pretty much had the street to ourselves then."

"Stick ball?"

He laughed. "Yeah. You were pretty much assured of a homerun if you hit to that corner," he said, pointing down the street. "And over there was the center of our universe," he said, indicating the red and white metal *Coca-Cola* sign above the darkened store.

"Rudy's and Tony's Luncheonette," she read aloud.

"I'll take you there tomorrow and introduce you to a New York staple—the egg cream."

"Is it anything like Eggs Benedict?" And when he laughed, she said, "Another of those queer expressions, like stick ball?"

"'Fraid so."

As they walked, she asked, "What are those peculiar Stonehenge things?"

"Fig trees," he said, matter-of-factly.

"It's getting so I don't know when to believe you. Must be some exotic flora."

"Nobody says flora around here."

"That's part of my charm," she said, leaning in and kissing him. "I've wanted to do that since we stepped from the car."

"What took so long?"

"Never mind. You were saying."

"They wouldn't survive the winter if they weren't wrapped in layers like that. You can usually tell by them where the Italians live."

"Then we must be in Italy," she said glancing around.

"Close. Some call it Little Italy, others are less charitable."

She nodded knowingly.

They continued toward the water. "As long as we're heading down memory lane, what's the story behind your name?" she asked.

"I wondered when you'd get around to that. There isn't much to tell."

"Let me be the judge."

He shrugged. "In ancient Rome men had three names. The second one identified them as a member of a specific clan, and served as proof of citizenship. For example, Julius Caesar was actually Caius Julius Caesar, which put him in the Julia clan. Anyway, at some point before I was born Mom got it into her head that she's descended from the Julias who occupied the Campania region, where Naples is. No one but she believes it, and we're not sure she really does, but she was so adamant that my father went along."

"That's it?"

"Yep."

She looked at him for a long beat. "It makes a good story."

Chapter Ten (1961)

"What's he into you for?" Julie asked Pino, Kelly's bookie.

"Exactly eighteen big ones."

Julie nodded. "That's good. Tell me when he hits twenty-five hundred."

"The rate he's going," the bookie offered, "that shouldn't be long. Probably another month."

The sooner the better, he thought, before asking, "How're you fixed for cash?"

"I could use an infusion," the man from Baltimore replied. "Not everyone's got your pal's bad luck. I took a few hits over the holidays with the college tournaments."

"You'll have it by the weekend. Meanwhile, remember this is between us."

"Fine by me," he said, his tone suggesting he could care less about Kelly's debt, as long as he didn't have to carry it.

Once back in Virginia, Julie phoned the president of the Tucson Merchants Bank of Commerce and Savings, in Arizona, using the number Testa had provided.

"Mr. Mendenhall's office," the secretary announced cheerfully.

"Please put him on."

"What is this about?" she asked.

"Just say Mr. Caesar wishes to speak with him."

"Mr. Caesar?" she repeated, wanting to be sure she heard it correctly. If it were any other name, she'd have been more resolute, and likely passed him off to one of Mendenhall's assistants. But she'd been sternly warned several days earlier by her corpulent boss to put this particular caller through immediately. He'd made that point the moment he strode into the bank when, rather than offering his usual greeting, he stood before her desk looking tense and out of sorts, telling her, "I'm expecting an extremely important call from a Mr. Caesar. I don't know when it will come, but whenever it does you are to put him through to me at once. Do you understand?" he said, before retreating to his office, where he continued brooding over the early morning call from New York, the caller telling him what he needed to do when Mr. Caesar contacted him. It had not been a pleasant conversation.

Now, three days later, she checked the name on the note she'd kept on her desk and said, "Yes, sir. He'll be right with you, Mr. Caesar." Then she ran to deliver the message.

"How long's he been waiting?" Mendenhall asked grabbing the phone.

When Julie had said all he had to, he asked, "Any questions?"

"No," the banker replied, "none at all. It's all perfectly clear."

* * *

It was mid-February before Kelly's bookie called again. "I got good and bad news," he said with an uneasy tone.

"Let's have it," Julie said, fearing his plans were in jeopardy.

"Our friend's been on a roller coaster. It started with a string of winners."

This must be the bad news, Julie thought. He hadn't counted on Kelly getting lucky.

"Then just when I figure he's about to get out of the hole, he lays on some heavy action which I'm happy to report turned south," the bookie said. "And that's when he doubled up."

"So what's the bad news?"

There was a brief pause. "That's it. He went over the twenty-five hundred."

Julie smiled. "What's he owe?"

"Four grand. Forty-one hundred, to be exact. It happened fast," he said, fearing he'd have to eat the difference. "If I turned him off he'd have taken his action down the street, and I know you didn't want that. He was like a dog in heat."

"Don't worry. You did right. I'll cover it," he said, before telling him what he wanted next.

* * *

Two weeks later, a Friday, Julie met Kelly at a small seafood restaurant near Baltimore's inner harbor. It was their first meeting since the celebration in Philadelphia. When he arrived, he found Kelly at the far end of the bar staring cheerlessly into a double Scotch on the rocks.

"How's it going, Mr. Commissioner?" he said setting beside him.

Kelly gazed up and, sighing, shook his head. "Not too good."

Julie looked surprised. "I don't get it. Last time we met everything was rosy."

"It's incredible how quickly things can turn around," he said. "I should've passed on this lousy promotion and stayed where I was."

"It can't be that bad."

"My whole life's wrapped up implementing phase two of our new program."

Julie clapped him on the back. "Cheer up. A little more work, a lot more prestige. It comes with the territory."

But he didn't cheer up, and throughout dinner the conversation lagged. Finally, tired of Kelly's sulking, Julie pushed his plate away and said, "Okay, enough already. I didn't drive up here to watch you brood all night."

Kelly shifted uneasily. "I'm sorry. I don't mean to be a jerk. It's just that I have a lot on my mind."

"All the more reason to put it aside. It's the weekend, relax."

"I suppose you're right," he said forcing a smile.

"There you go." But when Kelly didn't perk up, he said, "Is there something else?"

Kelly looked at him with moon eyes and nodded.

"Women trouble?"

"No, nothing like that."

"Worse?"

"Afraid so."

"Look, if there's anything I can do…,"

Kelly studied him, and for a moment Julie thought he was about to say something, but he gulped his drink instead.

"You sure you don't want to talk about it, Frank? Sometimes it helps to get it out. Get a different slant on it."

Kelly chewed his lower lip. "I really stepped in it this time."

"That bad?"

Kelly nodded. "A nightmare."

Julie waited.

His shoulders slumping, he said, "What's the use, you're going to find out anyway. I screwed up." Wringing his hands, he said, "I'm into the bookies again."

Julie took no pleasure in his discomfit, but this was business. "I thought that was over. What happened?"

"I wish the hell I knew. It all turned to shit so fast." Reluctantly, he told him, "I was laying down a few bets, nothing I couldn't handle with the new pay raise. I even had a string of wins, a few more and I could've squared things with you." Now, struggling to meet Julie's gaze, he said, "What with the new job and all, I guess I got careless."

Yeah, sure, blame it on the job, he thought. "How careless, Frank?"

"I feel like such a fool."

"Don't be so hard on yourself. It could happen to anybody. How much?"

"A bundle," he said, quickly adding, "But I was okay with that. I mean, all I needed was a few good wins and I'd be all right. Then, two weeks ago my bookie tells me his business went south. 'Too many big hits,' he said.

Told me his back was against the wall and without cash he'd have to go to the bank. You know," he sympathized, "sometimes even those guys get their nuts in a vise. Anyway, the thing is, he said I had to clear the books."

When Julie asked why he hadn't come to him, Kelly grimaced. "How could I after the last time? Instead, I leaned on my family for a short-term loan. God love them, they scraped up twelve hundred. That was two weeks ago. I promised him the rest in a week." Sweat was beading on his forehead. "I've been avoiding him since."

Julie shook his head. "Not a good idea."

"I know, I know," he said wiping his mouth. "The other night I spotted him outside my building."

"Did he see you?"

"No. I turned around and went back to the office and slept there." He was twisting his napkin. "I don't know what to do."

Julie asked, "What're we talking about? What's the bottom line?"

Kelly heaved a sigh. "Including the interest from the last two weeks," he said with a painful expression, "I'm down nearly four thousand."

"*Four thousand?*"

Kelly nodded grimly. "I told you it was bad."

"What about the twelve hundred?"

"I already gave him that. The balance is four thousand."

They sat in silence until Julie said, "I may be able to help you."

Kelly blinked. "Seriously? You can get that kind of cash?"

"It won't be easy, but, yes, I think so."

"Oh, sweet Jesus!" he said with a burst of energy. "You don't know what this means."

"I can guess. Besides, I'm sure you'd do the same for me if I were in your shoes."

"Oh, I would, you know I would." Then, thinking ahead, "When could you have it?"

He considered the question. "A day, maybe two," he said, marveling at how willingly Kelly accepted the offer this time.

More animated now, Kelly squared his shoulders, promising, "No more after this, I swear. This is my wakeup call. You do this for me and I'm off the ponies for good."

"I don't usually preach, but that's a wise decision. Meanwhile, I suggest laying low, maybe call in sick Monday."

"Good idea," he said, suddenly noticing his food. After a few bites, he asked again, "You're sure you can get it, I mean the whole four thousand?" And when Julie said he was fairly certain, Kelly grinned. "You don't know what this means to me."

Julie smiled. "I'm glad I can help." Then, looking around, he said, "You probably shouldn't be hanging around here. Why don't you go home and read a book. I'll call when I have it."

"You're the best," Kelly said, grabbing the check. "This one's on me."

Outside in the parking lot, they were sidestepping patches of ice and paying little attention to the three men coming their way. As they passed each other Kelly felt a hand on his shoulder, and suddenly his feet flew from under him.

"My glasses! I dropped my glasses," he cried as he landed.

"Fuck your glasses," the man said hauling him up and tossing him like a rag doll against a nearby car, the side mirror slamming into his kidney, pain shooting through him. "Where's the fuckin' money?" he said holding Kelly there, his steamy breath washing over him.

"No! Wait! It's taken care of, I swear," he said, unable to bring the face into focus. Then, waving blindly, "My friend, he'll tell you! Ask him," he cried before the heavy fist slammed into his stomach, and everything came up.

"Sonofabitch! Little bastard puked on me!" the man yelled, releasing his grip and dropping Kelly to his knees.

Now, clenching his stomach and struggling to breathe, he took a painful kick in his shoulder that had him rolling into his vomit, and then another that caught him behind the ear. "I'll have it," he sobbed, covering his head, "I swear."

"You're gonna get a lot worse you don't have it by Monday. You got that?" he said, his foot glancing off Kelly's ribs.

"Yes, yes. No more, please," he begged.

"This ain't nothin', you fuckin' deadbeat."

The assault took barely a minute, but it was like being hit by a truck. When the next blow didn't come, he raised his head and peered through his hands. The three men were shadows in the distance.

"Don't move, Frank. You're going to be okay," Julie said, handing him his shattered glasses.

Kelly looked at him and retched again.

* * *

His injuries improved over the weekend, but not his shattered psyche. Alone and distraught, he stayed locked in his apartment, lamenting the abrupt collapse of his otherwise well-ordered life. Feeling defeated, and lacking the energy to do much else, he lay on the sofa staring at the ceiling repeating a mantra of recriminations—*If only I'd quit when I was ahead. ...If only I hadn't doubled up. ...If only I'd stuck to my limit.*—until the light faded and the room grew dark. His only consolation came in knowing Julie was out there working his problem for him, but when Sunday passed without word he began to despair. It was well past midnight when, convinced Julie had failed, he dragged himself to bed clad in the same *Villanova Wildcats* shirt and gym pants he'd worn all weekend.

The room was black when the phone rang. Bolting up, he shouted, "I'm coming! I'm coming!" his hand swinging wildly in the darkness. "Hello!" he said, grabbing the phone.

"It's me, Frank. Sorry for the delay, but I've been trying to get the money."

He heard *trying to get the money* and groaned. "Oh, shit."

"Frank?"

"Yeah, I'm here," he said weakly.

"Well don't sound so glum. I got it and I'll bring it to your office by noon."

"You got it?! You really got it?!"

"I said I would."

Flushed with excitement, he shouted, "Oh, thank you, thank you. I can't tell you how much I appreciate this. I was so afraid…,"

As he ran on, Julie explained it was of necessity a short-term loan, but Kelly seemed not to care.

* * *

Winter yielded to spring, and, as promised, Kelly ceased betting, immersing himself in his work instead, the parking lot incident a distant but painful memory. And with each new triumph, the first person outside the agency he'd call was Julie, and together they'd celebrate, usually in Baltimore.

On one such occasion toward the end of April, Kelly found Julie less enthusiastic than usual. "Something wrong?" he asked.

Julie hesitated. "Actually, there is."

"What a klutz," he said thumping the table. "Here I'm rambling on about work. What is it?"

"It's kinda complicated."

"Hey, I thrive on complicated."

Julie stared past him for a moment, then nodding, he said, "Remember when I gave you the money I indicated it was a short-term loan?"

"Sure," he said, his tone suggesting otherwise.

"Well, that's the problem. That money's from my family trust fund, part of a stock-ownership deal my father set up with a bank out west."

"Uh-huh."

"We've used it over the years as collateral against short-term loans to prop up the family business when

114

necessary, and now the arrangement with the bank's about to change."

Kelly was leaning in close on his elbows, his brow creased. "That's where you got the money, from your father's trust?" And when Julie nodded, he said, "I had no idea."

"The problem," Julie continued, "is that the bank's board of directors has been struggling with a management decision of whether to remain regional or expand statewide."

"An interesting dilemma," he said, not making the connection.

"Well, I just learned they opted for expansion."

"Sounds like a wise decision."

"Sure, for them, but not us," Julie said. "Not at this time anyway."

"I'm not following you."

"They need money to expand. So to minimize incurring new debt they're recalling all outstanding loans. Those who can't come up with the cash will forfeit their shares."

Kelly blanched. "Oh, Jesus."

"I'm afraid he can't help us, Frank. We've been borrowing heavily against the stock, and we now have ninety days to settle up, or kiss our securities good-bye."

"I'll give you a check tomorrow, twice the usual payment."

Julie offered a weak smile. "Thanks, but we're going to need a lot more than that."

"How much more?"

"More than what you owe me. Like I said, we've been going to the well for a while."

"I'd give it to you if I had it."

"I know that."

"What're you going to do?" And when Julie didn't respond, he asked, "Is there someone you can go to, other family members, business partners?"

Julie shook his head. "There's no one." After a moment, he said, "But...,"

"But what?"

Julie paused. "I had an idea, but I'm afraid it's going to sound crazy."

"Don't be absurd. When you're in extremis nothing's crazy."

"Well... I've been thinking there may be a way out. It's problematic, but I think it can work, work for both of us."

"Come on," he said clapping his hands, "let's hear it."

"It's a wild idea."

"Tell me, already."

"If I'm right, it'll solve both our problems."

"All the better," Kelly said eagerly.

"It involves you," Julie said cautiously.

"Great. Now I get the chance to help you."

"But you haven't heard it yet."

"Doesn't matter."

Julie looked at him for a long moment. "I don't know."

"Out with it, for goodness sake."

"On one condition. That you listen to the whole thing before answering."

"Yeah, yeah," he said, "I'm all ears."

They were seated in the rear of a small tavern, away from the bar, the tables nearby unoccupied. Still, Julie looked around. Leaning forward, he lowered his voice and laid out his scheme. When he'd concluded, he told the stunned man, "If I'm right, the simplicity of it ensures its success." And when Kelly didn't respond, he said, "You said it yourself, there aren't enough experts out there to detect it, or anyone with more knowledge about the system than you."

Kelly's eyes were fluttering in disbelief.

"It's minuscule compared to the vast sums you disburse," Julie continued. "A drop in the bucket. The way I figure it, it'll be just another routine transaction."

Still, Kelly remained mute.

Sounding desperate, Julie said, "I need this, Frank. My family needs it."

Kelly removed his glasses and pressed his palms against his temples. "Never in a hundred years—make that a thousand years—could I come up with something like this."

"Who knows, *you might have* if I hadn't bailed you out," Julie reminded him.

"But even if it could be done—and I'm not saying it can—there's the issue of my public trust."

Julie's expression suddenly turned hard, his outburst startling Kelly. "Well, so much for friendship!" he said, tossing his napkin down. "My family's in deep trouble and you're worried about a few paltry crumbs that'll never be missed. Be a fucking man and just say no, for christsake!"

Kelly reddened. "Now hold on," he said, looking around. "I didn't say no."

"Not directly," he said pushing from the table. "I got the message. Thanks for nothing."

"Calm down, please," Kelly implored. "You must admit this goes far beyond a friendly loan."

"*Friendly loan?* How about I placed my family in jeopardy to save your ass *and* your fucking job, and you hand me a line about public trust? You think those scumbags in Congress diverting millions to their cronies share your sense of *public trust?*" he said, spitting the words out.

"Look, I'm sorry. I didn't intend to minimize your dilemma. Forget what I said about public trust. Suppose we focus on your idea instead, okay?"

"Go on, I'm listening," Julie said knotting his arms across his chest.

"Well, for one thing, you can't take somebody's social security check because he dies. In most instances there are dependents—usually spouses—who continue receiving those payouts. If just one check fails to arrive we hear about it immediately."

Julie unfolded his arms. "What about when there isn't a spouse or dependent? What then?" he said, still angry.

"Then our district office notifies us and we stop the checks."

Julie considered that. "How many of *those* death notices—when you terminate the payout—do you estimate you process a month?"

"I don't know, couple of thousand, I suppose."

"What's the average amount of those checks, a rough estimate?" he asked, his anger waning.

Kelly scratched his chin. "Probably two, two-fifty each."

"That's upward of half a million a month, six million a year."

Kelly paled. "Jesus!" he exclaimed, his voice falling to a whisper, "You want to steal *six million*?"

"Why not, if that's what it works out to be?"

Kelly fell quiet, confusion and fear etched in his face.

"Look," Julie continued, "I don't have many options. If I can't come up with something my family winds up in the street. Are you saying it can't be done?"

"No," he admitted cautiously, "I didn't say that."

"So, it's feasible?"

"I guess. Hypothetically."

"Explain it to me," Julie said more gently now.

"You mean hypothetically?"

"Whatever."

"Well, without getting too technical, the IBMs we use—the 1410s, 7080s and 705s—are tape-oriented and programmed in a machine assembly language that only a few workers have the skills to interpret. And since most programmers don't have the requisite skills beyond transposing the data from one form to another, the odds of anyone detecting what you propose are admittedly slim to zero. So, in that regard, it can be done."

"Go on."

"Another factor in your favor is that the tremendous pressure we're under to get the checks out on time forces us to devise ways of bypassing our own software. Plus, we lack a system of documenting our programs, and nor do we have time to develop one."

"Let me get this straight. You're saying you're already altering your software programs?"

"That's right."

"So, if you wanted to, you *could* make a few changes here and there and do what I'm suggesting?"

"It's conceivable, provided we code the social security numbers of the deceased without survivors so they remain in the system an extra month before deleting them."

"It's that simple?"

"Technically, yes." Then he quickly added, "But that doesn't address the problem of what to do with those checks. You'd have to assign an additional code directing them somewhere, and that's where your scheme falls apart, cashing them without attracting attention."

"What if that could be done?"

Kelly shook his head. "That isn't likely."

"For the sake of discussion, let's say it is."

"Then those social security numbers drop from the rolls the following month and no one's the wiser."

"And the month after that?" Julie asked wanting to be certain Kelly understood this wasn't to be a one-time diversion.

He shrugged. "Once the program's established, repeating it would be automatic, as simple as re-routing a train before it reaches its final destination. All that's required is to set up a permanent detour for the checks before inactivating the numbers."

"And how secure would that be?"

"Very," Kelly assured him. "Once the program's part of the system the only person who'll know it's there is the one who installed it."

"What're the odds of it coming to someone else's attention, say because it's a new procedure?"

"Can't happen," he said, shaking his head, "because no new social security accounts are being created. It would simply be recorded as the final transaction on existing accounts. You know," he said with a quick smile, "it's really quite clever. And, the timing's perfect, too."

"How so?"

"Because something like this would've been detectable a year ago. Now, with our new system there's no paper trail for auditors. All the data's buried on reels of innocuous computer tape." Then he added, "But of course there's that problem of where to deposit the checks, which, as I said, would surely raise a red flag."

"What if they were routed through a bank in Arizona, say, not to be cashed, but to be re-routed?"

"Arizona? Like the bank connected to your family trust?"

"Yeah, like that one."

"I suppose if they were diverted from there to a large enough network, one that extends beyond that region, it'd work okay."

"Does this mean you'll do it?"

"I thought we were speaking hypothetically."

"Forget that. Will you do it?"

Kelly squirmed in his seat. "You're asking an awful lot."

"Jesus, put yourself in my place."

Kelly bit his lip. "Who else would be involved?"

"I'm not being a smart ass, but I can't give you names. These aren't people you and I normally deal with. But if you're worried about anyone knowing of your involvement, you needn't be. This is strictly between you and me."

Kelly looked hard at Julie. "You mobbed up?"

121

Julie shook his head. "I'm not, but I know some people."

"This is pretty scary."

"You'll be out of the picture, I promise. You're name will never come up."

After a long silence, Kelly asked, "If I were to say yes, what's my cut?"

"I figure we'd split five percent of the gross." And when Kelly blinked, "I know it doesn't sound like much, but if your estimates are correct, we're looking at around…"

"Twelve thousand a month," Kelly said. "And the rest goes to *these other guys*? Doesn't that strike you as grossly out of proportion?"

Julie agreed. "But we can't do it without them. They have the access to banks and other financial institutions. Besides, it'll be divvied up a hundred ways, with someone getting a cut every time it's moved. And it'll be moved a lot. Whereas ours comes right off the top."

"And how would we get it?"

"Once the checks are processed our share goes directly to numbered offshore accounts. One for each of us."

"You've pretty much thought this through."

"There was no point coming to you with a half-assed idea," he said without apology.

Kelly nodded. "Where off-shore?"

"Grand Caymans. It's perfectly safe and only you'll have access to your account." Leaning across the table, "You make this happen, Frank, and we're going to be very wealthy."

There was a long silence. Finally Kelly sighed. "Okay, I'll help you."

* * *

Kelly phoned Julie several weeks later, he sounded buoyant but nervous. Whispering, he said he'd devised a program and was ready to include the data in the tapes going to Treasury. The checks, he said, would be in Tucson on the third of the following month. Then he reported that he'd underestimated the monthly average of decedents without dependents. He said he'd reviewed the data and instead of two thousand, as he'd originally thought, the average was closer to thirty-five hundred.

"Altering the tapes was easier than I expected," he said. "When you say *go,* the new program is activated and becomes a permanent part of the existing one. Thereafter, as far as the government's concerned, everyone in this category will have lived one month longer than he actually did."

"That's pretty funny," Julie said.

But Kelly didn't laugh. Instead, he said, "And should anyone care to check the numbers, which isn't likely, the procedure ensures the recorded deaths corresponds to the death notices on file in our district offices."

"What're the chances of someone spotting the one-month extension?"

"No one can do that without knowing precisely what to look for and where to look for it."

"I'll be in touch," Julie said, and hung up.

* * *

Two days later Julie and Gava met in Fort Lee, New Jersey, not far from the George Washington Bridge. "It's more than we expected," Julie told him.

"How much?" asked Gava.

"Around eight hundred thousand per month."

"You did good," the older man said, his weak eye rolling lazily. "Very good."

"That's gross, of course. Our boy gets his two and half percent off the top, as we agreed." And when Gava frowned, he reminded him, "He knows the rules—every dime goes offshore. Is there a problem?" he asked, noting Gava's displeasure.

"I'm thinking that's a lot for one guy. What's he gonna do with two-fifty a year? You see what I mean?"

"It's his show, Don Paolo. Without him we get zip."

"We could put a gun to his head."

Julie shook his head. "You needn't worry. I've got him on a short leash."

"I don't know. That's a lot for someone not in the organization. We're going to need every dollar."

But Julie wouldn't yield. "You'll have plenty," he said, not knowing Gava's plans. "The population's increasing and aging. Things can only get better."

"And you're sure no one's gonna pick up on this?"

"Positive. They're running seven days a week; twenty-four hours a day to ensure those checks are received by the third of every month. As soon as they meet one deadline, they're busting their tails to make the next one. It's a zoo down there, and the few monitors they have are too busy preventing breakdowns to think about anything else."

Still, Gava wasn't satisfied. "What about the ones writing the checks?"

"That's the sweet part," Julie explained. "Social Security doesn't write the checks. They compile the data, enter them on computer tapes, and send the tapes to Treasury, which is the only agency authorized to issue the payments. The way the system works, Treasury has no way of knowing what's right or wrong with the tapes. Their only job in the process is to run them through the check-writing machines while relying on the folks entering the data on the tapes to be correct."

Gava heaved a sigh. "Sounds too good to be true."

"It'll work," Julie assured him.

"If it plays out like you say, your share's fifty a month."

Julie smiled and thanked him. It was about what he'd expected.

* * *

In July, over $850,000 in Social Security checks arrived in Tucson. Once they'd been dispersed around the country, Mendenhall transferred $21,000 to Kelly's Caymans' account. Julie's share passed through the Caymans to two other banks before arriving at a numbered account in Liechtenstein. Most of the rest Gava claimed.

CHAPTER ELEVEN (EARLY 1962)

Ordinarily, Julie would've opted for the wing chairs by the stone fireplace in the Metropolitan Club's lounge, but seeking privacy, he steered Jeffries to a corner, away from the other members and guests.

"Jacob Goodmann's doing great things on the Judiciary Committee," he said as they drew on their cigars. "The guy's a dynamo, ferreting out reticent witnesses and gathering crucial testimony on mob influence in the unions. They'd never have done as well without him. Wouldn't you agree?"

Jeffries leaned into the soft club chair. "These are marvelous," he said, rolling the Cuban between his fingers. "Getting harder to find." Then, shrugging, "I suppose he's doing a fine job. Sounds like you think he's ready for a promotion. Is that why we're here instead of Georgetown?"

"Am I that transparent?"

"The way you track these guys you should be working for *Roll Call*," he said of the Capitol Hill newspaper. "You got your fingers in more shit than the Kennedys. Is there anything that doesn't get by you?"

"You overestimate me."

"I doubt it. To be honest, I haven't a clue about what's going on over in Judiciary other than what's in *Roll Call,* and what that pompous chairman spews at his press conferences." He shook his head. "I despise the little prick."

"Then take my word for it, Goodmann's doing a bang-up job." He'd known Goodmann from law school; a diligent but average student who'd later signed on with the U.S. Patent and Trademark Office, and likely would've remained there had Julie not recommended him to the high-profile post of assistant counsel to the House Judiciary Committee. That was two years ago, and now with a key sub-cabinet slot available at Justice, Julie saw yet another opportunity for him.

"What've you got in mind?" Jeffries asked, setting his cigar in the marble ashtray.

"There's a slot over in Justice, Special Counsel and Chief of Staff to the Assistant Attorney General of the Criminal Division."

"Nobody's ever gonna accuse you of thinking small."

"Think about it," he said, signaling the waiter. "If Bobby Kennedy's serious about tackling the Mafia, Goodmann's his man. He's got the background and the moxie."

Jeffries' attention was suddenly drawn to a shapely Asian woman being escorted into the lounge by one of the members. "I suppose," he agreed, without shifting his gaze.

"He's got the contacts and he knows the issues," Julie said. "Besides, Kennedy doesn't need another politico on his team, not for that position." He paused when the waiter approached with their drinks. "Goodmann's the right man and you're the one who can deliver him," he said when he'd gone. "Are you listening to me, Bob?"

Jeffries had been tracking the woman as she crossed the room. Now, shifting his gaze, he said, "I hear you. And if I didn't know better I'd swear you're building a shadow government."

"Well, what do you say?"

"I'll see what I can do for your Mr. Jacob Goodmann." Then, casting a hungry look across the room, he said, "Whadya say we mosey on over to Georgetown?"

* * *

Several weeks later Julie met with the powerful chairman of the House Ways and Means Committee at the elite all-male Cosmos Club on Embassy Row. He'd scheduled the meeting earlier, while delivering the requisite ten thousand dollars to the congressman's aide, the price of obtaining the chairman's undivided attention over a quiet dinner.

"Mr. Chairman, thank you for coming," he said, greeting the Texan as he stepped from his chauffeured car.

"Always a pleasure, son," the tall man replied, his basso voice resonating in the marble entryway, the firm handshake, business-like and brief.

The nods and greetings directed at his guest as they passed through the lobby gave Julie the odd sensation of hosting the congressman in his own home. The feeling stayed with him up the carpeted staircase and in the private dining room with its solitary table and white-gloved waiter. Unlike the main dining room, there was no menu here. The chef knew the chairman's preference for fresh game and the precise way to prepare and serve it.

It was customary not to discuss business over dinner, the chairman preferring to devote his attention to the meal prepared for him. Whatever Julie had to say would have to wait until they'd moved to the ornate salon, with its Belgian tapestries and vaulted cherub-decorated ceiling. Here, tuxedoed attendants moved silently across Persian carpets delivering premium tonics and cigars. His guest took the initiative by selecting two chairs in a favored corner.

Ten thousand dollars didn't buy much of the Texan's time, and once seated, Julie began. "It appears the president's wasting no time implementing his platform, Mr. Chairman," he said, mindful of the man's seniority and influence.

"It's always best to ride a fresh horse when entering town, son."

Julie's concern that evening was the fledgling space program, which the Democratic leadership, with Kennedy's urging, had agreed to augment by appropriating the first installment of a twenty-five billion dollar, multi-year commitment, designated the Apollo Lunar Program; an astounding increase over the seventy-seven million budgeted five years earlier in response to Sputnik.

"There's a highly qualified former Air Force logistics officer by the name of Michael Fitzhughes, Mr. Chairman, who's ideally suited to oversee NASA's Contracts and Grants Division," he began, initiating the agreement that would cost Gava an additional fifty thousand dollars.

* * *

It was no coincidence Julie's agenda mirrored Kennedy's ambitious New Frontier platform, a massive spending spree that included the newly-established Food Stamp Program—a federal giveaway aimed at eliminating the raw deprivation and squalor Kennedy had witnessed in Pennsylvania and West Virginia's coal regions during the election campaign—where he arranged for Gerald Dymond, a mid-level bureaucrat, to be elevated to a key position. In the same way, Henry Hatters, a misplaced systems analyst in the National Guard's Congressional Liaison Office, found himself promoted to the post of Special Assistant to the Deputy Assistant Secretary of Defense for Logistics and Acquisitions. And so it went, relying on Jeffries and other contacts, and Gava's deep pockets, Julie succeeded in moving several others into important jobs around town, most without their knowledge.

* * *

"Why here?" Nunzio complained, when they met at a New Jersey Turnpike rest stop. "You know I hate leaving New York."

"Better get used to it," Julie said. "There's a lot happening outside the Bronx."

"So now you're a citizen of the world. Well, to hear Gava talk, maybe you are," he conceded. "I never seen him like this before, all stirred up over these deals you're making."

"That's why we need to talk. It's time you knew about a guy named Goodmann."

* * *

Two months later, Goodmann was working late, as he usually did, when he took his first call from Nunzio.

"Mr. Goodmann," the caller said, "you don't know me but I've been referred by a friend who wishes to remain anonymous." Thereafter, he spoke quickly, without pause. "I got some information I can only deliver to you and nobody else, information that'll be very helpful to you."

"Who the hell is this?!" Goodmann said, certain this was a prank and not finding humor in someone whose voice he didn't recognize having access to his private line. "I don't know how you got this number but when I find out I'll have your ass," he said before hanging up.

When the phone rang moments later, he picked it up and immediately said, "You're pushing it, pal."

He was about to slam the phone down again when he heard, "Hang up again, asshole, and I'll come over and break your fucking legs."

Goodmann froze. No one he knew would carry a joke this far. "Who is this?" he said guardedly.

"Like I said, none of your fucking business. What is your business is what I'm going to tell you. Now, I got this number and your home number. One way or the other you're gonna hear what I got to say. You decide, and make it quick. I'm not hanging on this goddamned phone all day. So what's it going to be?"

"I'm still here," he replied more cautiously.

"Good. I understand your reaction. With all the nut cases running around you gotta be careful, but I'm not one of 'em. What I gotta say comes from inside, and if you play ball you can bring them to their knees."

"Them?"

"The organization. The mob," he said, impatiently. "Who do you think I'm talking about?"

"Who is this?"

"Don't be stupid. I tell you and I'm dead. Now pay attention. I'm giving you information nobody outside the organization knows, including those FBI *cafones*, and no strings attached. You interested, or what?"

As absurd as it sounded, Goodmann wanted to believe it was true. He'd known informants who'd come in offering information, mostly of questionable value, and generally to save their own hides, but never an insider, as this caller claimed to be, and certainly no one offering it freely and without being coerced.

"Well?" Nunzio said impatiently.

Vowing to crucify the perpetrator if this turned out to be a joke, he said, "I'd be a fool not to accept your offer. When do we start?"

"Right now, pal," Nunzio said, and then launched into an overview of the secret organization, which he indicated was built around more than two dozen families. Occasionally, Goodmann interjected questions but they were largely ignored.

"Let me get this right," Goodmann pressed. "You said *twenty-four families? Twenty-four?*" It seemed inconceivable the government's intelligence could be so far off.

"You heard me," Nunzio replied before going on about the powerful commission and how it controlled its members down to the lowliest soldiers. He also explained how territory was divided and sub-divided around *free zones* like Vegas and Miami, where families operated freely provided they didn't encroach upon other families. Forty minutes later, he concluded by revealing to the bewildered lawman the centuries-old code of honor, obedience and silence, which he said no member dared break.

Goodmann wrote furiously, laboring to capture every nuance and detail. Attempts at prying names loose were put off with assurances of future phone calls. Goodmann's first task, the caller said, was to verify what he'd been told so that when he called again there'd be no doubt about the veracity of further disclosures. To Goodmann's astonishment, the caller reaffirmed his intention to talk only with him. Attempts by anyone to alter that arrangement, he threatened, would put an end to the deal.

"You got that?" Nunzio demanded.

"It's very clear."

His last words before hanging up rattled the young attorney. "Another thing," he warned. "Be careful who you talk to and what you say about any of this. These guys are connected and if anybody thinks you're tapped into a rat, you're dead."

To his astonishment, the conversation ended as abruptly as it began, with Goodmann staring at a sea of hastily scrawled notes and sensing he'd just grabbed a tiger by the tail. Alone in his office, he was at once frightened and elated.

Prior to the call he'd been at his desk for hours, pumping himself with coffee. Now, his bladder ached for relief, and he raced for the men's room. He hadn't gone far when Nunzio's warning had him running back and snatching up his notes and locking them away.

He slept fitfully that night, and was back at his desk early the following day poring over department briefing papers and organized crime reports, most containing unsubstantiated claims and references, but nothing as specific as what the caller had revealed. He noted, too, that the first suggestion of a national criminal organization anywhere near the size and scope intimated by the caller had surfaced in 1957, when a curious New York State trooper discovered mobsters from across the country at Joseph Barbara's Apalachin estate. Prior to that, no federal agency other than Treasury's Alcohol, Tobacco and Firearms Unit had taken such allegations seriously.

He puzzled how an organization described by the caller as *bigger than U.S. Steel* could operate with impunity without the government's knowledge. The answer, he reasoned, had to be its code of silence, and Hoover's longstanding refusal to acknowledge an organized criminal network.

Wanting to understand how they'd established a foothold in America, he worked backward to early archival accounts of the notorious Black Hand Society that emerged in New York at the turn of the century and later spread to Chicago. From there he searched arrest records of such men as Johnny Torrio, ruler of New York's infamous Five Points Gang in Manhattan's lower East Side, and Joey D'Andrea, head of the Sewer Diggers and Tunnel Miners Union, and labor hoodlum Vincenzo Cosmano, and Jake "Greasy Thumb" Guzik, Torrio's bookkeeper, all predecessors of Capone and Luciano. Next, he examined FBI intelligence reports and, more recently, transcripts of the McClellan Hearings, looking for unguarded remarks that hinted at or substantiated the caller's revelations. Next, he searched Treasury and ATF files. It was a tedious process, but one that seemed to establish Nunzio as a credible source. Now, he could only wait for the next call.

* * *

Months later, after the names of selected low-level Sicilians had been provided to Goodmann, Gava summoned Julie to Lake Carmel. "This thing with your friend in Washington is working good," he said. "Our Brooklyn cousins are starting to feel the heat. I hear talk of indictments."

They stood by the water's edge, a light wind rippling the surface of the otherwise calm lake.

"Me too," Julie confirmed, "with more to come."

Gava nodded. "The more the better."

"What's next?"

"With the feds on them, the families need help unloading their merchandise, which is one of the things we need to talk about." Stooping, he picked up a flat stone and, rubbing it clean with his thumb, drew back and flung it low across the water. It took three long hops and sank. "I must be getting old. I used to get five, six skips."

"But you got good distance," Julie offered, before asking how he intended disposing of the other families' stolen goods.

"Depends how much has to be moved. There's the regular way," he said, referring to what was sold out of private mob social clubs, and what the soldiers bought from the bosses for ten cents on the dollar and then re-sold.

Julie had learned that fencing was a way of life in the organization, with everyone at every level profiting in the flourishing black market. Even he received a cut of what his men moved, though, admittedly, it didn't compare to the large-scale trade in New York.

"The way I see it we need a better system, something more efficient."

"And that's what you want me to figure out?"

"Yeah, something that won't draw attention to the operation. We do it right, it could be a money maker."

It didn't take Julie long to resolve the problem, and several weeks later he phoned to say, "Concerning that issue we discussed by the water, I have a solution."

"I'm listening."

"Can you establish a legitimate company licensed in West Virginia or Pennsylvania, and not connected in any way to anyone we know? It's got to be clean."

"That's easy," Gava replied. "What'll it do for us?"

"Provide access to a big customer."

"Who's that?"

"The U.S. Navy."

Gava laughed. "It'll be done."

Within months, the new company, a wholesale distribution center, was providing merchandise to the Navy's Bureau of Supplies and Accounts for its global network of base exchanges. And by November, similar arrangements were made with the much larger Army and Air Force exchange systems. It was a profitable deal for everyone. Hijacked and stolen goods came in the front door and went out the back door with very little of the overhead expenses incurred by legitimate suppliers.

But not all Gava's schemes worked as smoothly. One in particular nearly brought him down.

At the time, Vito Genovese was the most potent force in New York. His dominance over the largest and most disciplined army served to keep the other bosses from acting against him despite the fifteen-year sentence he was serving in Atlanta's federal penitentiary. Reasoning his removal would create a power vacuum that would generate infighting among the Sicilians, Gava decided to target the old don by alerting Goodmann of how he was running his family from prison.

The phone call came on a sweltering Friday evening, when most of Goodmann's colleagues were headed for the beach. It was shortly past six, the time Nunzio usually phoned; excepting the time when Goodmann had been out ill and the call came to his home, upsetting him deeply. Beyond that one consistency, Goodmann never knew when the calls would come, or where the tipster's leads would take him. In this instance, he was astonished to hear Nunzio finger a man he identified as the boss of all bosses.

Armed with this new information, Goodmann wasted little time setting up surveillance ops at the prison, but he grew careless and in his haste, word slipped out alerting Genovese. Fortunately for Goodmann, the news didn't deter the over-confident don, who, as the mob's main source of heroin, was determined to keep the pipeline open rather than risk losing his source of power. From wiretaps in the prison visitors' center the feds soon learned of the next shipment and its route and, with Interpol's aid, seized the entire cache in Marseille, where, had they known of his existence, they might've captured Genovese's French supplier as well. And while the seizure was a minor setback for Genovese, the portion of Gava's plan that generated tremendous public scrutiny, and nearly undid both men, began with a series of mistaken assumptions within the prison.

Aware of the Fed's increased interest in him, Genovese suspected the leak had originated from a close associate and, for reasons known only to him, he mistakenly assumed fellow prisoner Joseph Valachi, a barely literate soldier, had turned, and so ordered his murder. Upon learning of his death sentence, Valachi began moving around the prison with extreme vigilance, carefully distancing himself from other inmates in common areas. When the daily pressure of survival became too much he brutally beat another man to death, falsely thinking he'd been sent to execute him. Now facing the death penalty and certain death from his peers, he broke the code of silence, offering to tell all he knew.

Brought before Senator McClellan and the Permanent Investigations Subcommittee, the elderly hood proved a captivating and dramatic player despite his inability as a lowly soldier to disclose anywhere near what Nunzio was passing to the feds. Yet, his grandfatherly face and gravel voice filled the airwaves, and America listened with rapt attention to the broken English of an authentic mobster describing his structured life within the secret society.

Fortunately for Gava, Valachi's experiences had been limited to Brooklyn, and there was no mention of the Bronx family across the river.

Chapter Twelve (1963)

The guest list had been carefully crafted in January and the invitations mailed in late-March.

Julius Caesar Vittorio, Esq.,
requests the pleasure of your company
at a house-warming party
Saturday the twenty-fifth of May 1963
beginning at seven o'clock in the evening
at
Rugby Hall on the Severn River

"Frank, we'll have some business to discuss," he informed Kelly when he called to accept, "so plan on staying overnight. If those Navy weather forecasters are right," he said, referring to the academy's pre-graduation festivities, "we'll take the boat out the next day."

"Count on it," Kelly replied. "By the way, what prompted you to take over that old dinosaur?"

"Nikki. The old place reminds her of England. I didn't see it at first, but now that she's finished with it I'd have to agree. Besides, it was just sitting vacant and I figured what the hell, I can afford it."

There was silence.

"What's wrong?" Julie asked.

"I was thinking of what you said about watching my lifestyle, and here you are renovating this mansion."

The comment didn't surprise him. He'd anticipated Kelly would want to dip into his share of the skim one day. "We already had this discussion," he said. "Unlike you, with your fixed government salary, I can show enough legitimate income to justify the expense."

"I haven't forgotten," Kelly replied, not sounding very pleased.

"Look, I know it's frustrating, having the money and not being able to spend it how you want, but we can't get careless now. Things will be different once you leave the agency. I'll even help you get started, I promise. But that won't be for a while." Adding, "This isn't the time to cut the operation short."

"I'd like to be young and healthy enough to enjoy it."

"You will be," Julie assured him, while deciding he needed to do more to bind Kelly to him.

* * *

The task of restoring Rugby Hall had been monumental, requiring Nikki's constant supervision. Still, she embraced it with enthusiasm. The turn-of-the-century Tudor landmark, set on cliffs high above the Severn River, had stood empty and forgotten for years until Julie spotted it from the river and purchased it from the county. Strangely, its isolated location—far off the main road—had contributed both to its deterioration and preservation. Unsheltered and exposed to the elements, its exterior had suffered, while the interior looked much as it had during its halcyon days as a boys' prep school in the late-forties.

Having paid pennies on the dollar for it, Julie spent heavily restoring it. Now, nearly a year after commencing the project, and a week before the party, he and Nikki were wandering through the house surveying her contributions.

"I thought we'd never finish," she said with an air of satisfaction.

"I don't know how you did it, but you really captured the essence of this mausoleum," he told her.

She laughed. "Having a blank check certainly helped." It was a gentle reminder of their disagreements throughout the lengthy restoration; she trying to rein in expenses while he insisted on top quality materials and workmanship no matter the cost. In each instance he prevailed.

"I can't turn a corner without seeing you," he said as they entered the paneled solarium, the afternoon sun angling in through the original crimson and blue stained glass windows and the river far below them. "You're as much a part of this house as the walls."

Smiling, she said, "That's how I planned it. Now, whichever room you're in you'll think of me."

"I have a better idea," he said.

* * *

A sentry on the main road directed guests to the partially hidden lane that dipped and curved past newly planted corn fields and pastures, and which ultimately brought them to the stately house, where Julie greeted them beneath the arched porte-cochere. Few, if any, had known of the mansion, and they marveled at the sweeping view as their cars were whisked away by uniformed attendants.

When Julie finally joined Nikki in the garden, they sought out the VanDorens, who they found seated in a quiet corner beside the low wall.

"Well, young man," the admiral said, gesturing toward the house, "you've certainly come a long way since we met."

"Thanks to you," Julie replied.

"Somehow I doubt that. But we're delighted to have played a role, no matter how minor." Then, changing the subject, "Do you know the story behind this old fortress?"

"You mean, that it had been a private school, and for a brief time afterward a restaurant?"

"Well, that part's common knowledge," the admiral said. "I mean the part about the lumber baron from up north building it for his first wife."

"Darling, Julie has guests to attend to," Miriam said with a gentle nudge. "He doesn't have time for such nonsense."

"Won't take a second, dear. The poor lady died before moving in and he never set foot inside. Years later the school came along and bought it." Then, lowering his voice, "Some locals swear her spirit settled in. They even claim to see her up there in the window at times. Which is why they call this old place, *The Gray Lady.*"

"That's wonderful," Julie said with a laugh. "I love those stories. You've just added another chapter to the old place."

"Don't pay him any mind," Miriam said. "It's nothing but old bar talk. This is a lovely house and you've done an absolutely marvelous job infusing new life into it."

"Thanks," Julie said, "but Nikki deserves full credit."

"Seriously," VanDoren said, "I've always admired it, and feared someone would come along, level it and divide the property. Now that would've been a tragedy. We're delighted you took it. It'll be good having you in the neighborhood."

"I'm happy to know that, because we have a surprise." Turning to Nikki, he said, "Why don't you tell them? After all, if it weren't for them...,"

Nikki reddened. "I'm not very good at announcements." Then, drawing a breath, "Julie's asked me to marry him and I've accepted. I've been biting my tongue all evening. We wanted you to be the first to know. We haven't told anyone yet, not even our families."

Miriam leapt up and threw her frail arms around her. "That's wonderful! We're so happy for both of you." And as they showered the young couple with good wishes, others nearby joined the circle, and soon Julie and Nikki were shouting answers to "When's the big day?" and "Where?"

"June," Julie replied, while an energized Nikki, said, "New York and England. Two ceremonies."

As word spread, Julie broke away and went to the patio, where he cut off the band and signaled the caterer. Taking the mike, he said, "If I may have your attention. By now most of you already know what I am about to say. So much for surprises." As he made the formal announcement tuxedoed waiters marched from the house bearing large silver trays of champagne.

"Congratulations, you scallywag!" Jeffries said sidling over to him. Then, whispering, "I guess this means no more visits to Georgetown."

Julie shook his head. "It definitely means that, you horny toad. I'm afraid you'll have to find another cruising buddy."

Jeffries shrugged. "It won't be the same."

"I'm sure you'll manage," Julie said as one of VanDoren's classmates came over and threw an arm around his shoulder, thereby freeing Jeffries to pursue a redhead who'd caught his eye.

"I've known Nikki since she arrived here," the man said, clapping him on the back. "You're a damn lucky fellow. If I were younger I'd have given you a run for your money."

"Well, I'm glad you aren't."

Glancing at the house, he said, "Too bad you bought this old place, though. It's a beauty, but I think mine would've been more suitable for you two."

"Had I known it was on the market I might've considered it," Julie told him.

"Actually, it isn't, not yet, anyway. I only just decided after this past winter. Can't take many more like it. We're heading south, to Key West. Got a cozy place near the naval station there."

"Never too far from your shipmates, eh?"

The old sailor smiled. "It's all we know. I've always admired this place but to be honest, I think you two'll be bouncing off the walls. It's more a fortress than a house."

"I guess that's why I like it. But don't count me out on your place."

The man cocked an eye. "It's not polite to yank an old seadog's chain."

"I wouldn't do that," Julie assured him. "It's something I've been thinking about for awhile, owning a house in town. How about it, will you give me first option?"

Studying him, he said, "If you're serious, count on it."

"Never more so," Julie assured him.

"I don't know what you've got up your sleeve, young man," he said, extending his hand, "but it's a deal."

"How's next month?"

"Give me a call," he said before moving away.

"What was that about?" Nikki asked, as she approached. "Old Bill looks ecstatic."

"I offered to buy his house."

"That isn't nice. You shouldn't tease him."

"That's what he said. But I'm serious."

"Whatever will you do with it?"

"You mean, whatever will *we* do with it." Then, leaning in, he whispered, "Our secret?"

She giggled like a schoolgirl. "Yup."

"A private club. This town needs a place where legislators and lobbyists can meet other than the bars down on Main Street, and his place—right on the corner of Maryland and King George—is perfectly situated."

She shook her head. "It's a fine idea, but it can't be done. The Historical Society will never allow it."

"We'll see," he said with a wink.

"Seriously," she warned, "I know them. They can be very obstinate, especially to outsiders."

"I'll make them an offer," he said with a confidence that aroused her. Then, seeing Kelly approaching, "Let's discuss it later."

She dug her nails into his arm. "Later? The instant we're alone I plan on violating you, Mr. Vittorio."

"Hold that thought," he said as Kelly neared.

"Another coup!" Kelly said, grasping their hands. "How do you guys do it? First this incredible house, then the wedding announcement. What's next?"

"That's what we need to talk to about," Julie said.

* * *

The following morning the sky was clear and the river calm. While cruising past the academy, Julie turned to Kelly and asked, "You heard of Food Stamps?"

"You mean those little blue letters on the sides of beef?"

"You're in the right church, but wrong pew. Both come under Agriculture, but this is one of Kennedy's pet projects. Started about two years ago, it provides food to needy families."

"A noble undertaking," Kelly said, lifting a beer from the cooler.

"Just like social security."

Kelly's head snapped around.

"Relax," Julie told him, "they can't hear us."

His voice tense, Kelly whispered, "I can't help it."

"Just listen, okay?"

"Do I have a choice?"

"It began as a pilot project in West Virginia and seven other states, and now serves over a quarter million families."

"Kinda small," Kelly said, thinking of his vast constituency.

"Which is why no one's really focused on it."

"No one but you."

"That's because it's got potential. Not like your operation, but big enough for us."

"Whoa!" Kelly said, straining to keep his voice down. "What do you mean *us*? What have I got to do with any of this? Besides," he said, his eyes darting aft, "we've already got ours."

"Like it or not you're going to have a lot to do with this program. The folks in charge are concerned about fraud and want to minimize it before the program gets larger, which it most certainly will."

"What the hell's that got to do with me?"

"I'm about to tell you."

"I can't wait," he said with a sigh.

"They're moving into your territory and by next year anyone applying for food stamps will have to provide their social security number." Noting Kelly's confusion, he said, "Don't you see what's happening, Frank? Another agency's about to create a data bank using *your* numbers."

As they neared Kent Island Julie altered course, allowing them to pass down the flat coastline. "From your reaction, I assume Agriculture hasn't come to you about this yet?"

Kelly shook his head. "This is the first I heard of it. No one in my organization's talking to other agencies about converting to social security numbers. That is, except for DoD, where they're considering doing away with military ID numbers. But that's down the road."

"That's interesting," Julie said. "We'll have to keep an eye on that, but today let's talk about food stamps."

"You talk, I'll listen."

"The way I see it, if properly set up, this change they're implementing will give you access to their accounts."

Kelly shook his head. "I'm not following you. We're not equipped to distribute food stamps."

"Forget about distributing them. I could care less who gets them. What I care about is merging the two programs."

"Why the hell would we want to do that?"

Julie gauged the distance to their destination and slowed. He'd hoped to have this discussion wrapped up before reaching port.

"Remember when you told me about being ready for change? Well, here comes another wave. Today it's Agriculture, and from what you just said, Defense won't be far behind. It's happening, Frank, the government's moving in your direction, depersonalizing us with numbers. It won't be long before we're nothing but a row of ciphers."

Kelly looked sheepish. "I think the teacher-student roles have been reversed."

"Hardly," he said with a warm smile. "The point is you can't have these agencies using your data without the right controls in place."

"What kind of controls?"

"A formal policy that establishes inter-agency protocol for sharing data, one that allows access to your system while protecting the integrity of the system," he said, steering for Kentmorr Marina.

"I never thought about it."

"Well you'd better start, because you don't have much time."

"What's the rush?"

"The policy's got to be crafted and in place *before* they come to you, or they'll accuse you of stonewalling them, and then you'll have a messy turf war on your hands."

"You make it sound imminent."

"It is imminent, which is why you have to get your people working on it now. It's the government way, nobody questions existing policy. They may not like it, but they won't question it if it's already on the books."

"Maybe you should be running the agency."

"Doesn't pay enough." Then, noting Kelly's expression, "What?"

"Perhaps it's time to pull the plug, get out before these other agencies become too involved. We've had a good run."

"We can't, not yet. There are too many people in it." And when Kelly frowned, he said, "Frank, just do as I suggest, okay? We'll talk about getting out later. "Oh, and one more thing, I've been thinking we should have a program that captures and stores the numbers we use, some type of retrieval system."

"What on earth for?"

"For later on."

"Later on?"

"To skim the food stamp program."

"Jesus! Where's this going to end?!"

"With us being very rich," Julie assured him. The marina was in view, and as they turned into the narrow channel, he said, "Incidentally, I'd like to buy a company that provides computer support to the feds. Can you locate one that's on the market?"

Frowning, he asked, "What're you up to?"

"It's just something I want to do."

"I'm beginning to feel like I've entered the eye of a hurricane."

Julie smiled. "Don't worry, Frank, I won't do anything to jeopardize our arrangement. Just get me the info and I'll take it from there."

"There aren't many around."

"I figured that. See what you can do. I'd like to make an offer by the end of summer. And of course, you'll be a partner."

"I can't do that! It's illegal."

"I should've said, a silent partner, with your twenty percent going offshore." Then, turning, he announced, "We're here, ladies! Hope you're hungry."

Later, on the return, Kelly sat with his date in the stern, neither of them talking much.

Chapter Thirteen (1963)

The tree had been decorated weeks earlier, yet the mood in Rugby Hall was as bleak as the weather. Alone in the living room, Julie stoked the dying fire and watched a string of embers shoot up the chimney. As he was learning, the old house was often drafty, especially on cold nights when the fireplaces acted like funnels, sucking out heat from the house.

As it had across the nation, Kennedy's assassination in Dallas the previous month left a lingering sense of loss that wouldn't be dispelled by the holidays. Still, like the rest of America, Julie and Nikki proceeded with their plans, attending requisite parties and exchanging greetings and gifts, but with an emptiness that often left both giver and receiver wanting.

While Nikki slept upstairs, he settled in his chair and watched the fire, wondering what the future held. There had been so much turmoil this past year—the Berlin crisis, the Cuban missile standoff, angry civil rights battles, a growing U.S. involvement in Indochina and, closer to home, the flood of rumors linking Lee Harvey Oswald's killer, Jack Ruby, to the mob.

"Oswald was a fruitcake and so's that cowboy Ruby," Gava had replied without hesitation, when Julie asked if he thought the organization had been involved in either of the two slayings. "Nobody likes the idea of a loner snuffing the president so they figure it's a conspiracy, and who better to blame than us," he said dismissively. "It's all bullshit."

And when Julie persisted, asking if were possible one of the bosses had acted independently, perhaps Genovese, with all his problems, Gava ended the discussion. "Forget it!" he said. "It wasn't us."

But Julie hadn't forgotten. Instead, reflecting on the Sicilian creed—*Never hurt your enemy, but someone your enemy loves*—he reasoned that killing the president was the perfect way of striking at his brother Bobby who, with Goodmann's task force, was creating havoc among the families. If that were so, then by connecting Gava to Goodmann, they were all culpable, even he. It was not a pleasant thought.

He needed a drink, and as he went to the liquor cabinet he glimpsed their framed wedding photo and smiled. It may not have been a good year for the Kennedys, but it had been an exceptional one for him.

There had been the two weddings, one at St. Theresa's in the Bronx, and the second soon afterward in England, followed by an exquisite European honeymoon and, upon returning, the purchase of the Maryland Avenue house, which Nikki had expertly converted to a modest version of an English gentlemen's club—once he'd donated thirty thousand dollars to the Historic Annapolis Foundation. And finally, there was the acquisition of the two computer service firms.

"Both are on the block," Kelly had informed him in September.

"Why are they selling?" he'd asked, wanting to be certain they met his needs.

"The owners are typical eggheads, lots of technical smarts but no business sense. Now they're insolvent."

"Why, is business falling off?"

"To the contrary, they have plenty of work, but the overhead's killing them. They foolishly locked themselves into high-end leases, expensive furnishings and equipment, and excessive salaries. And now they're in a hole they can't get out of. Nobody told them the government won't let them roll those expenses into their overhead, so they have to eat it."

"Have they tried cutting back?"

Kelly nodded. "Sure, but they're in too deep. Another six months and they'll have to close down, which makes their mistakes your gain."

"Which of the two do you like?" Julie asked.

"I've done the analysis and I recommend either one, both have solid government contracts."

It was an easy decision. Julie purchased both, merged them and retained one of the original owners as chief operating officer.

In October, as he'd predicted, the project managers at Agriculture sought Kelly's assistance with their Food Stamp Program.

"And you provided them a copy of your regulations?" he'd asked when Kelly informed him.

Kelly nodded. "Yep. I said it was all spelled out for them—the who, the why and the wherefores—plus the requirement that I chair the working group."

"Any problems?"

"Not a whimper. They're delighted to have us do their work for them."

Yes, Julie mused, as he poured himself a drink, it had been a very good year.

Chapter Fourteen (1964)

Gava summoned Julie to New York in February. "We have to talk," he said, his tone more anxious than usual."

"When?"

"Day after tomorrow."

For these quick, unscheduled meetings they began using LaGuardia Airport's General Aviation hangar, enabling Julie to fly in out the same day.

"He's over there," Reni told him as he stepped from the charted single-engine plane, pointing him toward the black Lincoln in the shadow of the building.

"What's up?" Julie asked when he climbed in, closing the door against the drone of engines.

"Joe Magliocco's dead. Heart attack," he said, of the man who'd enjoyed a brief reign over the Profaci family after the latter's death from cancer the previous year, and who'd been feuding with the Gallo brothers over the past several months.

"Should I feel sorry?"

"You should feel glad. The old bastard's been a ball-buster from day one. Nothing but trouble."

"Then I'm happy for you," he said, curious why such news warranted a hasty trip north.

"This is the first big change in the commission," Gava explained. "With Magliocco out, the crown passes to Joe Colombo, who I can work with. And, more important, he doesn't trust Gambino or Lucchese," he said of the other bosses. "Joe also knows if he doesn't make an alliance with somebody soon they'll cut him out."

"And that somebody's you?"

Gava puffed his cigar, the ash bouncing off his knee to the floor. "I have to get to him before the others. And the only way is with cash, which he needs bad."

"In that case, you'll be pleased to know about our next skim."

"Like the one we're in?" he asked anxiously.

"Not as big. Not yet, anyway." He explained, "It's a new government assistance program with virtually no accountability. So far, it's been a clean operation, with only a few cheaters among the merchants at the local level."

"This thing got a name?"

"The Food Stamp Program."

"Never heard of it."

"Not too many folks have," he said, before telling him how the president was pushing Congress to make it permanent. "It should pass soon, with initial appropriations around seventy-five million. Publicly they say it'll eventually reach four million people at a cost of four hundred million, but they're low-balling it to get the bill passed. Actually, it'll be closer to ten million people, which'll put it around a billion dollars. But that'll take a few years."

"Those fuckers'll lie even when telling the truth's to their advantage," Gava said. "So how do we get ours?"

Rather than burdening Gava with details about fluctuations, like seasonal unemployment and inflation, that enable families to qualify for the stamps, he simply said, "Since there's no way of accurately predicting how many families will need assistance from year to year, they're establishing an annual two percent sliding buffer to keep the program solvent."

"And that's how we get ours?"

Julie nodded. "We insert our data into their buffer, and as the budget grows, so does our take. Which is what we're doing now, setting it up."

"We?"

"Kelly."

"You're putting a lot on this guy's shoulders. You sure this is the only way?"

"We can't do it without him," he replied. And when Gava questioned the notion, he said, "Maybe we can make some changes later, but we need him now."

"What's our take?"

"Small at first. There's about three hundred thousand families in the program now, but that'll change dramatically with the new law."

Gava grunted. "The sooner the better. We need Colombo on our side."

Julie didn't respond.

Later, as his plane rose and turned south, he looked down at the city and considered a Gava-Colombo alliance and doubted the Sicilians would tolerate such an arrangement.

CHAPTER FIFTEEN (1965-1966)

As Julie had learned, the tempo in Annapolis, unlike other Chesapeake Bay communities, was determined by events rather than seasons; the most disruptive being the academy's weeklong graduation and commissioning festivities in June that drew thousands of visitors from across the country. Thereafter, a run of boat shows, regattas, football games and homecomings kept the town active through early December when the pace finally slowed, but only briefly. In January, the state legislature was back in session, bringing with it an army of political hangers-on, lobbyists and hookers.

Located just two short blocks from the State House, Julie's exclusive Maryland Avenue Club quickly became a magnet for the rich and powerful, with hard-drinking pols and lobbyists shuffling into the cozy oak bar and small dining rooms nightly.

It was a busy time, what with the new computer firm and this new venture, and he failed to notice the not-so-subtle clues coming from Nikki, until she confronted him one blustery night in March. Unlike the storm, which had been building for days, she came at him quickly and without warning.

It was one of the few evenings he'd made it home for dinner. They were in the library with their coffee, the marble coffee table between them.

"We need to talk," she said in a tone that gave no hint of the issues troubling her.

"Sure. What's on your mind?" he said.

"I've lost one husband and I don't intend losing another."

His eyes widened. "What're you talking about?"

"I know you're up to something."

He was tempted to say, "Of course I'm up to something. I'm always up to something." Instead, he said, "Could you be more specific?"

"I'm talking about the club, among other things."

"What about it?"

"It's supposed to be a legitimate business."

"It is," he said lightly. "Why would you think otherwise?"

"Don't lie," she said, setting her jaw. "If you love me, you won't lie to me."

"Of course I love you."

"Then tell me what's going on."

"Look," he said, "I don't know where you're going with this, but I assure you we're operating a legitimate business."

"Then you won't mind telling me who those men are on our corporation papers, and why I haven't met them."

"Is that what's bothering you?" he said with a reassuring laugh that did little to calm her. "You haven't met them because listing them was a formality to satisfy the city. We needed two corporate officers who've been town residents for at least five years. VanDoren hooked me up with a couple of friends, and in exchange I pay them an annual stipend. It's not illegal and the reason you don't see them around is because they have nothing to do with the club's operation."

But she wasn't mollified. "And what of the other goings-on?"

"What goings-on?

"Spying on our patrons, for one. What's that about?"

"*Spying?* Don't be ridiculous."

"I asked you not to lie to me. I know what they're up to, those New Yorkers you hired. They're spying on our members."

His tone smooth and easy, he said, "What gives you get that idea?"

"Stop it! Stop treating me as a fool!" she said, slamming her coffee down and spilling it. "I've overheard them and I know what they're doing." And when he didn't respond, "Well?"

"I don't know what you heard, but whatever it was, you're mistaken. Nobody's spying on anyone."

"Julie," she pleaded, tears welling, "Like it or not I'm involved, and that gives me the right to know what you're doing."

"And I'm telling you the club's a legitimate operation."

She shook her head. "What've you've gotten us into?"

"Please, calm down."

"How can I when I know you're not being truthful?"

He looked at her for a long moment and shrugged. "All right, maybe the boys do hear something and we talk about it. It's no big deal."

She was shaking her head. "It's more than that. They're collecting information."

"And what if they are? Listening to some boozed-up legislators babbling out of school isn't a crime."

"They're doing it for you and I want to know why." And when he didn't reply, "Am I being foolish expecting an honest answer?"

"It's not important," he repeated. "You're getting worked up over nothing."

She stared hard at him. "Tell me and let me be the judge."

"I can't get into it."

Her eyebrow shot up. "What's that supposed to mean?"

"Trust me, sweetheart, you really don't want to know. So can we just drop it?"

"No, we can't drop it. You either tell me or it's over between us."

"What?! An hour ago I came home, we kissed, had a lovely dinner, everything was fine. Now, because of some perceived indiscretions at the club, you tell me our marriage is in jeopardy? What the hell's going on?"

"I'll tell you what's going on. It's not just a few indiscretions, as you prefer to call them. It's your refusing to bring me into your world, where I have every right to be. Furthermore, it's more than the club. You're living two lives and I'm part of only one of them. We're at a crossroad and it's time to set things straight between us, starting now, tonight. I need answers, not more lies."

"I haven't been lying," he argued.

"I'm talking about lies of omission."

He heaved a sigh. "There's nothing to tell."

"Please don't do this," she pleaded, tears now wetting her cheeks. "All I'm asking is that you bring me into your life, to trust me," she said coming over to him.

"But I do trust you," he said, taking her hands. "I'd trust you with my life."

"Then tell me about the men who come here, the ones who can't possibly have anything to do with your work," she said of Monte and the others. "Who are they? And while you're at it, what's behind the phone calls, the ones I'm not supposed to overhear, and the sudden trips to New York and Philadelphia and God knows where. Stop pretending, and please tell me."

Again he shook his head. "It isn't what you think."

"That's the problem. You don't *know* what I'm thinking. You don't know anything about what I'm thinking," she said, her voice cracking, "because you've shut me out. You pretend none of this other business exists and worse, you expect me to as well."

"Nikki, if there was something to tell you, I would. Honest."

"Please don't use that word," she said pulling away. "I've been telling myself that one day you'll realize I'm the one person you *can* confide in, but that day never comes," she said brushing her cheeks. "Instead, I find myself knee deep in your muck. For God's sake, *trust me*, Julie. I'm tired of pretending I don't know about the bundles of cash circulating through our house, the whispered conversations with those men, and your business with Frank.

165

Startled, Julie asked, "What business?"

"There!" she said. "I've hit upon it."

"I asked you, what business?"

"I don't know exactly, but it's something you prefer keeping between yourselves."

"Who have you been talking to?"

She gave him a pitiful look. "You don't get it. I haven't talked to anyone. I'm not a fool."

"Nikki," he said, taking her arm, "this is far more complicated than you think. Please let it go."

But she wouldn't. Insisting instead, "You *have* to talk to me."

"I *can't*. Not about this."

"That won't do. That won't do at all," she said rising.

"Nikki, come back!"

"Not till you're ready to trust me," she said over her shoulder.

A moment later the upstairs door slammed and the house fell quiet, leaving him to wonder how much she really knew. Sighing heavily, he pushed up from the chair and trudged upstairs.

"Come on, Nikki, open up," he said through the bedroom door.

"Not till you tell me the truth."

"How about we discuss it tomorrow?"

"Now," she insisted. "I'm tired of waiting." And when he didn't reply, she said, "Well?"

"I need to go to the club for an hour or so."

"You might as well spend the night there. You aren't sleeping with me."

"We'll talk later," he said, certain she'd be more reasonable in the morning. But he was mistaken. The note on the kitchen table said she'd phone in a few days, hoping by then he'd know he could trust her. She'd packed some clothes and left without saying where.

That night he tossed till dawn.

* * *

"Come home and let's talk," he told her when she phoned a week later.

Watching her step from the car, he judged from her appearance that it hadn't been a good week for her either. He noticed, too, she'd come without her suitcase.

They met at the front door in what began as an uneasy truce, with him telling her he was glad she was back, and Nikki pausing in the center of the foyer with an uneasiness that had him thinking how quickly relationships can deteriorate.

She didn't respond, but followed him instead into the library, where she stood stiffly by her chair.

"Nikki, for God sakes, this is your house, please sit down." And when she did, he asked, "How about a drink?"

"No," she replied from the edge of her chair.

And when he said, "Mind if I have one?" she answered with a shrug.

"Nikki, I want to do whatever's necessary to make things right between us," he said, "but I fear what you're asking will set us apart rather than mend things."

"I thought we were going to talk," she said, her hands locked firmly in her lap.

He looked at her for a long moment. "We are, but there's a proviso. You can't tell anyone. This must stay between us. Our lives depend on it." Again silence. "You still want to hear it?"

"If this is a trick…,"

"No trick. All I ask is that you not disclose any of what I say."

"You needn't worry," she assured him, "which is exactly what I've been trying to tell you."

"One question. Have you mentioned anything about Frank and me to anyone?"

"Oh, Julie," she sighed, "I don't really know anything, and more importantly, I wouldn't if I did."

He gulped his Scotch, thinking, this is the last thing Gava wants. "I'm dealing with men who might kill us if they knew what I'm about to tell you."

Her expression suggested she was waiting for something more, and when it didn't come, she said, "You're serious!"

"Yes." Then, wishing he'd been more tactful, "We're not in any imminent danger—not if we play by the rules."

"Whose rules?"

"I'll get to that."

"It's the *Mafia*, isn't it?" she said, and knew immediately she was right.

Recalling the anxiety he'd felt that day in the garden seven years earlier, when this whole business had been dumped on him, he proceeded carefully. "In a sense."

"What kind of answer is that? Either it is, or it isn't."

"It's not a term they use."

"Nevertheless, you're one of them?" To his wonder, her tone suggested she didn't find the notion objectionable.

"Not really. I'm associated with them—in a distant way—but I'm not what you'd call a member."

"I'll have that drink now," she said. And when he delivered it, she took a long swallow and followed it with another.

"Silence and discretion," he continued, while she eyed him from over the rim of her glass, "that's all that's necessary. As long as we keep our mouths shut no one will bother us." She drained her glass and held it out. When he returned it to her he told her about the Maryland Club, how he'd conceived of it as a source of privileged information.

"What type of information and for what purpose?" She was leaning back, her legs crossed, listening intently.

"There are advantages to knowing of contracts for big projects like the nuclear power plant they're talking about putting south of here in Calvert County, and the airport expansion, and new bridges and highways, and waste treatment plants. It's all extremely valuable if you know about them long before they're made public and while the deals are being negotiated."

She listened in silence as he ticked off other projects being pushed by special interests, that if implemented would commit huge sums over the coming decade, and what that information meant to certain people in Philadelphia and New York.

After another drink he told her of his arrangement with Monte and the others, and how it tied in to their visits to the house, and how it had all evolved after his father's death, and why he'd allowed himself to be brought into the organization. He told her about Kelly and the skims they'd devised, concluding with his own acquisition of the computer service firm and his plans for it.

"Well," she said when he concluded, "you've been busy."

"You could say that," he admitted with a tight grin. "I'm making some people a lot of money." Then, holding her gaze, he asked, "So how's this affect us?"

"I'm not going anywhere," she said, topping off their drinks. "You need someone you can trust, and I may be your only true ally."

Julie's relief was palpable.

Chapter Sixteen

Several weeks later Julie was back in New York.

"It's time to strike again," Gava told him. "With the old man sick," he said of the failing Vito Genovese, "the Sicilians are starting to make moves." Then he explained, "Genovese understood power—how to get it and keep it. He made Joey B strong and played him against the others. Now that's he's on the way out they'll go after Joey, and we're going to help."

Joseph Baratta, alias Joey B, was a shrewd don with a large disciplined army, perhaps the largest in the New York region, and the likely successor to Genovese.

"Why target him?" Julie asked.

"For one thing, he wants to make the organization invisible by moving into legitimate businesses. He figures it's better to walk away from some operations while we're in control than have them taken away later."

"But that's what you want?"

"Sure, but not yet. There's still plenty to be made."

"So why not form a partnership?"

"This ain't Wall Street," Gava reminded him. "Besides, Joey ain't interested in sharing power, especially with a Neapolitan. There can be only one boss. Even the commission bends to one man.   No," he said shaking his head. "He'll change everything, and those who don't go along are out." Though alone, Gava lowered his voice. "We should be okay as long as they think it's Sicilian against Sicilian."

"And if they suspect otherwise?"

He shrugged. "Then we're tomorrow's sausage."

It was a disturbing image; one Julie preferred not to linger on. "How'd he become so powerful?" he asked.

"When Genovese closed the door to new members after the Apalachin fuckup, Joey brought in soldiers from Agrigento, tough guys who don't rat out someone from their hometown, or switch sides." Then, frowning, he said, "It's going to be a mean war. Genovese was in charge too long—since Luciano was deported. What you got now is a pack of hungry wolves."

Before they were finished, Gava said, "Once the bodies start falling we call your friend Goodmann."

As events unfolded, it didn't take long for war to erupt. It began unexpectedly in mid-July, with Baratta launching a dramatic frontal assault while his enemies were negotiating a loose alliance. Moving with military precision, his men snatched his rivals' *consiglieri* from their beds in a combined pre-dawn raid. Had the stakes not been so high, his boldness might've brought everyone to the table without a single shot. Instead, allied by necessity, his opponents retaliated in kind by launching a swift counter-attack against four of Joey's main bases—one for each man kidnapped. In the hours before midnight, when his men were sure to be around, they set off four powerful bombs, leveling two Brooklyn social clubs, a major warehouse and distribution center on Long Island, and his prized retreat in Tucson. In all, seven soldiers, three Mexican servants and a trove of commercial food products were blown apart. There was to be no negotiating.

From there, it quickly turned into a grim war; one sensationalized by eye-catching headlines, graphic stories, and politicians clamoring for public order. In the midst of it all Nunzio phoned Goodmann.

"How's it going, counselor?" he said when Goodmann picked up.

"Hello, stranger," the lawman said immediately recognizing the voice. "It's been awhile," he said, mistaking the caller's informal tone as a sign of amity. And, in a failed attempt at humor, "I was beginning to think you were among the casualties."

"You think getting shot at's funny?" Nunzio snapped back. "Maybe somebody should come by your house and pop a few through the window."

Goodmann stiffened. "I hope you aren't threatening a federal officer."

"Up yours, you little weasel! You're so hot to play in our game, then maybe you should start checking for bombs."

"Let's stay calm. Okay? Nothing to be gained pissing each other off," he said, the sweat building beneath his arms.

"You got that right," Nunzio countered.

"If I was out of line, I apologize," Goodmann said, vexed by the caller's quick temper.

Nunzio grunted. "You interested in what I got, or not?"

"Certainly," Goodmann replied, loosening his tie. "I'm always interested."

In the next instant Nunzio was telling him which Vegas casinos were mob controlled, their skimming methods, and how the cash was delivered and to whom.

This unexpected bonanza, arriving in the midst of one of gangland's bloodiest wars, confirmed what Goodmann had long suspected but had been unable to prove. "This is very helpful," he said, "but I need details. We can't get them without specifics."

"You'll get 'em," Nunzio promised before hanging up.

Aided by this new intelligence Goodmann pulled together a secret inter-agency task force aimed at scrutinizing the entire Nevada gaming industry and its vast interlocking corporate partnerships. He further dispatched an army of inspectors to search the personnel files of each mob-controlled casino. It was a massive undertaking that extended his already long days late into the night, often leaving him barely enough time to race home for a cold meal and a few hours sleep.

It was during one of those intervals, after waking in the predawn hours, that he found an envelope in his dresser that set his heart pounding. His hands trembling, he stared down at the plain white envelope and the word *BOOM* scrawled boldly across it. For the first time in his dealings with the faceless informer, he questioned what he'd gotten himself into.

"What're you doing?" his wife muttered as he fumbled in the dark.

"Just getting a handkerchief, dear," he whispered in an unsteady voice. "Go back to sleep."

It wasn't until he'd dressed and was downstairs at the kitchen table that he tore open the envelope. Inside he found a single typewritten sheet of paper listing the mob's front men registered with the Nevada Gaming Commission along with the skims and payment schedules from each casino. Lower on the page were the casinos infiltrated without their owners' knowledge, and the names of mob men in each counting room.

Though he didn't expect to find fingerprints, Goodmann had the envelope and its contents checked anyway; there were none but his. Afterward, he stored the envelope, with its single word message, in his desk as a reminder to be more discreet in his dealings with the caller and more vigilant at home.

Armed with this latest information, he sought authorization for dozens of wiretaps, each requiring multiple signatures before being reviewed by a federal judge. Considering the volume of paperwork, leaks were inevitable. The first one revealed itself on a cool early October evening, two days before Joe Baratta was to be picked up on a secret federal indictment. As the don and his attorney approached his Park Avenue apartment building, two gunmen jumped from a waiting car and, after pistol-whipping his companion, forced the mobster into the car, leaving the bleeding attorney at the feet of the stunned doorman. Thus, with two credible witnesses looking on, Baratta disappeared into the night, prompting the *New York Post* to declare *Mobster Snatched on Busy New York Street!*

And while the incident was widely viewed as another escalation in the ongoing war, Gava knew better. With a rare mixture of admiration and frustration, he lamented to those around him that the old master had once again outsmarted the feds and the other bosses. But the setback was redressed days later when agents conducting simultaneous raids across the country picked up kingpins in New York, Providence, Buffalo, Chicago, Detroit and New Orleans, and in a second sweep soon afterward, landed the casino couriers and several lesser chieftains in Columbus, St. Paul, Denver, St. Louis, Nashville and Kansas City. Together, the raids sent shockwaves throughout the organization, ultimately forcing a number of families not inclined to deal in drugs to fund an especially large heroin shipment from Europe to compensate for lost revenues.

Again, Gava was ready for them.

When Goodmann's phone rang this time and the familiar caller asked, "Howyadoin', counselor?" he was overly mindful of not offending him. "I'm doing fine, thank you," the lawman replied.

"*Complimenti,* you've been busy," he said without alluding to the message left in his sock drawer.

"We couldn't have done it without you," Goodman conceded while fingering the envelope. "That last bit of information was critical."

"Yeah, but still you screwed up with Baratta."

"I don't know how it happened."

"It happened 'cause you're a bunch of clowns. How many times I have to say it, don't trust nobody?"

"But…," Goodmann protested.

"Save it. What's done is done. I got more for you."

Relieved, Goodmann joked, "At this rate we'll have to hire additional agents."

"You complaining?"

"No, not at all," he said, instantly regretting the lapse. "What've you got?"

"Heroin."

* * *

The following month, working with an elite New York police team, federal agents converged on Manhattan's Westside docks and, with minor resistance, confiscated fifty-one kilos of almost pure heroin concealed within a Buick Invicta offloaded from the transatlantic liner United States. They also nabbed several Brooklyn-based soldiers and three Frenchmen, in what the NYPD later termed the *French Connection*. The seizure, valued at over fifty million dollars, garnered major headlines and quick praise from many quarters, including the White House and New York Mayor John Lindsay.

* * *

In the months following his disclosure to the feds, Gava drew great satisfaction from watching his rivals' crews unravel, particularly Baratta's, which frayed quickly without his personal leadership. And though it took slightly longer, much the same happened in the other cities, where the bosses were bogged down preparing their defenses against a growing list of indictments. Lacking guidance and given the chance, many of their lieutenants were eager to make their own mark, often by responding with unbridled force when splintered rivalries quarreled over diminishing resources. By year's end, shootings and kidnappings were up as were arrests, allowing FBI Director Hoover to claim credit for shutting down criminal operations in Kansas City, Denver, Nashville and Pittsburgh.

Sensing the time was right, Gava let it be known he was available to broker a national peace, but the offer was harshly rebuffed by rivals in Miami, New Orleans and, most significantly, Chicago, all of whom saw the move for the power play it was. And while the rejection wounded his pride more than his reputation, he retreated quietly to the Bronx, feeling confident the day would arrive when they'd have to accept his assistance.

* * *

With hostilities continuing into a second year, Gava phoned Julie that spring, and asked, "How about I come see that castle I've heard so much about?"

Chapter Seventeen (1966)

Gava's black Lincoln traveled south along Ritchie Highway, the main four-laner linking Baltimore to Annapolis on this, the final stretch of a tedious journey, with Reni reluctantly holding to the speed limit and stealing glances at the heavy clouds. He'd been driving since early that morning, and the prospect of running into a thunderstorm at the end of the trip unsettled him.

Predictably, the rain came as he turned right onto Jones Station Road, large quarter-size drops that blurred his vision, causing him to swerve to avoid a delivery truck pulling away from a restaurant with a large wagon wheel out front.

"Didya see that?!" he said slamming the horn. "Goddamn idiot never even looked!" But no one replied. They'd grown tired of his grumbling miles ago. The narrow secondary road and its slow traffic didn't improve his mood any. Seeing clusters of tin-roofed shanties and roadside mailboxes, he said, "How the hell he'd ever find this place. Looks like fuckin' Dogpatch." Again, no response. When he spotted a lone horse taking shelter beneath a tree, he honked and grinned when it lifted its head and twitched its tail. "Least somebody's payin' attention," he said.

A few minutes later they came over a rise, and Nunzio, who was beside him, said, "There it is."

Reni peered at the edge of the road. "'Bout fucking time."

The wooden Rugby Hall sign, hand-hewn and flecked with faded blue paint from another era, was anchored to a pair of sturdy posts low and far enough off the road to be easily missed unless one had been alerted to look for it.

"You think he'd spring for a new one," Reni said easing off the road and nosing the car down the incline.

"That's the way he likes it," Nunzio said.

"Smart," Gava agreed from the rear. "He don't need to advertise."

Reni was assessing the short incline that might cause him to scrape the manifold if he weren't careful. Then, straddling the narrow road, he tapped the brake, allowing the car to roll gently until they were level. "These roads get any smaller we'll need a Jeep," he said.

They hadn't gone far when Nunzio barked, "Slow down before the goddamn stones come through the floorboard."

"It's this goddamned washboard we're on," he countered without slowing. "Sooner we get there, the better."

Finally, when he'd had enough, Gava said, "Reni, this ain't the friggin' highway. Slow down already. A couple more minutes won't hurt."

"Won't do any good," he said, but did as he was told.

Nodding at Gigi, dozing beside Gava, Nunzio asked, "You gonna wake him?"

"Let him go," he said of the older man.

"At last," Reni said when the woods peeled away and the road widened. Moments later they saw the old school sitting high above the river.

"There they are," Reni announced, spotting Julie and Nikki beneath the porte-cochere. "She's quite a looker."

"I'm nervous," Nikki said squeezing Julie's hand.

"Stay calm," he teased as the car pulled up. "These guys are wolves, they can sense fear."

"Oh, that's real cute," she said, releasing her grip.

"Welcome to Rugby Hall," he called as the men stepped out. "Too bad about the weather, but it should blow over soon."

"Nice spread," Gava said.

"A little off the beaten path," Julie replied while ushering them inside, "but we like it that way."

"Wouldn't hurt to have that road paved," Nunzio suggested.

"You must be Paolo," Nikki said extending her hand. "So pleased to finally meet you." She stood taller than Gava, but no one seemed to notice.

"Pleasure's mine," he said, his hand enveloping hers. "I heard many good things about you."

Nunzio, meanwhile, leaned into Julie, whispering, "Where's the john?"

"In a second."

"I'm sorry it's taken so long," she told Gava.

"Me, too. I shoulda come down sooner." Then, turning to the others, he said, "Allow me to make the intros. Of course, you already know your uncle."

181

"Hiya, sweetheart," Nunzio said kissing her cheek.

"And this is Gigi Mosca," Gava said of his elder lieutenant, the sleep still in his eyes.

"An honor, signora," he said with a short bow. "Thank you for opening your home to us."

"And this," the mobster said, drawing the last man into the circle, "is Renato."

"Reni's good," he muttered, his manner suggesting introductions were seldom made on his behalf. "Thanks for the invite."

"How about a drink?" Julie said, steering them from the coffered foyer into the living room.

"How about a john," Nunzio reminded him, and then rushed off when Julie pointed down the hall.

"*Bellisimo*," Gava said, taking in the furnishings and the expansive view of the opposite shoreline. "Very nice."

"Nikki deserves the credit for resurrecting this old mausoleum," Julie told them.

"You got real talent. Maybe you can do my place at the lake."

"I'd be honored," she replied sitting beside him on the sofa.

After dinner that evening, when they'd moved to the library, Gava signaled Reni and the man slipped away. When he returned moments later lugging a large elegantly wrapped box and set it on the coffee table, Julie asked, "What's this?"

"Finish pouring the drinks first," Gava replied.

Clearly, this was Gava's show. And when everyone had a glass, he raised his, and said, "*Amici*, many thanks for a terrific meal and your hospitality. On behalf of those of us who couldn't be with you on your wedding day, I offer a toast, which, though it is late, comes from the heart. To both of you, who we embrace as family, may you have a long, happy journey together. *Salute.*"

Nikki smiled. "Thank you, that was charming."

"Ditto," Julie agreed without concealing his curiosity.

"This," Gava said, nodding at the gift, "is for the house. But if you don't mind, Nikki, I think Julie should open it."

The red silk ribbon and heavy gold paper came away easily, revealing a sturdy crate with a hinged top.

"Where'd you get this, Fort Knox?" Julie joked.

"Better," Gava said with a thin smile.

"Whatya waiting for," Nunzio said. "Open it."

Julie raised the lid and peered inside. "I don't believe it!"

"Believe it," Gava said, clearly pleased with the response.

"What is it?" Nikki asked, leaning forward.

"Take it out, already," Nunzio said.

And as Julie reached in, Reni asked, "Need help?"

"I'll manage," he said, realizing too late it was heavier than he'd expected. Still, he withdrew the marble bust, setting it down again as Reni cleared away the container and its wrappings.

"Who is it?" Nikki asked.

"Julius Caesar," Julie replied. And to Gava, "This is incredible!"

"Hey," he grinned, "who better to have it than one of the great man's descendents?"

"Wherever did you find it?" she asked.

183

"In some warehouse where nobody appreciated it," Mosca told her.

"In New York?"

"No," he laughed. "Rome."

"You mean it's authentic?"

"Naturally," he said, surprised at the question.

"But how can you be certain?"

"Oh," he assured her, "we're certain."

"It was dug up over two hundred years ago," Gava explained. "When Charles III was building his Villa Campolieto in Herculaneum on the Bay of Naples— which used to be a Roman resort that was buried when Vesuvius erupted."

"A beautiful place," Nunzio offered. "You should visit someday."

Gava agreed. "Those Bourbons treated themselves good at our expense."

"It's unbelievable," she said, stroking the cool milky stone.

"You know," Mosca joked, "I see a resemblance."

Julie shook his head. "How can I thank you?"

"You did enough for a thousand statues," Gava told him. "You want more like this, you got 'em."

"It'll have an honored place in our home," he promised.

"Then we did good," he said to the others, as he withdrew a blue velvet jewelry case from his jacket. "And this, *bella*, is for you. For your hospitality."

"But…," she protested.

"No buts," he said, raising the lid to reveal a heavy braided gold necklace, and grinning as her eyes widened.

"It's magnificent!" she exclaimed.

"I think she likes it," Nunzio said.

"Here, let me," Gava said, looping it around her neck. "It's from Florence. They make the best gold."

"You're very generous," Julie told him, as Nikki moved to a nearby mirror.

"Nothing's too good for the wife of a Caesar. Besides, she's family."

Julie smiled. *If only you knew.*

* * *

By morning the storm had moved on, leaving behind a postcard perfect day. Warm sunlight reflecting off the river, a cloudless sky and the clean scent of new growth greeted them as they gathered for breakfast on the patio. Later, after Nikki left for the academy and they were descending the long stairs to the river, Julie nodded at the bulge beneath Gava's windbreaker. "You know," he said, "you really don't need that down here."

"We need 'em wherever we go," he replied. Then, studying the boathouse, he asked, "This come with the school too?"

Julie shook his head. "Just an old pier. I had it built when I replaced the stairs."

"Good place to dump somebody," Reni noted as they entered the shadowy structure, his voice echoing off the walls. "Just tie him to the pilings and let the crabs do the work."

The engine turned over quickly, filling the space with diesel exhaust. As they eased onto the river, Gava patted the gleaming wood. "She's a beauty, all right."

"I was lucky to find her. Bought it from an old admiral who lives over there," he said, pointing to the opposite shore.

"Get to use it much?"

"Not as much as I'd like."

Gava seemed to mull that over, then, peering over his sunglasses, he asked, "How about *commare*?"

The question surprised Julie, and he answered quickly. "Nikki's the only woman in my life."

"Come on," the boss insisted. "Guys always hunger for something different. It's how God made us."

"Not this guy."

He folded his thick arms and nodded. "Good. Keep it that way. Guys who screw around get careless."

They were heading up river, away from Annapolis, toward Round Bay, where Julie pointed out his former house.

"Big difference between that one and Rugby Hall," Gava noted. "That where you held school for that Charlie character?"

"Actually, over there," he replied, indicating the center of the river. "I'd forgotten about it."

"The important thing is he and the others don't forget." Then turning to the others, he said, "That's where Julie taught that little shit not to fuck with him."

As they looked over, Nunzio said, "Good spot for a swimming lesson."

Nikki was at the city dock when they arrived. "Right on time," she called.

Gava smiled warmly. "Never keep a lady waiting."

It was a short walk to the academy, and once there she led them on an abbreviated tour that concluded at the Maryland Avenue gate, a block from the Maryland Club.

"That was great," the three of them said enthusiastically, while Reni, who'd followed along in brooding silence, uttered a simple, "Thanks."

"I'm delighted you enjoyed it," she told them before bidding them farewell.

Julie smiled as he watched her head back to the Visitors Center. She'd been like a child since receiving Gava's gift, not wanting to take it off that night, and then putting it on again immediately upon rising.

"I could get used to this life," she'd told him while fingering it before her mirror.

"It's all about money," he'd said.

"You won't have to kill anyone, will you?" she whispered. And when he said he didn't think so, she smiled. "Then it's perfectly all right."

Julie had posted a notice closing the club for lunch that day, and had the chef serve one of Gava's favorite dishes, a spicy bouillabaisse, followed by pastries from Vaccaro's bakery in Baltimore's Little Italy.

"I can see how the members would feel comfortable here," Gava said. "Has Sonny been down yet?" he asked, of Sonny Bruno, the Philadelphia boss. And when Julie shook his head, he grunted. "Good. He doesn't need to know too much."

"He knows enough to get his share," Mosca reminded him.

"That's okay. We need him as much as he needs us," Gava replied.

"For now," Mosca added.

Later, while returning to the boat, Gava praised the academy's strict regimen, saying how necessary discipline was for an organization.

"Whatsamatter," Nunzio asked, noting Reni's sour expression, "you don't like how they handle those kids?"

Reni spit out his toothpick. "It's all bullshit. Just crack a few heads and the rest'll fall in line."

"Maybe they should make Reni the admiral," Mosca said, drawing laughs from the others.

"And in a week everybody'd be AWOL," Nunzio said.

Failing to see the humor, Reni stuffed his hands in his pockets and hastened his pace, saying over his shoulder, "You guys are a bunch of jerkoffs." And when Nunzio pressed the joke, shouting, "Come back, admiral," he increased the distance between them.

With just two skipjacks and a few pleasure craft in port, the harbor was quieter than usual, so too the bay, where the only activity was a squadron of Navy yawls tacking around a distant marker. With no other boats around, Julie steered a leisurely mid-channel course home while the others stretched out, their eyes closed and fingers laced across their stomachs. They'd just passed through the shadow of the old railroad trestle beyond Hospital Point when Gava raised his head and said, "Stop the boat."

"Here?" Julie asked.

"Yeah," he said from behind his sunglasses, the others now watching without expression.

"What's up?" he said shifting into neutral, the boat drifting forward.

Gava didn't answer, not directly, anyway. Instead, he said, "I like tradition because it's good for business. It's the same for us like it is for those midshipmen back there."

Not knowing where this was going, Julie nodded. "Yeah, tradition's good."

"You probably wondered why I brought Gigi and Nunzio along."

Actually, he hadn't until that moment, and so he said nothing.

"It's time to set things right," Gava continued. "Time to do what should've been done a long time ago."

Suddenly, Julie felt uneasy. Gava's comment along with his cool demeanor triggered images of his father— graphic images from police photos dropped on him soon after the killing by detectives hoping to shock him into revealing a name or two. Now that the skims were in place and the money was flowing, he worried that perhaps his time had come. *What do they need me for?* He glanced back at his uncle, but his face was as blank as the others.

"Today, we got a chance to take care of some old business," Gava said, seemingly unaware the current was pulling them back toward the bay.

Julie's hand was still on the throttle, the engine idling quietly, as he considered his options, which were few. There was the sheathed K-bar knife and flare gun, both within reach, but neither sufficient against four armed men. He might shift into gear and attempt a high speed run to the academy's sailing center where he'd seen a group of mids, maybe even knock Gava or one of the others overboard in the process, as he'd done with Charlie. Or, he might toss the ignition key overboard and swim the fifty or so yards to shore knowing they wouldn't shoot him out here in the open. In truth, none of the options seemed very promising.

"I told the other bosses," Gava was saying. "And they said this isn't the time, what with the feds and the war and all, but I said it has to be done."

Concluding that his best chance was swimming for it, he gauged the distance to shore again. When he looked back Gava was grinning.

"I didn't ask. Instead, I told 'em you're coming in. No more delays." And when Julie didn't respond, he asked, "Whatsmatter, you thinking we're going to do a Charlie number on you?"

"Why would I think that?"

Gava shrugged. "I don't know. But you could let go that throttle now."

Julie felt the heat in his cheeks as he let his hand slip away.

"You know we don't let just anybody in," the mobster said. "We want standup guys who're good for the organization. These boys," he said of the others, "are your witnesses. They being here makes it official. So, how you feeling about this?"

"I'm honored," he said, clearing his throat. "It's what I wanted from the start."

"You're father would be proud."

"I'm sure." *He must be spinning in his grave.*

"Coming in is like being married," Gava cautioned. "It means forgetting all other loyalties. From today on you have only one loyalty, the organization. Understand?"

He nodded.

"And you accept this without any reservations?"

"I do." *Except for Nikki. No one comes before her, not you, not anyone.*

"It also means being called upon to do things you never did before and probably never thought about doing."

"I understand." These weren't new concepts. He'd heard variations of them before, from classmates at La Salle Military Academy in Oakdale, on the Island, where many New York dons and ranking politicians sent their sons.

"We don't give this oath lightly," Gava warned. "Once you accept, it could mean killing somebody; somebody close, maybe in your own family," he stressed, his good eye locking onto him.

Again, Julie nodded.

"You already know this, but it's got to be said anyway. And that is, you can never speak of the organization or its affairs to outsiders. No exceptions."

"Naturally," he heard himself say, once more silently excluding Nikki.

"You understand, too, that you can't harm another member without the commission's approval."

"I do." *Except for my father's killers when I find them.*

"Wives and girlfriends are also untouchable. If you have to screw around, and I don't recommend it, do it outside the organization. There's nothing worse for morale. Ours is a business. We only succeed when we treat each other in a way that's good for business. Understood?

"Completely," he replied, while wondering about the internecine war Gava provoked and continued stoking.

There were other rules requiring that he behave in the proper manner, to come when summoned, to never steal

191

from other members, to never put anything in writing and, to always tell the truth—ironically, none of which seemed to apply to the man reciting them.

"Okay," Gava said when he'd finished, "hold out your hand."

As he did, he watched Mosca pass a miniature portrait of the crucified Christ to Gava, who, igniting it with his gold lighter dropped it into his palm.

"You swear before us to do all I have said, even if it costs you your soul?"

"I do," he replied, watching the paper curl into a flimsy ash that was quickly taken by a vagrant breeze. *Fat chance!*

Next, producing a pocketknife, Gava first nicked his palm and then Julie's. Pressing the two wounds together, he proclaimed, "Our blood is one. As of today you are family. Your enemies are our enemies and our enemies are yours. Then, embracing Julie in a sudden bear hug that set the boat rocking, he said, "Bravo!"

"Welcome aboard," Mosca said, thumping his shoulder.

"I told you you'd make it," his uncle said, with a painful arm squeeze.

Reni simply grasped his hand and smiled.

That night, as they lay in bed, Julie told Nikki of the ceremony and all it entailed.

"What's it mean?" she asked.

"Nothing," he said. "It's business as usual."

* * *

The following day, after she'd left for the academy, and the others had gone to Laurel racetrack, Julie took

Gava into the garden. With the sun warm on their backs and dew beneath their feet, they followed the curve of the cliff.

"Power's all in the mind," Gava said, his hands clasped behind him. "The longer we keep the others out of the picture the better," he said of his rivals. If their soldiers think they're coming back after things cool down, then they'll stay in control, but if they see they ain't…, Well, you can see how it works."

The message was clear: except for men like Vito Genovese, bosses didn't control their families effectively from exile, certainly not for long. Not even the legendary Luciano could retain power once he'd opted for deportation to Naples rather than jail in exchange for aiding the U.S. war effort along the city docks. Over the years others had tried wielding power from as near as Cuba and failed, as well.

At the far edge of the property, where the cliff jutted out like the bow of a ship, they paused beneath a large white oak, Gava sliding onto the bench Julie had brought from his father's garden. Gazing across to VanDoren's home, Julie wondered what the battle-tested admiral would make of this war. "Perhaps it's time to broaden our attack and consider other options," he said.

"You mean other than Goodmann?"

Julie nodded. "Now that he's in the senate, Jeffries thinks he's got a shot at the presidency."

The notion drew a snort. "So what else is new? All them scumbags think like that."

"True, but Jeffries is the one we're most interested in."

"He's nobody."

A warm breeze came up from the river, rustling the young leaves.

"But that can change. We have time. Johnson's not going anywhere anytime soon."

"How's this tie in with our problem?"

"I was getting to that," he said, deciding how best to soften the news he was about to deliver. "There are several anti-crime bills circulating the Hill, all aimed at overhauling the criminal code and expanding the feds' jurisdiction."

"And that's gonna make putting the Sicilians away easier?"

Julie nodded. "Any one of them will allow the feds to prosecute the bosses for crimes they oversee."

Gava blinked. "What! They wanna convict a boss for what a soldier does?"

"Exactly."

"How the hell they gonna pull that off?"

Julie explained. "In a nutshell, by changing the rules of evidence and redefining conspiracy and extortion in a way that links the bosses to the crimes, and then tying it all to foreign or interstate commerce to give them the jurisdiction they've been lacking."

"This is no good," he said, shaking his head while his right eye rolled skyward. "We gotta turn it around. We can't live with that."

"That's not possible," Julie said, citing several pending bills. "The best we can do is maybe delay them, but there's no way of keeping them from coming to a vote."

"This is connected to what we've been feeding Goodmann, isn't it?"

"Partly. The feds are frustrated. They got the leads but they're not getting the convictions they expected, so they're changing the rules. Then, too, there's all the open warfare."

"This isn't how I planned it," Gava said, his gaze shifting to some undetermined point between them.

"You can control only so much, Paolo. But I believe we'll be fine, provided we keep a low profile."

Gava looked up. "How's your pal Jeffries figure in this?"

Julie sat on the wall. "He's a player, someone we can use."

* * *

As they readied to return to New York, Gava took Julie aside and confided, "I'm giving Goodmann another fish, a big one. Joe Batters."

"This got anything to do with him not supporting your offer to negotiate a truce?"

"Sure. But it's also because he's getting too powerful," he said of Capone's bat-wielding successor. "We ain't careful, we'll be kissing his ass and paying for the privilege." He then disclosed how a large portion of the Chicago don's income came from Kansas City, where, with Batters' help, the boss there was running the operation from Leavenworth. "We'll play it like we did with Genovese. It's clean and it keeps the feds away from us."

"Why not a two-pronged attack?" Julie suggested. "In addition to alerting Goodmann, let's hit Batters with a congressional investigation."

"Whataya got in mind?"

"He controls the middle states pension funds, doesn't he?" And when Gava nodded, "That's something Jeffries is interested in."

"Could be a bumpy ride for everybody, us included."

"Not if we're careful."

"I'll think about it."

Before leaving, Gava said, "So that bozo wants to be president. Go figure."

CHAPTER EIGHTEEN (1966-1967)

Brian Moorehead eased his tan Mercedes into the designated *CCC Chief Operating Officer* space, cut the engine and leaned into the leather headrest with a long sigh. It was Wednesday, the day Julie came in for the monthly staff meeting and, by no coincidence, the day Moorehead reserved for lunch in the District. Today he'd opted for the Market Inn, a popular seafood house near Capitol Hill, favored as much for its generous cocktails as its fresh entrees. Now, sitting in the cool garage eleven stories beneath his office, he closed his eyes and surrendered to the lingering buzz from two vodka martinis and a half bottle of Chardonnay—his way of suppressing the tide of resentment that came with having to answer to an absentee owner heading what once had been his company.

As it usually did, the liquor rekindled pleasant memories, when he enjoyed the perks of ownership and country club lifestyle that went with it. Conveniently, it also blocked darker images, when he'd been under siege from battalions of creditors, and plagued by real and imagined ailments brought on by watching his company and his marriage slip away. Now, fortified with booze and the comfort of having his life in order again, he was certain that given more time he could've reversed the firm's downslide and salvaged it. Indeed, Brian Moorehead could easily rationalize nearly anything after these lunches.

Nor would he admit that without Julie there'd be no firm, no generous salary, and certainly no wife and family to welcome him home each evening. Now that he was debt-free and unencumbered, it was easy to believe he'd been duped into signing away his company by that New York dago. Moreover, he was convinced doing so had been a foolish mistake.

In that state of mind he could easily justify an occasional hit of cocaine, as well. And so, slipping his hand beneath the seat, he felt around for the old Prince Albert tobacco tin, and with a pinch of the white powder allowed his cares to slip away.

Since taking his first hit several months earlier, Moorehead had convinced himself such minor indulgences went unnoticed, and for the most part they did by his co-workers, but not Julie, who, with far more invested in the firm, was less inclined to overlook his mood changes and personality shifts than the laid-back staff. Still, he said nothing, which wasn't how he'd reacted when first learning of his sister's experiments years earlier.

"She's using marijuana?!" he'd shouted through the phone.

"It's just a little grass," Nunzio said after letting it slip. *"Don't tell me you never tried it."*

"No, never."

"Well maybe you should," his uncle replied. "Might do you some good."

"She's just a kid, ferchistsake!"

"Relax. They all do it."

"Not my sister!"

The following day he was back in the Bronx, waiting when she stepped from the train with her schoolmates.

Seeing him at the station, cross-armed and looking grim made her break from her friends. "What's wrong?" she'd asked, running to him. "Is it mom?"

It took a moment to reassure her everyone was fine.

"Then why're you here?" she asked, her girlfriends gathering around her.

"Say goodbye to your friends," he told her as he steered her to the street and a nearby luncheonette, where he pushed her into a booth. "What the hell're you doing?" he demanded.

"Doing? What're you talking about?"

"I'm talking about marijuana."

Her face brightened and she laughed. "Is that what this is about?"

"You think it's funny?" His slap drew a harsh look from the owner, an elderly man seated at the far end of the store.

"Mind your business," he warned him with a jabbing finger. And to her, "You hooked on that shit?" And when she didn't respond, "I asked if you're hooked on the stuff?"

Tears rolled onto her white uniform collar. "You don't understand," she'd said wiping her face.

"I understand plenty, and I'm here to tell you you're not screwing up your life on drugs. You go down that road and we're going to war."

She was massaging her mouth where he'd struck her. "You're too late."

"Whatya mean?"

"I mean I wish you'd called first. I could've saved you the trip and me a fat lip."

"Go on."

"I won't lie. I tried it. Everybody's doing it." As she spoke the afternoon sun danced off a passing bus, washing her in a soft light that underscored her innocence. "And I liked it," she conceded. "Liked it more than I knew I should, and that scared me. So I stopped. That was seven, eight weeks ago and I haven't touched it since. Nor do I intend to," she quickly added.

"Don't lie to me, kid."

"I'm not a kid and I'm not lying," she said petulantly.

"Where'd you get it?"

"Oh, Julie, it's everywhere," she said, making him feel foolish.

"And you haven't had any since?"

She shook her head. "Not a puff. Honest."

He studied her and warned, "I'll find out."

"I'm sure you will."

"God help you if I do."

"I believe you. But that isn't why I won't. I'm no fool." Then, forcing a smile, "I may not have Julius Caesar's name but I have his brains."

"Then use 'em, goddamnit," he advised, his tone softening. He then made her promise to call if ever the urge returned. "No matter when. You call, I'll be here for you."

Before leaving he suggested she tell their mother she'd taken a fall in gym class.

She touched her lip. "Yeah."

He was back at Rugby Hall that evening, and when he next spoke with Nunzio, he put the older man on notice to be more vigilant about his niece.

Julie smiled at the young secretary manning the reception desk at Contract Computer Consults. "I'm expecting some visitors, a few big, ugly guys. They should be here shortly," he said.

"Yes, sir," she replied with a laugh.

"I'm serious," he said. "Don't sign them in, and don't give them an escort." Then, before turning away, he added, "And stay out of their way."

"Yes, Mr. Vittorio," she called after him.

He hadn't gone far when he ran into three men talking idly in the hall. Stopping, he asked about a large contract he knew the government had recently put out for bid.

"Haven't heard about it," one replied. The others just shrugged. "Probably should check with Brian," the man said.

"I'll do that."

Julie found Moorehead in his office, a corner suite with a southeastern view of the Potomac River and the Maryland hills beyond it, his hands clasped behind his head and contemplating the skyline.

"Afternoon, Brian," he said knocking on the open door. "Shall we get started?"

"Oh, hiya," he replied, swinging around and pushing from his chair. "Be right there." A minute later he ambled up to Julie in the coffee room. "So, how's it going?"

"Not bad," Julie said. "You?"

"Same-o, same-o," Moorehead replied, taking the coffee Julie offered him.

The other associates, eight in all, including the three Julie'd encountered earlier, were already around the table when he and Moorehead entered the conference room and took their seats across from each other. "Okay," Julie said, setting his attaché case on the table, "let's get started."

With few exceptions these meetings followed the same format; they'd commence soon after Julie arrived, usually four o'clock, with Moorehead summarizing all that had transpired over the past month, the others filling in details as necessary. Today, there would be a change in routine. As Moorehead closed his notebook and the others, anxious to leave before the afternoon rush hour began, were pushing from the table, Julie drew them back.

"Not so fast, boys," he said. Taking a banded issue of that day's *Commerce Business Daily* from his briefcase, he tossed it down the table to Moorehead, clipping his coffee mug and spilling what little remained. "Open it," he said without apology.

"I beg your pardon."

Breaking from his usual easy-going manner, Julie frowned and said, "I said open it. Are you fucking deaf?" Everyone froze, including Moorehead. "Well, what're you waiting for?"

Clearly shaken, he picked up the newspaper and, removing the rubber band, unfolded it as he was told. "What about it?"

"What do you see?"

Not certain how to reply, he shrugged and said, "The usual announcements."

"Look inside."

As he did, a chorus of shouts erupted in the hall that had everyone turning toward the door.

"What do you see?" Julie asked, ignoring the disturbance.

"I, er, see several circled announcements," he replied while trying to make sense of the loud protests and what sounded like doors slamming. "Perhaps I ought to see what's going on," he said half rising.

"I know what's going on, and it doesn't concern you," Julie told him. "Now, sit down!"

"But…,"

"The only thing you need to concern yourself with is explaining why those contracts went to our competitors." Then, turning to the others, he said, "Any of you geniuses care to explain why we missed them?" And when no one came forward, "Come on. Forty pages of newsprint and I don't find one contract awarded to us." And when they dropped their eyes, he shouted, "Goddamnit, look at me! Six fucking months and not one major contract. You think I'm running a charity here?"

Then, turning on two of the men he'd spoken with earlier, he said, "How about you, Johnson, or you, Goff? And when neither answered, he asked a third man, "What've you got to say, Ferris?"

"I'm not following you," he replied.

"Well," Julie said leaning into him, "let's see if I can make it clearer. Why no fucking contracts, asshole?"

The man blinked. This was so unlike the easygoing, courteous Julie he knew. Lamely, he said, "We must've missed the announcements."

"All of them?!" Julie said incredulously. And to Moorehead, "Do you buy that, Brian?"

But Moorehead, whose attention was torn between the turmoil outside and Julie's tirade, could manage only a weak, "Excuse me?"

Julie slapped the table. "Pay attention! Every month I come here and you tell me everything's fine, no problems, we're moving along smoothly. Yet, when I ask these clowns a simple question they shrug and tell me, 'Check with Brian, he probably knows.' So, I'm asking, Brian, where are the goddamn contracts?"

From the hall, they heard, "You can't do that!" followed by a thud, as if someone had been shoved against the wall, but no one dared look away this time.

"Would another martini help you understand the problem?" Julie said without humor.

Licking his lips, Moorehead said, "I don't know what you mean."

"You're pathetic, Brian." Then turning to the other three, he said, "You're fired."

"What?!" Johnson cried.

"You heard me, you're fired."

"Contract acquisitions aren't our responsibility. Why fire us?"

"Because you're assholes, that's why."

Having recovered, Goff and Ferris protested, as well.

Cutting them off, Julie said, "This isn't about contracts."

"Then what is it about?" Ferris asked.

"It's about you three scamming me."

His face twisted, Johnson said, "Where ever did you get that idea?"

Julie looked at him and said, "You must think I just fell off a turnip truck. That I don't know you're running your own businesses out of these offices, on *my* time and with *my* equipment, instead of performing work I'm paying you to do."

"Oh, you're mistaken," Johnson protested strongly.

"Never bullshit a bullshitter, Johnson," Julie said withdrawing a manila folder from his briefcase and sliding it across the table. "Read it." And when he hesitated, "Go on, don't be shy. I want to hear you explain those phone logs, the stationery and invoices with *my* company address and phone numbers, along with those depositions from your clients. Go on," he said, tossing similar folders to Ferris and Goff, "show me where I'm mistaken."

As each of them peered into his file, Julie told the others, "You should know your colleagues here have put this entire company in jeopardy by running their own businesses on the government's nickel. Thanks to them we stand to lose every one of our federal contracts."

Outside, the commotion fell silent—disturbingly silent, for all but Julie.

"Oh, let me guess," Julie said with a troubling grin when the others looked up from their files. "You jokers didn't realize that our overhead—rent, materiel, salaries, the entire operation—is all expensed to our clients, which means we've been billing the government for work performed for your private clients. That amounts to defrauding the government, which is a felony. That's right, you idiots are looking at serious jail time, and I'm the one who can send you there."

"Oh, Jesus," Ferris groaned, his shoulders slumping.

Ignoring him, Julie turned to the door and called, "Louie!"

In the next instant the door swung open and all eyes were fixed on a menacing giant with arms as thick as his neck, and the dark shadow of a beard that made him look as if he'd stepped from the mines.

"Louie, please escort these bozos off the premises," Julie said. "The party's over, boys. If you hurry you'll find your belongings in the dumpster. That is if they haven't already been carted away. Hand Louie your keys and IDs, and get the hell out."

"Please," Ferris implored, "don't do this. We have families, mortgages, kids in school. Please. It won't happen again, I swear." Looking to Moorehead, he said, "For god's sake, Brian, say something!"

Moorehead, who'd been studying his hands and looking as if he feared he was next to face Louie, raised his eyes. "I'm sorry," he said.

So much for loyalty, Julie thought. "Get them out of here, Louie, before I turn them over to the feds."

Louie stepped into the room and the men flinched. "Move it!" he growled.

No one spoke as the three rose and shuffled out. Instead, they sat with their hands clasped, staring blindly into dead space.

Once Louie had closed the door, Julie looked at Moorehead and asked, "You think you can turn these misfits around?"

Realizing he and the others were being spared, he brightened and immediately said, "Yes! Yes, of course!"

"I'll give you six months, Brian, and not a day longer. You got that?"

"It'll be done," he said, his head bobbing.

"Or you're out of here, all of you." And when no one moved, he said, "Well, what the hell're you waiting for? Get to work!"

They were like school kids rushing for the door at the bell, the first ones pausing to be sure Louie wasn't waiting for them, the others crowding into them.

As Moorehead rose to leave, Julie said, "Find another desk, Brian. Starting tomorrow, it's my office."

* * *

Fear was an excellent motivator, and four months later CCC had landed several key federal contracts. And, while they were sizeable, they weren't the ones Julie sought. For those, he turned to people high in the procurement chain that used obscure technicalities to avoid the cumbersome competitive bidding process, allowing them to award coveted contracts to whomever they wanted.

* * *

Late one summer evening, well into Lyndon Johnson's second term, Julie brought Kelly to the office. They drove there after dining in Washington, Julie telling him it was time he had a firsthand look at the operation. After deactivating the alarm system, he led his friend down the darkened hall, flipping on lights as they went, the only sound the hum of the overhead fluorescents and the soft pat of their shoes.

"In here," he said stopping at a metal door and punching a code into the cipher lock that emitted a muted buzz before releasing the bolt. Once inside the small interior room, Julie said, "Take a look, Frank. This all came about because of you. Without you there'd be no CCC."

Kelly surveyed the rows of contract binders and programs, and shrugged. "I don't know about that. You're the driving force, all I did...,"

"Don't be modest. I know what you did, and now it's starting to pay off."

Kelly offered a tired smile. It had been a long day and he was anxious to see it end. "Mind if I sit?" he asked, pulling a chair from the metal table.

"You know what this represents?" Julie said, his voice alive with excitement.

"Well, if volume is any indication, it appears you've acquired a good chunk of the fed's workload."

Julie grinned. "A damn good chunk, my friend— payrolls, acquisitions, subsidies, foreign aid programs, bulk fuel services, loan repayments—it's all here in these programs and spelled out in contract after contract."

"I'm very happy for you," Kelly said in earnest. "You've done well."

"No, Frank, *we've* done well."

"All I did," Kelly reminded him, "was find the companies. You bought and merged them."

"You saying you don't want your share?"

"I'm saying I don't deserve any credit," he said still uncomfortable with an arrangement that had put him in conflict with his government position.

Sensing his concern, Julie reassured him, "Relax, no one knows about our partnership, and no one will."

"If they do, I'm finished."

"Stop worrying. You're a rich man, and you're about to become a lot richer."

"Yeah, a rich pauper. What good's money when I can't spend it how I like."

"We've been over all that. It won't be long."

He let out a dry laugh. "That's easy for you to say."

"It'll be worth it, I promise."

"Okay, okay, he said, stifling a yawn. "So, why'd you bring me here?"

"Always looking ahead. Give me a minute, will you."

"Go on, enjoy yourself, but remember I have to be in the office tomorrow."

"I'll be quick." Then pointing to a set of binders on a nearby shelf, he asked, "Ever hear of the Elementary and Secondary Education Act?"

"Can't say I have."

"I'm not surprised. It's only just been signed into law. The important thing is it's going to transform HEW's office of Education, where we administer their training, purchasing, construction, and grant distributions. When it kicks in our workload'll triple."

Kelly managed a smile. "That's wonderful."

Then, indicating another binder, he said, "And with these contracts, we disburse and collect seventy-two million dollars in student loans for Health and Human Services."

Kelly whistled. "Nice."

"If you think that's good, just wait till the welfare programs are up and running. You gotta love Johnson and his Great Society."

Kelly nodded. He'd been a longtime advocate of social reform.

"Here's another plum," Julie announced, selecting three other binders, all labeled *Housing and Urban Development*. "Public Law 89-174 is about to elevate the Housing and Finance Agency to cabinet status, the brainchild of two Floridians—Congressman Dante Fascell and Senator Bob Jeffries."

"Fascell I heard of, but not Jeffries."

"You will. We also have him to thank for this contract," he said of a thick binder. "Tech support for the Model Cities Program."

"Like Levittown?"

Julie shook his head. "Inner-city projects, rent subsidies and low-interest mortgage loans for unqualified buyers."

"Where are you going with this?" Kelly asked, checking his watch. "I know you well enough to know you didn't bring me up here just for this. There's something else."

Julie just smiled. "In a minute," he said selecting another binder. "Here's one of Kennedy's legacy. Voucher payments for job training." Then, extending his arms, he said, "We're into more shit than you can imagine, Frank. Highway safety, interstate commerce, air traffic controller employment vouchers, federal railroads, urban mass transportation payments."

"All first-rate projects," Kelly conceded, the yawns coming regularly now.

"But nothing like this baby," Julie said, showing him a row of binders labeled with the stylistic black and white NASA logo. "Thanks to the Soviets and their five unmanned spacecraft orbiting the moon we're throwing a ton of money at the Apollo Moon Project."

"They aren't up there alone," Kelly reminded him. "We got Surveyor I."

Julie shook his head. "Not good enough. We have to get a man up there before they do."

"No doubt with CCC's help," he said.

"Thanks to Jeffries we're tracking NASA projects and paying sub-contractors in fifteen states. The program's so big we had to open offices in Cape Kennedy and Houston."

"I'm very pleased for you. Can we leave now?" Kelly asked behind heavy eyelids.

"First, tell me what you think about it."

"Why don't you tell me what I'm supposed to think, you're going to anyway."

"Fair enough," Julie said taking the chair across from him. With his elbows on the table, he leaned forward and said, "I want to know how to skim our share?"

Kelly blinked. "You must be kidding!"

"Frank, you think I pulled all this together just for the contracts?"

"But you've got an enormous amount of work here. Other firms would kill for it."

"I don't care about the work. The real money's in the skim."

Kelly looked at him and shook his head. "This is insane. When's it all going to end?"

"Not for a while, I hope. It's too soon."

"You know," Kelly reasoned, "if you back away when you're ahead, it isn't quitting."

"I can't. It's not my call, Frank."

"Jesus, don't they have enough already?"

"Forget about them and tell you'll work your magic here."

"What's it going to take to satisfy these people?"

His grin falling away, Julie said, "You know it doesn't work like that. We're committed, and now we have to produce."

"You mean *I* have to produce. What if I say it can't be done? What then?"

"I'm not sure I can make them believe that."

"You realize," Kelly said shaking his head, "you got half the government in this room."

"A quarter, a half, what's the difference? It's all the same concept, isn't it? We alter the programs and insert the skim."

Kelly was rubbing his head. "Aren't you concerned it might blow up in our faces?"

"How can it, if we follow the same procedures?" Julie argued.

After a silence, Kelly said, "I don't have a choice, do I?" And when Julie didn't reply, he said, "I can't be in two places at once. Who's going to monitor the changes once they're made?"

"I'll take care of that. You just tell me how long it'll take to make them."

"I don't believe this," he said with a heavy sigh. Then, looking around, he said, "It depends on the programs and how they're set up. I can't tell you without knowing what we've got here."

"Right now I'll be happy with a guess."

"Always in a hurry," Kelly said.

"I have people to answer to."

"What've you got us into?"

"Just tell me how long."

Kelly shook his head, thought a moment, and said, "At a minimum, three, four months, quite likely longer."

"I was hoping for less."

"I'm sure you were," he said without humor. "You'd better have a goddamned sophisticated network in place to absorb it all," he cautioned. "There'll be a shit-load of money once it starts flowing."

"It'll be ready when you are," Julie said. "Banks, drop boxes, security firms, investment houses—it'll all be there."

As they rode the elevator Kelly turned and said, "What if I'd said no?"

Julie looked at him and smiled. "But you didn't."

"A few years are all we need," Julie said once they were in the garage, "then we slip into the shadows."

Kelly nodded, but he didn't believe it, not for a second.

Chapter Nineteen (mid-1967-1968)

The intrusive click on Moorehead's intercom before the caller's voice came through was driving him mad. In the tomblike silence of his smaller and far more modest office, it had become as irritating as fingernails on a chalkboard. At first he tried ignoring it, and when that failed he lowered the volume, but that made hearing the caller difficult. Next he relocated the machine across the room, but the click was still audible.

One afternoon, after a three-martini lunch, he yanked the damn thing from the wall, but it was replaced the following day. Deep down he knew it wasn't the insistent click he resented so much as what it came to represent—the leash to which he was now tethered to Julie—and, worse, the bitter reminder of his humiliating loss of authority.

It was August when he was jarred by that sound that would have him on eggshells for the next several weeks.

Click.

"Brian, can you break away? There's someone I want you to meet."

"Be right there," he replied, grabbing his jacket and heading for his former office, where he found Kelly standing before the large window, the light behind him obscuring his features.

"Brian, this is Jon Peters," Julie said from behind his desk; another irksome habit. After all he and the others had done to atone for past sins, the man continued distancing himself from them.

"A pleasure," Kelly said, extending his hand.

Moorehead stepped forward. "Likewise," he said, noting the stranger's expensive clothes. Then, with a closer look, "You look familiar. Have we met before?"

Kelly shrugged. "I don't think so. I'd remember."

But Moorehead persisted. "I've seen you somewhere."

"Perhaps around town," Julie suggested. "Or likely, you saw us together. Jon's one of my partners."

This was the first he'd heard of any partners. "Maybe that's it," he said with an uneasy feeling.

"Jon'll be looking over the operation during the coming weeks. Evaluating our procedures—software, protocol, contracts—the whole enchilada."

Julie's flat tone implied nothing out of the ordinary, but to Moorehead the announcement sounded like a death knell, the end of his tenure at CCC. "I didn't realize we had problems, certainly none we can't handle in-house," he said.

"Now don't get defensive, Brian. Jon's a sort of efficiency expert."

"Efficiency expert?" he said, studying the man. "What kind of efficiency expert?"

Julie ignored the question. "He won't get in your way. Right, Jon?"

Kelly smiled. "You won't know I'm here," he assured Moorehead, who kept shifting his gaze between them.

"Well," he said, licking his lips, "you'll call if I can be of assistance?"

"I'll do that," Kelly replied.

"Jon'll mostly work out of this office, but he's bound to pop up anywhere. So, alert the others without alarming them," Julie said.

"I'll try not to be too disruptive," Kelly added. "I know how folks get nervous when outsiders come around sticking their noses in their affairs."

Moorehead didn't respond.

"Tell 'em I'm not interested in assessing productivity or rating performances. That's Julie's area. My goal's simply to see how we can better serve our clients."

"Oh, you're one of us," Moorehead said, a little easier now. "I thought you might've been one of those Wharton MBA wonks."

"Just the opposite. I'm far more comfortable with technology than with people."

"I'll be interested in your assessment," he said, not liking this one bit.

The notion of an outsider, even a partner, reviewing his work set him brooding. Later that day, as he left for home he passed Julie's partially open door and saw Peters alone, hunkered over a stack of contracts. For an instant he considered stopping and bidding him goodnight, but reasoning he was trouble, decided the less he had to do with him the better, and continued on. He ate little that evening and slept fitfully.

Over the next few weeks he struggled to recall where he'd seen Peters before, and finally it hit him. It had

217

been at a technology trade show in Las Vegas, where he'd given a talk about some government program. But that bit of information did nothing to diminish his misgivings. Noting that Kelly was in before anyone and remained long after the others had left, he began wondering if he had a life outside the office. He was like a shadow on the wall— there but not there. If he wasn't sequestered with mounds of contracts, he was running programs in the mainframe room, always alone and never once seeking assistance. One evening, pretending he'd forgotten something, Moorehead returned near midnight to discover Peters in the secure room pouring through the NASA binders. When he offered assistance, Peters glanced up, smiled, and politely refused.

A tense seven weeks passed before Julie summoned Moorehead back.

"Sit down, Brian," he said, motioning to one of two heavy leather chairs in the center of the room, while he remained at his desk, the very desk Moorehead had purchased what seemed like a decade ago.

They were alone, Peters was off somewhere. Perched on the edge of the chair, he thought, this is it, it's over. He's giving me the ax.

"You've been doing a fine job keeping everyone focused," Julie began.

Okay, Moorehead thought steeling himself, here it comes. But he couldn't sit there and let it happen. Taking the initiative, he began jabbering, saying what needn't be said, and doing it with an intensity and speed that only served to emphasize his fear.

"Thank you, but it's more than me, you know. I mean, I've got a good team now. Everyone dedicated to making CCC a success. All highly motivated men. That fire you lit under them," he said, purposely excluding himself, "really got their attention. Got everyone focused again. Not a slacker among them, not a one." He wanted to stop—knew he should—but couldn't. "They're pulling a hundred percent. I wouldn't change a thing. They'd go to the moon and back for you. No slackers. Oh, I already said that, but you know that."

Julie almost felt sorry for him. "True," he said bringing him to a halt, "but you deserve much of the credit."

Moorhead blinked. Had he been mistaken? Perhaps he wasn't being fired. "That's very kind," he said cautiously. "I've learned a lot from you."

And when Julie said it took a big man to admit that, Moorehead felt his face warm. "It's just the beginning," he said less tentatively. "We've got the momentum now to keep charging."

"Good," Julie said, his thoughts more on Moorehead's observations about Kelly's work there. "These several weeks must've been frustrating, having to watch an outsider intrude on your turf," he said.

"Perhaps a tad disconcerting," he conceded.

"Just a tad?" Julie said.

Forcing a smile, he admitted, "Perhaps more than a tad. But I figured it's your show and if you think I should know you'll tell me." And when Julie nodded, it wasn't clear if Julie was agreeing that it was his show, or that he was about to disclose what Peters had concluded from his visit.

"Did you and Peters get a chance to talk?"

"No, not really. Whenever I offered to help he declined."

"Help him how?"

Moorehead shrugged. "I figured I could provide some clarity."

"And?"

"And nothing. He thanked me and said he'd let me know if he needed my assistance."

"And did he?"

"No."

Julie studied him a moment. "Well, Jon's not shy. I'm sure he would've asked if he had a need." Then to Moorehead's surprise, he said, "He had nothing but praise about how you've structured the operation."

"*Had*?" he said leaning forward. "He's done here?"

"Pretty much. I expect he'll be gone in a day or so."

"So, should anyone ask, it's business as usual?"

"Yep."

"No changes?"

"What type of changes?"

Moorehead shrugged. "I don't know—personnel, policy, operational. All that work, there's bound to be changes."

"Perhaps a few, but nothing significant. Certainly nothing that needs to be addressed now." Then, rising and coming around the desk, he said, "You know, I've been thinking it's time we took a breather. God knows, we've certainly earned one."

"A breather?" he said, fearing the ax again.

"Yeah. Loosen our togas a bit."

"Our togas?"

Julie smiled. "We've been working without a break for months. Hell, it's past Labor Day," he said as if just realizing it. "Summer's over and we're still at it."

Moorehead thought back several months, to that black Wednesday when Louie and his cohorts had descended on them. It had been a horrible experience. Since then he'd spent precious little time with his family.

"I was thinking we might get together in Annapolis Saturday," Julie continued. "Get out on the water, maybe cruise the bay."

"Gee, that'd be swell. The kids'll love it."

"No. No kids or wives. We'll do it with the families another time. We need time away from the office, the two of us. What do you say, you up for it?"

What could he say? Moments earlier he'd been expecting the worst, and now the man was opening his home to him. "That would be fine, a boy's day out. I've never been sailing."

"I'm not a rag sailor, that's for guys who like to work. This is pure relaxation, which is what we're entitled to."

"Sounds even better."

"One more thing," he said, when Moorehead stood to go. "I'm increasing your salary, and if we end the year as I expect you can count on a fat bonus, as well."

Moorehead returned to his office wondering how he could've been so mistaken about his stature in the firm.

Fully rested, he rose early Saturday feeling far better than he had in months, kissed his wife and headed for Annapolis. The morning was bright and clear with a hint of autumn in the air. He crossed the Severn River and headed north to Jones Station Road, where he nearly missed the entrance to Rugby Hall. The sun grew stronger by the time he reached the house and he could feel the heat rising from the river. It was a fine day, he mused, pleased at finally forging a bond with Julie. The door opened and his eyes widened.

"You must be Brian," Nikki said.

"And you're Nikki," he said, accepting her hand.

"Please come inside. Julie's getting the boat ready." She wore linen Bermuda shorts and a sleeveless blouse.

He followed her into the kitchen, admiring her silky sun-bleached hair, the curve of her legs, and her musky perfume.

"You'll have some breakfast, won't you?" she asked.

"Sure," he said sitting at the table set for three, fresh flowers in the center.

"Julie's told me about the work you're doing," she said handing him a cup of coffee. "He says you're the backbone of the firm."

"He's being overly kind," Moorehead replied. "It's really the other way around. He's the driving force," he said trying to keep his eyes from washing over her.

At one point, bending to a retrieve rolls from the oven, she turned and caught him staring and responded with an amusing smile that both embarrassed and aroused him. Later, when her hand brushed his while re-filling his cup, he imagined she might be hungry for companionship. It was a pleasant fantasy that kept him looking for other signals.

"It's too bad you're not coming with us," he said when she joined him at the table.

"Perhaps next time," she replied with the same arousing smile.

He was thinking how pleasant it was sitting there, the two of them, the river glistening in the distance, when Julie came up from behind and startled him.

"You made it okay," he said. "We picked a good day, wind's light and the water's calm."

Nikki noted the flash of disappointment, and saw it again after breakfast, when Julie leaned in and kissed her as they readied to leave.

"What do you think of her?" Julie asked as they left the boathouse.

"She's a wonderful gal," Moorehead replied, glancing back at the bluff.

"She is that, but I meant the boat."

"Oh, it's a real beauty." His thoughts were still back at Rugby Hall when they reached the city dock.

"Brian, meet Gino," Julie announced when Esposito, the Maryland Club manager, climbed aboard. "You guys get acquainted while I steer around these rag sailors," he called over his shoulder.

"Where're we going?" Moorhead asked Esposito as they headed toward the bay.

"Not far. Down the coast a ways," he replied while handing him a beer from the cooler he'd brought.

Moorehead thought it early to start drinking, but he took it anyway, and by the time they'd reached Herring Bay they'd dusted off a six-pack between them.

"There it is," Esposito said nodding toward Deale, one of the fishing villages dotting the bay. And when Moorehead glanced at the idled charter boats alongside the wharf, he said, "No. Over there," indicating an anchorage about fifty yards off a point of land.

Shielding his eyes, Moorehead saw the sleek yacht amid several boats, and his pulse raced. Two bikini-clad women were waving at them from the bow.

"Oooh-eeee," Esposito sang, "get a load of those casabas."

Moorehead just stared.

"I think I know how Columbus must've felt," Esposito said when the women undid their tops and jumped in.

A moment later Julie cut the engine and they drifted to the yacht, the two swimmers coming up beside them. And as Julie tossed a line to a waiting crewman, Esposito leaned over the stern and, telling her she was too big to throw back, helped the large-breasted one aboard.

Not knowing what to do, Moorehead stood there watching, until jarred by the other swimmer.

"Well?!" she cried.

"Huh?"

"There's a million jelly fish in here."

Feeling foolish, he quickly bent and, grasping her smooth arms, pulled her up, the water splashing on him. She was a head shorter than he, evenly proportioned, with the well-toned figure of a gymnast, and smelling pleasantly of coconut lotion—all lovely attributes. But what he focused on mostly were her breasts.

"Thanks," she said shaking her short dark hair, the droplets hitting his face.

"You're, uh, welcome," he said, thinking he'd suddenly been transported into a Fellini film.

"You got a name?" she asked with a fetching smile.

He was still gazing at her dark nipples when Julie called from the yacht to say he'd catch up with them later. Moorehead watched him head for the bridge, where a well-tanned man in a skimpy European swimsuit and gold necklace was frowning down at them.

"Who's he?" she asked of Julie. "He's kinda cute."

"Oh, just a guy I work worth," he replied. "What's with the greaseball up there? He doesn't look too happy about you being here. You two connected?"

Her smile disappeared. "He owns the boat, but I wouldn't use that term around here if I were you."

"Why, is he the jealous type?"

"Are you worried?"

"Should I be?" he said, looking to see if they were still being watched.

"First answer my question," she said snaking her arm around his waist. "What's your name?"

He said, "Brian," guessing she was in her early twenties.

"Would that be Irish or Scotch?"

"Would what be Irish or Scotch?" The warm dampness of her body against his, made concentrating difficult.

"Your name, silly."

"Does it matter?"

"It might," she said with a dimpled grin.

"What's your preference?"

Her smile widened. "Well, I'm kinda partial to Scotsmen. They're so virile, if you know what I mean."

"I believe I do, and you're in luck," he lied, checking the bridge again, and pleased to see both men gone. "And what's yours?"

"Call me Carol. You married, Brian?" she asked nodding at his wedding band.

"Sorta."

She laughed. "You mean she is, but you're not."

"That's one way of putting it. Is that a problem?"

She shrugged. "It might be for her, not me."

"So, Carol, what about that gentleman up there with my friend?"

"That's better. He's a pretty tough cookie." And when Moorehead frowned, she said, "But don't worry, I'm a free agent." Just then the boat rocked and she tightened her hold. "Well, whatayasay, Brian, shall we join the others?"

He looked around and was surprised they were alone.

"Why not," and taking her by the waist, lifted her onto the ladder.

Inside, the smoke was thick and pungent. A few couples were swaying to a bossa nova, the others were gathered at a long bar across the room. Conversations were low and intimate, and no one looked their way as she led him to the bar and angled a space for them.

Moorehead looked around, expecting to see Esposito, but couldn't find him.

"Here," she said, handing him a frosted glass.

"What, no paper umbrella?" Then, tasting it, he smacked his lips, declaring, "Mmmm. Tequila."

"You like it, laddie?"

He answered with a long swallow. "What else is in it?"

She shrugged. "It's the house special. Whoever's tending bar makes his version."

Just then someone squeezed in beside them, pressing her into him.

"You got one friendly boat here," he said.

She winked. "Gets friendlier the longer you're aboard."

"Not to mention the service," he said when another drink appeared.

"That gets better, too," she promised. "It all gets better."

He pushed away his empty glass, took up the full one and drank. "This is potent stuff."

"Doesn't seem to affect you."

"Sweetheart, I believe you could make a rubber band hard."

The edges of her mouth turned up. "I'll take that as a compliment."

"You can take this, too," he said taking her wrist and pushing her hand down between them.

"Hey!" she shouted pulling away. "What the hell're you doing?!"

Heads turned and suddenly he was the focus of attention.

"Is there a problem here?" someone asked.

"Nothing I can't handle," she said fixing Moorehead with a cold stare and looking as if she might swing at him.

Standing there under her gaze, his shoulders sagging, he could think only of Julie and his job. One word of this and he could kiss it goodbye. Swallowing hard, he said in an unsteady voice, "Please..., I'm truly sorry." But the words seemed not to reach her. "I didn't mean to offend you," he continued. "I thought we were..., I mean, between the booze and the way we were talking and pressing against each other..., Well, I got aroused and I thought...,"

"You thought I was a pushover!" she said louder than necessary.

227

"No, no. Honest. I didn't think that at all. I'm sure you're a fine young lady."

Before he could say more she was laughing.

"What…?! Why're you laughing?"

The sparkle back in her eyes, she said, "I wish I had a camera. You should see yourself."

"You mean that was a put-on?"

Coming to him, the warmth back in her voice. "Relax, cowboy. I was just having some fun." Then, slipping her hand where he'd put if before, she said, "Where's your friend?"

"He went back into his shell," he said, relief turning to anger. Then, gulping his drink, he said petulantly, "That wasn't funny."

"We're not all doormats," she said, in what was a clear reference to his wife. When his mood didn't change, she pressed into him again, saying, "Come on, Brian, don't be a grouch."

"It was embarrassing," he said, his excitement returning.

"I'm feeling movement. Does this mean you forgive me?"

Before he could reply there was another drink at his elbow. "This guy getting paid by the hour or the drink?"

"Empty glasses are against the rules," she told him.

"There are rules?"

"Why do you ask?" Her eyes were mischievous again. "Are you a rules man?"

Grinning, he said, "Uh-uh, the opposite. I'm a rules-baker. Make that a rules-*breaker*."

She giggled and he laughed with her. "I think I've had enough house specials. I'm beginning to feel airborne."

Pretending a frown. "I thought you were a Scotsman."

"All right, one more then," he said signaling for another.

"That's my bonnie lad." And when he finished it, she took his hand and led him to a nearby sofa, where she pushed him down and fell on his lap. "How's this, cowboy?" she said, placing her arms around his neck. "Still feel airborne?"

"No, but I'll tell you what is airborne," he replied.

"No need to."

"You're…, er…, not going to embarrass me again, are you?"

Putting her lips to his ear, she whispered, "Only if you'd like me to." Then she kissed him, her tongue pressing in on his.

"Wow!" he said when they'd pulled apart. "Where'd you learn to do that?"

"You ain't seen nothin' yet," she said, kissing him longer and harder.

After a while he slipped his hand beneath her swimsuit, and then winced when she stiffened. "Not another rejection," he said, almost pleading.

She smiled. "I think you've had enough rejections, sweetie. It's time we got serious," she said standing. Then, pulling him up, "Let's go."

"Where to?"

"To paradise."

Down below, the first cabin she tried was locked, but not the second.

229

"Say, this is elegant," he said taking in the paneled stateroom. Then, grabbing himself, he said, "I hafta whiz."

"In there," she said, pointing to the bathroom. "Hurry back."

When he returned he found her stretched across the bed, a packet of white powder balanced on each nipple, a third, lower down.

"You want it before or after?" she asked tilting her head.

"Howbout during?" he said, tearing at his clothes.

"I like that," she said swinging her feet to the floor.

Without a word, he stepped forward and watched with delight as she powdered his erection.

"Be still while Carol works her magic," she murmured bending to him.

Moorehead closed his eyes and did his best to make the moment last. But she was far more skilled than he imagined, and soon he was on his toes, shuddering uncontrollably.

But she hadn't finished with him. "Lie next to me," she said. Then, dusting herself with the remaining powder, she guided his head down, telling him, "Enjoy yourself, laddie."

The spell was broken when Esposito pulled the black satin sheet away. "Wake up, pal, time to go," he said, shaking him.

"Wha..?" Moorehead said, blinking him into focus.

"How ya feelin', pardner?"

"Gino," he mumbled through the lingering taste of coconut, "what the hell happened?"

"Who you kidding, you animal?" he said tossing Moorehead his clothes. "Sounds like you ruined that little heifer for life. No one's ever going to satisfy her like you."

"She said that?" he said, pushing himself up.

"Would I lie?"

Suddenly he wanted more. "Where is she?"

"Give the kid a break, you beast. Besides, she's already ashore with the others."

"Ashore?"

"The crab feast, and if you don't move your ass we'll miss it." And as Moorehead struggled with his clothes, he asked, "So you like the white stuff?"

"Uh?"

"Snow White. Coke."

"I know what you mean," he said guardedly.

"You like it?" And when he didn't reply, Esposito shrugged. "Hey, what you do is your business."

"What's that mean?"

"It means we both work for the same man, which means I ain't saying anything to nobody."

The slight motion of the boat was making Moorehead queasy. "So this stays between us?" he said, fumbling with his belt.

"I like my job, too."

"What about the girl? Carol?"

"Don't worry about her. We had a little talk and she's savvy."

"You're sure?"

Esposito nodded. "Yeah, she's cool."

Moorehead sighed. "I guess I owe you."

"Forget about it."

"No, I mean it. Thanks."

"It's no big deal." Then taking several packets from his pocket, he said, "Here, it's primo. A gift between friends."

Moorehead shook his head. "I can't."

"Why not?"

Moorehead shrugged.

"Go on, take it," he said, pressing them into his hand. "What're friends for? Besides, I get all I want any time I want."

He hesitated. "Just between us, right?"

"Who am I gonna tell?"

Moorehead looked at the packets, then shoving them in his pocket, said, "It's damn good of you."

"Call me anytime. I got a reliable source from New York. High quality, reasonable price, and always available."

Moorehead went into the bathroom, threw water on his face and emerged with a grin. "You know," he said, squaring his shoulders, "life is good."

Esposito laughed. "Better than you know. Now let's get some grub, I'm starving."

Once ashore, they found newspaper-covered picnic tables laden with pitchers of beer and mounds of steamed crabs. And while Moorehead went off searching for Carol, Esposito told Julie, "It's done."

* * *

It was mid-November. Nixon was forming his new cabinet, and Julie was in the cold lifeless hills of Lake Carmel.

"Everything's in place, Paolo," he said of Kelly's alterations to CCC's programs. "We're ready to begin."

They were walking under a heavy sky, leaves crunching beneath their feet, their hands deep in their pockets and two bodyguards trailing behind. The older man in heavy woolen slacks, matching cap, and down hunting jacket, took several paces before asking, "What's your guess on the take?"

"It's complicated," Julie told him. "It depends on how soon the feds spend the money. He then explained, "It's not like Social Security or food stamps, where they disburse a given amount per month. With these programs the amount'll vary from quarter to quarter. It's mostly determined by spending cycles, but don't worry," he assured him, "ultimately we get our share."

"I don't like ultimately. Give me a number."

Julie shook his head. "It differs with each program. For example, with the Small Business Administration, first we send unsecured loans to ghost companies, and when the program shows those loans are eighty percent repaid we use the data to create more loans to ourselves, and so on."

"I hear you, but I still want a number."

"Like I said, it's complex. So complex Kelly had to create a separate program to monitor the skims. The important thing, Paolo, is whenever the government spends a dollar we get our share."

Gava stopped and turned, his lazy eye adrift, the other, cold and hard. "No, Julie, the important thing is we're in a fucking war, and wars cost money. So give me your best shot."

Julie sighed. He didn't know. "Conservatively, a hundred million a month."

Gava went silent for a long moment, then he smiled. "Better not let anything happen to Mr. Kelly, or that other meatball."

"Moorehead," he said.

"Yeah, him."

"They're both under control," he assured him.

CHAPTER TWENTY (1968-1969)

Vowing never to repeat the debacle at Joe Barbara's upstate farm in Apalachin, Gava had purchased his own safe haven on the outskirts of Hawthorne, a tiny community north of the city. The spacious farm house and outbuildings stood away from prying eyes, at the end of an unmarked lane in the center of fifty acres of apple trees. As an added precaution, the property was deeded to the caretakers, Gava's second cousin and his wife, John and Alma Russo, while the orchard itself was leased to local growers.

In the icy days of February, two weeks after their supreme leader Vito Genovese's diseased heart finally failed him; Gava called a summit of ranking bosses. It was the first gathering of its kind since Barbara's 1957 fiasco, and, understandably, it drew an uneasy band of men. And while all agreed it was needed, none much cared for being summoned by a Neapolitan. Yet, they attended. Of the twenty-four families that monopolized America's underworld two years earlier, only eighteen were present. The others, in such disarray, were either represented by more powerful allies or had suffered enough losses they could no longer be considered families.

Unlike Barbara's conclave, which drew fifty-five dons and under bosses and their entourages, along with uninvited New York State troopers and a lot of unwanted news media, Gava's was limited to the eighteen bosses. Here, too, he was vigilant; staggering their arrivals and departures through several gates around the property, all guarded by men dressed and armed as hunters. And whereas Barbara had taken over the local hotel, reserving a hundred rooms in his name, those responding to Gava's call would not remain anywhere near Hawthorne overnight. Nor did he order hundreds of pounds of steaks and other delicacies from local shops, as Barbara had. As he reminded them, this wasn't a social event.

The afternoon shadows were long by the time they arrived and had settled around a single table. And while there were several pressing issues confronting the warring factions, the most delicate one, and the reason they'd consented to meet, was to select Genovese's successor.

Gava knew this wasn't going to be a cakewalk. Those in attendance were an uncompromising lot of veterans who'd fought the hard fight and survived. Yet, on this day, even the usually confident ones were uneasy, their expressions as dark and severe as the winter night closing around them.

"Let's take care of first things first. We need to talk about Joey B," he said, of the still-absent Sicilian. "He has to go. He's got no business being on the commission."

Immediately, Johnny Dekes, the aging Detroit boss, was on his feet defending Baratta, on whose friendship he relied as a counterbalance against the more powerful Chicago outfit. "Hold on a goddamned minute!" he protested. "This is bullshit," he told the other New York bosses. "Without Joey you got complete control. You can't take him out, so you want us to do it for you," he said looking around for support and finding none.

"Okay," Gava said, his voice rising. "You want Joey to keep his seat? Fine! Let's give him the fucking seat. Tommy!" he shouted, summoning a flat-faced soldier from the adjoining room. "Bring me a chair and put it here," he ordered, indicating the space beside him.

The man nodded and returned with the chair, backing cautiously from the room.

"*Bene*! Here it is," Gava said. Then, addressing the vacant seat, he said, "Joey, you got something you wanna say? No? Okay. Then your pal Johnny does. Go on," he said to the man across the table. "Ask Joey for his advice about anything. And while you're at it, be sure to ask for some dough to cover you while the feds beat your brains in. Or maybe you should ask him to stop the war he manipulates from wherever the hell he's hiding. The bloodiest fucking war in our history that keeps us from doing what we're supposed to do. Go on," he urged, grabbing the chair and rattling it.

Dekes' powerful fists remained clenched before him, his dark eyes smoldering. Refusing to be drawn in, he said through clenched teeth, "It's your show, Paolo."

Holding Dekes' stare with his good eye, the other floating wildly, he went on, "Maybe you should ask Joey for protection from the niggers and spics moving into our territories. You know, the ones we can't control anymore because we're too busy fighting each other and dodging the fucking feds."

George Vercessi

When Dekes failed to respond Gava flung the chair against the wall behind him, sending bits of plaster to the floor. "So much for Joey's advice."

"That's a nice piece of showmanship, Paolo. Next time, do it with Joey in it," Dekes challenged. "Now, if you finished your little act maybe we can talk about the problem." To the others, he said, "You know Joey'd be here if the feds weren't hounding him like a dog. Everybody here understands the need to go in the shadows till things cool down. This ain't the first time a boss went in hiding, and his absence shouldn't be used against him." To Gava, he said, "When the heat's off, and it will be, he'll be back stronger than when he left."

"Yeah, and at our expense. Please, Johnny, don't insult us," he said, modulating his tone. "We're talking survival here. Joey isn't the solution to our problems. And if he was, how long do we wait, and what're we supposed to do till then? Be honest, Johnny. Is he hiding from the feds or waiting out the war he started?" Looking around, he said, "He's divided and weakened us, and if we don't get off the dime and take action we'll be sucking hind tit while those street punks move in and take over what's left of our business."

Having put them into this quagmire, Gava knew the pressure they all faced. He also knew that under different circumstances they'd have challenged him for his boldness, as Dekes was doing. But with their cherished anonymity peeled away and the feds on their backs, and the organization in turmoil, these aging dons, some in declining health, were feeling uncharacteristically vulnerable.

"Paolo speaks for me," interjected an elderly Brooklyn boss, one who'd come to rely increasingly on Gava's support. "The way we're heading we're gonna be extinct. This thing with the feds isn't like when Dewey and Kefauver came after us. I don't know how the bastards do it, but they got over six hundred indictments. Nobody's safe today. And what the feds don't do to us, we do to ourselves with this war. It's time we face facts and make changes, or it's over for us. *Finito!*" he said pounding the table.

"Who more than me wants change?" the Denver boss quickly added. "I'm out millions, but is dumping Joey the answer? I'll be honest, I don't know. But I do know Paolo's been a good friend. I say we listen to what he's got to say."

Nodding his agreement, the San Diego don lamented, "If this shit keeps up I'll be kissing those wetbacks' asses and paying for the privilege. There's deals going down I can't get a piece of because of the feds. Paolo's right. Either we make changes now or start talking Spanish."

Gava listened placidly as each man voiced his frustrations. And when they'd finished, he told them, "There's a way out of this hole we're in. I been talking to my cousins in Naples and I got the okay to offer support to anyone who wants it, deep support for as long as we need it." And when the others looked at him skeptically, he said, "That's right, they'll underwrite our losses till this mess blows over." Adding, "But only if we stop the fighting. They talked it over with your people in Palermo and they all agree this has gone far enough."

The room fell quiet as they considered the implications of such an arrangement. And when someone asked how this could be, that the Camorra chieftains were willing to insert themselves in the organization's affairs, Gava said they saw this as the only way to recoup what they'd lost in the process. What he didn't say was that he was financing the arrangement. But he did say the offer wasn't without conditions; most notably, that the Neapolitans expected he would assume Genovese's position within the organization. As expected, this last piece of information set them arguing again, and for a while it appeared the offer would be rejected. But Gava's supporters held firm, and one by one the opposition yielded until only Joe Batters, the powerful Chicago boss, remained. In the end, even he conceded. The decision made, it then fell to Batters, as the longest sitting boss, to ask, "On behalf of the others, Paolo, will you agree to serve?"

Gava nodded and all present swore their allegiance.

Perhaps fearing Baratta's reprisal, they opted not to vote him out, as Gava had proposed, and as a conciliatory gesture he didn't push the issue. Instead, he laid out his unorthodox plan for keeping the organization from further unraveling.

He began by decreeing, "The war is over. Two years is enough. Our cousins across the sea will support only those who make peace. The others are on their own."

As with any imposed treaty the pronouncement was greeted with subdued enthusiasm, particularly among those with scores to settle. Still, they agreed. Even Baratta's outlawed clan, to whom word would be sent explaining the arrangement and all it entailed, would be spared if they fell in line.

Not surprisingly, his next pronouncement proved the old warriors still had fire in their bellies.

"To survive and prosper we must embrace change," he told them. "The old ways of doing business are over. Starting today, one of my men will be a member of each of your families. It would be good not to ignore him."

Again there were protests, with some threatening to walk out. But Gava listened patiently, and when they were through, he said, "I've heard you, now hear me. You argue for what is good only for you and your own families. That, my brothers, is a recipe for anarchy. Unlike you, I want what's good for all of us, but we will fail before we begin if we leave here expecting to do business as usual. Right now there's too much bad blood. What we need is buffers, people to run interference, and my people can do that. Without them in place the peace won't last a week. Now, if anyone has a better idea put it out there."

A few tried, but he rejected their logic, arguing, "You think Naples is going to pump cash into your pockets without guarantees?"

In the end, they consented, some more reluctantly than others. And while it was a victory, he knew it would be short-lived if he didn't win over the few hardcore dissenters. Those he couldn't persuade, he'd feed to Goodmann.

CHAPTER TWENTY-ONE

The peace, though tenuous in some regions, was still holding nine months later when Gava left for Naples. Predictably, absent the shootings, the war had slipped from the headlines. Further, without Nunzio guiding him, Goodmann's task force had become far less intrusive. What most concerned Gava now were rumblings from some *padrones* in the Italian countryside—thus the journey.

Months earlier, Neapolitan emissaries had judiciously suggested a summit between the Camorra kingpins and their Sicilian and Calabrian counterparts. Like most dealings in this strange land of the *bella figura*, where maintaining one's stature was vital to the process, negotiations had been lengthy and often tedious. Finally, it was agreed. The factions would meet in Benevento, a village sixty kilometers west of Naples. And while the site confirmed the Camorra's new prominence in America, it had little bearing on how the groups functioned in Italy, where historically the only times they joined forces were to combat more powerful enemies, as they had with Mussolini's oppressive central government some thirty years earlier.

Gathered within the Camorra chieftain's mountain fortress, they were as grim as the heavy mist shrouding the valley below. For this first meeting, they followed a protocol that accorded each man, including Gava, equal status.

"It isn't business as usual," Gava began, mindful of his mission. "As you know, we're moving out of some areas and into more legitimate operations. That's the first step. Soon afterward we'll transfer some business to groups on the fringe of our territories, those that now live off our scraps."

"Why?" asked the Sicilian from LaStidda, the Mafia branch rooted in Baratta's ancestral town of Agrigento.

"Because we're going to need partners," he told them. "Those little shits are hungry and I want to bring them to the table while it's still ours."

"And what do we get in return?" asked a thickset man known to his countrymen as the *Beast*, because of his success in infiltrating his opponents and savagely eliminating them. Among the Sicilian contingent, he was the most powerful.

Gava's view of inner-city gangs differed from many of his peers back home, who mistakenly believed they could be controlled by force, a belief shared by their Sicilian countrymen. "More than we give," he replied. "America's changing and soon our cities will be sewers. You can forget about law and order because it won't exist. Believe me when I say it's best to make these changes while we're in control, because the longer we wait, the more it'll cost us. The gangs today are made up mostly of penny ante punks. If we wait for them to organize we lose everything. By doing it now we do it on our terms."

"What're you giving away?" the Beast pressed him.

"To start with, the street action, including the drug trade."

"That's crazy! We'd be fools to let it go," argued Nicola Spina, known throughout his native Calabria as *The Supreme One* for his position as head of the 'Ndrangheta syndicate there, and whose New York and Florida families relied heavily on the lucrative cocaine and heroin trade.

"We won't lose anything. We're just going to step back a little," Gava told him. "We'll continue controlling the source. Drugs are spreading, and everyone's looking the other way now, but that'll change when the drugs reach into the white neighborhoods. Then the feds'll step in. And as you know, once they do, they make headlines. And the easiest way to get headlines is to pick up dealers. I don't want our people getting rolled up with the spics and niggers.

"Nor can we get into turf wars with them. They're a bunch of *pazzos* who use thirteen year-olds for triggermen because they get prosecuted as minors," he said. "Think of the headlines when we start blasting pimple-faced kids. No," he said, "better to make deals now with the clubs we want to do business with, and help them eliminate the competition. It don't matter who sells the shit on the street, 'cause in the end they buy from us. But more important, they'll take the heat."

"I have no problem with you managing things in America," Spina replied. "You want to put the punks between you and the cops, that's your business as long as it doesn't reduce our income."

"Your income will grow," Gava assured him. Next, he spoke not of murder, or extortion, or family warfare, but of the organization he envisioned that one day would function as a shadow government, much as it did in Italy. His message was simple; it was time to shift from force to subtler, less obvious means of control. "We're already on our way," he told them, "and you can join us and enjoy great wealth and power, or you can follow the old ways."

"We already gave you our backing. That is why you are the leader," the Beast said. "What more do you want?"

"There are still some who fight me. Sicilians listen first to Sicilians, and to succeed in America I need your full support."

"And what do we get in return for this peace you seek?"

"Power unlike any you've known before."

There were ten at the table—four Sicilians, four Neapolitans, the Calabrian and Gava.

"If we agree, who controls the operation?" The question came from a wiry Sicilian who'd sat quietly till then. He was younger than the others, closer to Julie's age, with pockmarked skin and penetrating eyes set beneath untamed eyebrows. His rumpled appearance was meant to make him seem like a simple man of the land, when in fact he rose from the crowded streets of Palermo and was every bit as savvy as any New York boss. In his brief tenure heading his organization, he had extended his influence beyond Sicily, into northern Italy, Hungry, Austria, Yugoslavia and Malta. Of them all, it could be said he was closest to Gava's equal.

It was the question the Neapolitans had expected, the very reason for this meeting. And while directed at Gava, it was answered by their host, the Camorra chieftain, a burly giant of a man, broad as a door is wide and as tall, who, like the Beast, enjoyed mythical status throughout the region. Always in hiding, he was a master at changing his appearance. And despite his size, it was rumored he could walk through a regiment of *carabinieri* and not be recognized. On this day his cropped jet-black hair and full beard enclosed his square head like a helmet, and when he spoke it was in the raspy voice common among the poor who'd grown up in cold, damp environs.

"We do," he answered through stubby brown teeth, indicating everyone at the table. "Paolo's organization will be as powerful as we allow it, but we are the ultimate decision-makers."

"You say *we* freely," said the Beast.

"When decisions must be made, they will be made by us at this table," he assured them. "Whatever happens in America happens with our blessing."

"And what of their commission?" the Sicilian asked.

"It continues with Paolo at the head, but it will no longer be used to set family against family. Those days are over." Then, spreading his huge hands out before him, he asked, "Gentlemen, are we in accord?"

Spina, the Calabrian, said he'd go along.

The Sicilians allowed the man from Palermo to respond, and he too consented.

With all in agreement, the Beast said, "So be it. We are one."

Chapter Twenty-two (1969 – 1970)

Summer began cool and wet, then cruelly reversed itself in early July, turning much of the east coast into a brown tinderbox by August. But Julie didn't care. He was enjoying his latest acquisition, the *Lady N*, purchased from the Naval Academy when a larger vessel was assigned to the superintendent, one capable of handling increased protocol requirements levied on him by Nixon's aggressive foreign policy initiative that brought unprecedented numbers of VIPs to Washington, and thus to Annapolis. As a frequent guest aboard the old boat, Julie had moved quickly when the admiral announced plans to dispose of it.

Built in Holland before the war for a wealthy Philadelphia merchant who later turned it over to the U. S. Navy, the handsome fifty-footer was outfitted with distinguished brass fittings, teak decks and hand-rubbed mahogany fixtures. Julie's first act after acquiring it was to strike the original name and re-christen her. Thereafter, he and Nikki explored the Chesapeake Bay, cruising far north to Perryville at the mouth of the Susquehanna, and south to Solomons Island, where the Patuxent River joined the Chesapeake, which was where they were intending to go when he'd been summoned to Lake Carmel.

The evening before meeting Gava, he and Nunzio stepped from the house to the carpet of lawn that had been his father's garden. Where vegetables had grown, there were now intersecting footpaths boarded by English boxwoods. Even the revered cherry tree had fallen to the ax, replaced by a natural stone fountain similar to ones found in the atriums of Italian villas. And along the far side, where the fig trees once grew, were cone-shaped cypresses, chosen by his mother because the ancients had used the wood to encase cherished items for posterity. "The Pharaohs used them for coffins, and the Greeks and Romans for urns for their war heroes. This is how I wish to honor your father," she'd said of the stately sentries.

"What's this meeting about?" Nunzio asked, peeved at not being informed of its purpose.

"I guess we'll find out tomorrow."

"Remember who you're talking to," he snapped, still smarting from Gava's overly cautious way of parceling out information since taking control.

"All I know is it has to do with last year's summit in Hawthorne," Julie said.

"I know all about Hawthorne," he said. "I was there, remember? Tell me something I don't know."

Julie smiled. "Let's wait."

"You know," his uncle said, "you're starting to remind me of your old man."

"What's that supposed to mean?"

"It means I get the feeling you don't trust me."

"And why wouldn't my father trust you?"

Nunzio looked at him and shrugged. "What the hell do I know."

"Well, you wouldn't have said it if there hadn't been a problem."

Less concerned with the past than tomorrow's meeting, he conceded, "We had our differences sometimes, that's all."

"What sort of differences?"

"It ain't important. Tell me about tomorrow."

"All I know is he wants to talk about the deals he's been making," he said, as Nunzio withdrew his Camels and coaxed one from the pack.

"You mean the business in Benevento?"

"That's my understanding," Julie said, noting how small the sleek gold Dunhill looked in his uncle's hands.

"So how's that fit in with tomorrow?"

"It was no small achievement, getting them to come together."

"No shit, Dick Tracy. But how's that tie in with the Hawthorne meeting?"

"I can't say."

"Can't or won't?"

"Look, you know he's got this vision of how the organization should move forward. No doubt that's what he wants to talk about."

"Yeah, yeah, I know all about his vision. What I'd like to know is the changes he's planning," he said in a clear reference to his own long-held desire to move up in the organization.

"If I knew something I'd tell you." As they reached the edge of the garden, he said, "Tell me about Paolo and my father."

Again, Nunzio shrugged. "What can I say. They were like brothers. They respected each other, and no matter what happened they backed each other. That is, till they got their own territories."

"And?"

"And, what?"

"What happened then?"

"What do you think? Things changed. They always do. That's life."

"How?"

"Figure it out. They're out there hustling with their own crews, and naturally a rivalry develops. Nothing serious, a friendly kinda thing."

"A *friendly* rivalry?"

"That's what I said."

"And how'd you fit in?"

Another shrug. "Your old man would bust my chops, saying I should be working for him instead of Paolo. Said it wasn't right having his brother-in-law with the competition. That's when I reminded him it wasn't my call. Still, he didn't like it." After a moment, he said, "We were under Big John DeVito then. Fat John we called him, but never to his face. Now there was a tyrant."

"What do you mean?"

"The bastard controlled everyone's lives. You want a new car, you check with him and he tells you what to buy and who to buy from. He had to have a piece of everything. You want a house, he tells you what neighborhood. The only thing he didn't do was sleep with your wife on your wedding night like that greaser Ippolito in Chicago."

"A boss actually did that?"

He nodded. "That was years ago, but not to guys in the outfit. If that bastard saw someone in the neighborhood he wanted, you gave her to him."

"What happened if the guy objected?"

"She became a widow," he said, flipping his cigarette away.

Julie shook his head. "Unbelievable." After a few steps, he asked, "What about DeVito?"

"One of his tricks was playing everyone off each other."

"Must've done wonders for morale."

Nunzio nodded. "Talk about not trusting nobody. The old bastard even brought in soldiers from Naples, and then sent them back when they got too comfortable. He was always watching," he said touching a spot beneath his eye, "and shaking things up."

"How'd he and my father get along?" he asked when they'd reached Nunzio's shiny black Buick Electra hardtop, the only model he'd drive since learning it was the one Luciano preferred in his exiled Naples.

"No problem. He had a lot of respect for him, and for Paolo, too. Said they made a good team."

Julie studied his uncle. Despite his assurance, he suspected the rivalry hadn't played out as well as he'd have him believe. "What happened to DeVito?" he asked as Nunzio climbed in and started the engine.

"Caught a bullet in Miami," he replied before driving away.

* * *

Neither man spoke much during the drive north, Julie because he was thinking more of Paolo and his father, and

Nunzio because he was still sore at being shut out. When they arrived at the lake, the temperature was refreshingly cool, the scent of pines reminding Julie of the Severn and his postponed cruise with Nikki.

"Who's here?" he asked nodding at the cars beside the house.

"The Caddie's Gigi's," Nunzio said. "I don't know about the others."

They were walking to the house when Gava pushed open the door. "'Bout time," he called. And as they drew closer, "You're lookin' good," he said to Julie.

"You're looking pretty fit, yourself," Julie said of his even tan and easy manner.

The man heaved a sigh. "Things can always be better, but for now I'm happy. How's the new boat?"

"You heard about it?"

"I hear everything," he said winking at Nunzio.

"She's a beauty. Come see it."

"Maybe I will," he said, leading them through to the porch, where they found Reni and Gigi, the lieutenants from Chicago and Detroit, and two Camorristi from Naples, mobsters who'd become permanent members of Gava's crew as part of the deal forged in Benevento.

"First we eat then we talk," Gava said, motioning to the loaves of bread and cold cuts on the sideboard.

As they ate, Mosca pointed to the clouds gathering at the head of the valley. "In Napoli we call those *peccorini*, little lambs," he told Julie. "They bring rain. Soon we'll have a storm, but it won't last long."

Julie studied the distant puffs of cotton and the otherwise clear sky and, deciding rain was unlikely, replied between bites, "In case you haven't heard, we're in the middle of a drought."

"Don't matter," the older man said, eliciting smiles from his two countrymen, "it'll rain."

Julie looked again. "I doubt it."

"A grand?" he said.

Julie shrugged. "You're on."

"That was a sucker bet," Nunzio said, brushing food from his mouth.

"Fuck the rain," Gava said, pushing his plate away. "We got more important things to talk about." Then grinning, he said, "Today's the start of a new era. Thanks to Julie, we're moving into another phase." More clouds gathered as he told them of deals struck with the Sicilians and Calabrians, and how it all tied in to the Hawthorne summit. Soon heavy drops were pinging off the roof, and when Julie looked up he saw a curtain of rain moving down the lake toward them, the wind stirring up whitecaps before it. Closer in, boaters were rowing frantically for shore. Moments later, the languid willow at the edge of the property bent while its branches snapped out furiously. No sooner had those closest to the screen dragged their chairs away, and it was over. Scattered across the yard were leaves and torn branches. And with the sun came the distant shouts of children from the opposite shore.

Julie glanced at Mosca, who smiled. Nunzio simply shook his head.

Gava, meanwhile, continued. "It's time to think about the future, to make sure we keep the power we worked so hard for," he told them. "Me and Gigi, we talked," he said motioning to Mosca, "and we figure it should be like

Chicago, back when everyone thought Nitti took over from Capone, but it was Paul Ricca who was boss. And because they kept it quiet it went like that for years. It's going to be harder to pull that off today," he admitted, "but we gotta try. And the best way is to have somebody already in place and ready to take over when it's time, somebody in the shadows." Pausing, he said, "We figure that should be Julie. He's our best shot at holding on to what we got and keeping the feds out of the picture."

"And the Sicilians," added Mosca.

"Them too," Gava said.

Julie met his uncle's gaze and smiled, knowing he'd have some explaining to do during the ride back that evening.

"The problem is these computers," Gava went on. "As Julie can tell us, there's no escaping 'em. Once they tag you, you're in 'em for life. It's not like when they didn't know a soldier from a capo. Now everybody talks to everybody through these fucking machines."

"When do we tell the others?" the man from Chicago asked.

"In time," he was told. "For now, this thing with Julie stays between us."

As he listened, Julie was reminded of old tales in which names held serious power, and simply knowing a creature's name enabled one to control it.

Nodding at the two Camorristi, Gava told them, "Soldiers are coming from Naples. They'll work in legitimate businesses and have nothing to do with the organization. They're here to be used only by bosses with my blessing, and if a job turns messy they'll be back in Naples before the feds can ID them. Things are going to be different. We're running a cleaner operation. No more shoot-em-ups, like before. These guys are professionals."

Next, he said, "It's time we talk about putting our man in the White House. Somebody with a sense of obligation, not like that Kennedy bastard."

"Johnson was no prince, either," Mosca reminded him. "Look what he cost us. I don't mind paying," he said, "but when they forget where it comes from it pisses me off."

"They're all the same," Nunzio said. "This bum Nixon included."

"Which is why we need our own guy," Gava said.

"I don't see it happening anytime soon," Julie told them. "Whether you like him or not, Nixon's a two-term president. The voters don't oust incumbents during a war, not even an unpopular one like this one. And this war isn't going to end any time soon. On the positive side, it gives us time to position our man."

Chapter Twenty-three (1970)

When Gava asked Julie several months later, if he'd heard of Moshe Lipsky, he replied, "Who hasn't?"

A Russian Jew, Lipsky's connections were legendary, and his standing within the organization rock-solid. An early member of the notorious Amboy Dukes in Brooklyn's Brownsville section, he and his pals, Longy Zwillman, Lepke Buchalter and Bugsy Siegel, had earned a reputation as ruthless killers under the banner of Murder Incorporated. With ties to another clique of Russian Jews, Capone's archrival, Detroit's Purple Gang, he went on to join forces with Albert Anastasia, Lucky Luciano, and later, Vito Genovese, allowing the Italians to run things while he oversaw their gambling operations, the Vegas and Reno skims and their offshore drug money. As a loyal member of the Genovese family, he held a seat on every major council until Gava took over and let it be known he didn't trust him.

Thereafter, with his support within the organization waning, Lipsky began calling in markers in a futile attempt to strengthen his position, which further incensed Gava, who accused him of dividing and weakening the organization. Lacking an army of his own, he could either continue calling upon his dwindling allies for support, or retire. The choice was made for him when he learned of a pending federal indictment, and he quietly disappeared like his former ally Baratta. But unlike Baratta, he surfaced in various European cities exhibiting an opulent lifestyle before disappearing again and finally settling in Jerusalem. There, he immediately began an aggressive campaign for Israeli citizenship and the criminal immunity that came with it. His strategy was simple; make large contributions to key charitable organizations and ensure each donation received the appropriate publicity. But the Israelis didn't respond as he'd wished. Instead, embarrassed by his self-serving stunts, and continued pressure from the U.S. Justice Department urging his return, Prime Minister Golda Meir was forced to expel him as an undesirable.

Lacking other sanctuaries, and assured by his former allies that the fix was in, he willingly strode into the FBI's arms at Miami's airport. Three months later he appeared before a federal judge where, after a series of mistrials, he was convicted under the new RICO act.

It was while he was out on appeal because of poor health, and once again making demands of former associates, that Gava confided to Julie, "We have to clean house, but not the usual way. If we screw up he can hurt a lot of people, including yours truly." And when Julie hesitated, Gava asked in a tone suggesting he might be persuaded otherwise, "You think we shouldn't put the old bastard out of his misery?"

"No, I think we should," he replied. "He definitely knows too much." Surprisingly, the decision hadn't been a difficult one, and he marveled afterward at how easily he'd sanctioned Lipsky's execution, wondering when he'd crossed the line.

"Okay. He's dead," Gava said with finality. Then studying him, he asked, "So, what's bothering you?"

"I was just wondering if anybody ever retires from this outfit."

"Sure, sometimes."

"And the other times?"

"This is important, so remember it," Gava counseled. "People don't get killed for no reason. Those who die deserve to die."

Why did my father deserve to die?

Several weeks later he read that Lipsky had been found dead in his Miami Beach apartment, an apparent suicide victim, and he thought no more of it. An earlier time he'd have wondered, likely even cared, whether the man had left behind a wife or mistress, or any loving person.

Soon afterward, while Nixon was petitioning Congress for sixty million dollars to fight organized crime, Joe Colombo, the Profaci family don, was countering a series of federal indictments by publicly accusing the government of targeting him because of his heritage. And when Gava objected, the dapper Brooklyn boss refused to back off.

"You must stop this, Joe," he told the charismatic mobster, after one of his many appearances on national television. "We don't need this kind of attention."

"You're mistaken, my friend," the unflappable Colombo argued. "The only way to win this fight is by taking it to the press, like they do with us. You watch, they can dish it out but they can't take it. We're just starting to make things uncomfortable for them. Trust me on this," he said in his soothing tone, "we will prevail."

"You're not listening, Joe," Gava said with unusual restraint. "You keep this up you'll queer a lot of deals for us."

They spoke at length, and when they'd finished Gava accepted Colombo's promise to ease up. But after several weeks, when he failed to do so, Gava, both hurt and angry, called Julie in and, together, they decided to send Colombo and the rest of the organization a clear message; a message which was delivered on the twenty-eighth of June, while Colombo and fifty thousand co-celebrants gathered at Columbus Circle to kick off the second annual Italian-American Unity Day Rally.

At 11:45 A.M., fifteen minutes before the event was to commence, twenty-five-year old Jerome Johnson, a black photographer from New Brunswick, New Jersey, who'd been filming the powerful don, stepped forward and pumped three 7.65-millimeter bullets into him. Colombo went down immediately, a slug lodged in his brain and blood gushing from his neck and mouth.

That evening's television news led with the events at the base of the gaily-decorated Christopher Columbus statue, and the ensuing melee, when four additional shots pierced the humid air. Gruesome footage showed Johnson's lifeless body on the sidewalk, a .38-caliber nickel-plated Smith & Wesson beside him.

Asked about the unexplainable absence of Colombo's bodyguards and who the second shooter might be, one high-ranking police official replied tersely, "Those are good questions, but I don't have any answers."

In the days following, the police announced that the gun used on Colombo had been reported stolen nine years earlier. As for Johnson, his assailant was never identified, nor did his background suggest he was a professional killer, despite the masterful way he stalked and gunned down his victim.

"The sonofabitch survived," Gava lamented to Julie afterward over dinner in Pelham Bay.

Colombo was still in a coma when his Italian-American League disbanded and faded into obscurity several months later. He would eventually die without coming out of it.

CHAPTER TWENTY-FOUR (1971)

In what would be their first discussion on the subject, Julie arranged to meet Jeffries at the exclusive Georgetown Club in Washington, an unassuming townhouse in a row of similar homes on upper Wisconsin Avenue, distinguished only by its small brass plaque beside the street level door. He'd reserved a private room, where they could dine without distractions, specifically the female kind.

"Well, what do you think?" he asked after laying out his plan. "Can you commit?"

"Naturally I'm flattered that you'd even think of me this way," Jeffries replied. "But what's the urgency?"

"The clock's ticking and I need to know." And when he didn't respond, Julie reminded him, "I'm on your side."

"Of course I'm interested. Who wouldn't be? But no one's going to take such a commitment seriously now, not at this stage. I don't want to be another Harold Stassen," he said of the former Minnesota Governor and perennial presidential candidate. "Besides, I haven't even looked that far ahead."

"It's time you did."

Jeffries shook his head. "What's all this about? Why the rush?"

"There are people who want a change, people eager to support someone who's simpatico."

"That's half the people in this town, and all of them wanting someone who'll play ball with them."

"But none as powerful as organized labor."

"And they really want me?" he said skeptically.

"They want someone they can trust."

Frowning, he said, "I don't get it."

"You know how the system works. Organizations put feelers out and then they narrow the field."

"So this is legitimate, and you're their point man?"

"Why's that surprise you? You know my ties to labor."

"Because *I'm* not affiliated with labor," he reminded him. "I don't have any kind of record that would draw them to me."

"Don't worry about that."

Jeffries laughed. "Yeah, right."

"I'm serious. That's not a deal-breaker."

Jeffries studied him. "One of us is being very naïve. But for the sake of argument, let's say it isn't you. What're they looking for?"

"It's quite simple. They want someone with an open mind who won't screw them later." And before Jeffries could ask why, he said, "They're worried."

"Worried? What've they got to be worried about? They got industry by the balls."

"Times are changing. They're losing clout. Union memberships are at record lows and declining."

Jeffries' shrug indicated that wasn't his problem. Still, he asked, "Why me, when they can choose from a field of contenders?"

"I'm only the messenger."

"Who else are they looking at?"

"My understanding is right now you're it."

"And you believe them?"

Julie nodded. "I do. You're the man they want."

"It doesn't make sense."

"Stranger things have happened in this town."

Jeffries squinted across the table. "I want you to be totally honest. How do you assess this proposal? Are they fishing, or is it the real McCoy?"

"You know me, Bob. I wouldn't waste your time or mine if it wasn't genuine. They're prepared to do whatever's necessary, which means throwing everything behind their candidate."

"Just what type of support are we talking about?"

"I need to know if you'll commit first."

He shook his head. "I can't do that till I know what they expect of me?"

"A commitment to run, and your support when you're in office."

"That's it?" And when Julie nodded, he squared his shoulders and said, "If they're looking for a lap dog they better look elsewhere. I'm my own man, always have been. I won't be a stooge."

"No one's suggesting that. Like I said, all they want is someone they can trust to do the right thing, someone who won't screw them." Adding, "If you sign on—and I don't see anything wrong with being pro-labor—you'll have a blank check."

Still unconvinced, he asked, "And if I do, how do you envision making the leap from where I stand to being a credible advocate for labor? I mean, while I'm not anti-labor, I certainly haven't been out there leading any charges."

"We have time to fix that, which is why they want an early commitment."

"You'll have to explain that," he said. "I'm just a dumb ole southern boy."

"Sure. Dumb like a fox," Julie said. "We'll start by expanding your base beyond Florida by having you introduce a series of pro-labor bills. It doesn't matter that they don't go anywhere. The point is that you're there on the Hill advocating for them, which brings you over to their side, and which qualifies you to address their regional and national conventions. Later, when word gets around that your participation at fundraisers attracts the big donors, it won't take long before the party bosses are flying you around the country to support fellow Democrats. And at every appearance they'll guarantee substantial contributions. As you know, it's all about money."

Jeffries shook his head. "Sounds ambitious, maybe too ambitious."

"Of course it's ambitious! We're going for the gold. But it's doable, and once the party sees you can generate the bucks, you'll need a stick to keep them away."

"I wish I shared your confidence."

"You will once the money's flowing. So," he said after a moment, "What's it going to be? You in or out?"

Chapter Twenty-five (1972)

It was summer, and a number of heavy hitters were traveling far and wide, notably Secretary of State Kissinger, who was busy negotiating a failing Vietnam exit strategy, while closer to home, Jeffries was racing between political fundraisers before heading for Miami to endorse George McGovern and his running mate Tom Eagleton at the Democratic nominating convention. Gava, meanwhile, was also on the move. But unlike the others, he kept a much lower profile. Slipping into Italy via Switzerland—his preferred route—he was met near the border and driven south to Naples and then on to Benevento. Julie followed in mid-August, taking a Pan Am flight to Rome, where he checked into the exclusive Hotel Eden, overlooking the haute couture shops of Via Condotti at the foot of the Spanish Steps. The following morning, boarding the Rapido, he quickly found an empty compartment and settled in for the two-hour journey to Naples, and his initial meeting with the Benevento commission.

Gava had said the Sicilians he'd be meeting were as ruthless as they were powerful. That they'd eliminated over five hundred of their own in a bloody internecine war that enabled them to form the super-secret *La Cupola* commission in Palermo, which had recently captured the international heroin trade from their rivals in Marseilles. "These are dangerous men," he'd cautioned. We must not reveal too many details of our operations or they'll come after them, too."

He was reflecting on such an eventuality when the train rolled out of the seaside town of Formia and the door to his compartment slid open.

"*Permesso?*" the stranger asked with a smile. Trim and neatly tailored in a bleached muslin suit, he carried only a newspaper and a loosely wrapped package.

Julie looked up in surprise. With most Italians away on vacation the train was practically empty, and he wondered why he'd chosen this compartment. When he hadn't responded immediately the man looked around, as if to say, there's plenty of room for both of us.

"Sure," he finally said. "*Si accommodi.*"

But instead of entering he moved aside, allowing a shapely young woman in a gauzy summer dress to precede him, her perfume, a heady lilac fragrance, instantly filling the compartment. And while her manner was tentative and less confident than his, she offered a warm smile as she moved to the opposite seat, while he placed his package in the overhead rack.

Once settled, she smiled again before turning to her magazine. Taking the seat beside her, her companion immediately lost himself in his *Il Mattino*, Naples' major daily newspaper.

His attention now diverted from the Sicilians, Julie leaned back and watched the passing countryside. Several times he felt the woman's gaze, and each time caught her studying him with a curious expression before quickly dropping her eyes.

No one spoke, and all remained tranquil for the remainder of the journey, that is until they neared Naples, when she grew fidgety, flipping pages without purpose while crossing and re-crossing her legs. Soon afterward, as they left Pouzzoli, the station before Naples, she rose and, stepping to the door, nervously began smoothing her dress while her companion continued reading. Then moments before pulling into Mergellina, she slid open the door and, with a final glance at Julie, disappeared down the corridor, which was when her friend cast aside his newspaper and retrieved his package, allowing the wrapping to fall away.

"This is for you," he said in perfect English, holding the automatic inches away from Julie.

I'm going to die he thought as images of old news clippings of his father's bloody body ran before him. *I'm going just like him.* But the shots never came. Instead, the stranger tossed the gun down beside him, saying, "You might need it." Then, like the woman, he was gone, the door sliding closed behind him.

Julie remained seated, unable to move. His mouth had gone bone dry and his heart was pulsing blood through his ears like the ocean. It wasn't until the train jerked forward again and he glimpsed the pair heading for the stairs that he grasped what had happened. This is Gava's doing, he thought grabbing the gun, a nine-millimeter Beretta, and checking to see if it was loaded. It was, and he immediately chambered a round.

Gripping it beneath his jacket, he darted for the door, and scanned the corridor. A handful of passengers were at the far end of the car, none looking his way. Expecting others might still be in their compartments, he hung back several minutes once they'd pulled into Napoli Centrale to be certain all had departed. Then, shoving the gun inside his belt, he grabbed his suitcase and headed for the platform. Finding it deserted, he approached the dimly lit tunnel leading to the main concourse and waited by the entrance for the last footsteps to fade. To his distress, the tunnel curved to the right, preventing him from seeing if someone were waiting in the shadows. Determined to be vigilant, he took a breath and edged forward, hoping to make himself less a target by keeping to the inside wall. Twice he imagined a human sound and froze, but no one appeared.

To his relief, the usually hectic concourse was quiet, with only a few holiday travelers milling about, none looking particularly suspect—but then, neither did the couple in his compartment. Cautiously steering a path around them, he quick-stepped it to the entrance, the gun heavy on his hip, where he expected to find the escort Gava had promised.

When he reached the canopied entrance there was no one, not a soul. Out beyond the station, the city was deadly quiet. He'd been to Naples before, but never during the peak summer holiday. Now, absent the crush of people, the city looked curiously enchanting. Puddles from an early shower glistened like scattered gems across the broad Piazza Garibaldi. While off to the left, without the usual shroud of exhaust fumes, the dark medieval towers of Castel Nuovo looked oddly benign. The clear air even made Mount Vesuvius and the surrounding mountains seem closer. For a brief moment, viewing the ancient port city as it might've been centuries earlier—with its grand palaces and Greco-Roman architecture—it was easy to forget the immediate threat of danger. But that moment quickly passed when a vagrant he hadn't noticed edged up beside him and, in a tired voice, asked, "*Sigaretta?*"

His hand darting beneath his jacket, Julie spun and stared at him. "Jesus!" he stammered, his heart pounding again.

If he'd noticed the weapon, it didn't seem to register. Instead, gazing through flat eyes, the man raised two fingers to his lips, repeating, "*Sigaretta, per favore?*"

"No," Julie said, pressing the gun back into his waistband. "*Non fumo.*"

Nodding, the beggar turned and drifted toward a knot of drivers milling around their taxis at a distance, and in that instant Julie realized the scene wasn't right. The cabs weren't queued up in the taxi zone at the entrance near where he stood, nor was anyone else around him—no porters, vendors, or urchins—no one but the beggar. And now he was gone.

Standing out there alone, a perfect target, he recalled Gava's admonition about the Camorra's grip on Naples providing no guarantees, and he snatched up his suitcase. But before he could retreat inside, a pair of dark Alfa Romeos raced to the curb, and in the next instant an ursine man had jumped out and was rushing toward him.

With fewer than a dozen paces between them, Julie reached for his gun and saw the man's eyes widen.

Raising his hands, he called out, "*Albo lapillo, Don Julio! Albo lapillo!*"

The phrase he'd argued against as an unnecessary precaution sounded sweet, almost musical. "It means *white stone*," Gava had told him at the time. "To the Romans it signified happiness or good fortune," he'd said, explaining how the ancients assessed each day and marked it by dropping either a white or black pebble into an urn which they then tallied at month's end.

"*Sono Gianni*," the thick-faced Neapolitan said hastily as he came up to him, his eyes sweeping the area. Short and squarely built, he bore an ugly white scar along his jaw line. "Sorry to be late," he said seizing the suitcase, and revealing his own weapon beneath his windbreaker. "We must leave *subito*."

As the cabbies looked on they turned and ran, his escort directing him to the lead car, and slamming the door once he'd jumped in.

"*Benvenute a Napule, Don Julio,*" the driver said raising his fist to his cap, while the one with the suitcase hustled back to the second car.

Julie nodded in return, and in doing so spotted a shotgun in the passenger well, and a semi-automatic pistol and two grenades on the front seat. Before he could comment the second driver honked and they were off, speeding through the city without regard to traffic signals. Within minutes they were on the Autostrada, where they settled into the fast lane, and held it by tapping the bumper of anyone foolish enough not to yield. And while that occurred only twice, it was enough to leave Julie as rattled as the other drivers.

It was his first visit to Benevento, and he knew only that they were heading for the Camorrista chieftain's retreat somewhere in the region, a fifty-kilometer journey that should've taken less than an hour, and likely would have, had they proceeded directly from the highway rather than taking a series of erratic detours through the countryside. It was on their second pass through town that the driver explained as best he could the need to ensure they weren't being followed.

"We must be *molto* careful," he said over his shoulder.

"*Si, capisco*," Julie replied.

Minutes later they were zipping through a lush valley where the driver suddenly hit the brake and took a sharp turn, putting them on a gravel road that had them jouncing through low-lying fields toward the mountains.

They hadn't gone far when he stopped without explanation.

"What's going on?" Julie said with alarm. And when the driver didn't respond, he asked, "*Ce` problema?*"

"No problem. *Sono amici,*" he replied, pointing ahead.

Straddling the road about twenty paces away were three men, each cradling a shotgun.

"Friends?"

"*Si.*"

Julie looked back at the vacant expressions on the men in the second car. Friends my ass, he thought with a sinking feeling, as he whipped out his gun. I've been set up.

"*No, Don Julio! Tutto posto!* Everything okay! You no need that," the driver implored.

Julie wanted to believe him. It was the first time he'd shown any emotion. But he couldn't chance it. "Insurance," he said as the trio drifted toward them.

"*Per favore.* Not a good idea."

Julie looked at him for a long moment. There was genuine fear in his eyes. "You better be right," he said, slipping the gun beneath his jacket again. Meanwhile, the one in the center stopped and leveled his weapon at them while his comrades came down both sides of the car.

"*L'Americano?*" the one beside the driver asked leaning down, the other watching him.

"*Si,*" he replied.

The man looked back at Julie without expression, and as their eyes met he offered a slight bow and touched the brim of his hat. Then, stepping aside, he thumped the roof and waved them through.

"Soon we be there," the driver said as they drove away, the tension still in his voice.

"I hope so," Julie replied, wiping his palm across his trousers. When he looked back the men were gone.

They went about a half mile before the narrow stream they'd been following veered off to the left, and soon the road rose in a lazy switchback that took them high above the valley, providing a spectacular view that ended abruptly when they turned into the shadow of the mountain and onto a perilous bone-jarring road that looked to have been chiseled from the rock against its will. Undeterred by the steep grade or the blind curves, or the lack of a guardrail, the driver held to a constant speed, steering with one hand and shifting with the other. On several occasions Julie was tempted to instruct him to slow down, but remained quiet lest he distract him.

At about the time the air turned noticeably cooler the landscape also changed, with pines and firs, many rooted among moss-covered boulders, replacing the sturdier oaks and chestnuts they'd seen earlier. In places where the forest thinned, Julie glimpsed the neighboring mountain ridge and guessed they were nearing the summit. Sure enough, the grade leveled and they emerged on the edge of a field that had been burned clear, providing those up ahead an unobstructed view of their approach.

"We are arrived," the driver announced, stopping and waiting for his comrades, who wisely fell back to avoid the shower of stones they'd been kicking up in their wake.

"What's that?" Julie asked, pointing to the iridescent wall surrounding the compound.

"The villa," the man replied, not understanding.

And when they began moving again, he asked, "Why so slow?"

"Too fast, and they shoot," the driver said, indicating the stone towers at the corners.

"You're joking," Julie was tempted to say, but resisted when he saw the rifles tracking them.

As they waited before the steel-plated gate, Julie understood why the wall appeared to glow in the distance. It had been the sun reflecting off countless shards of glass embedded in it. He smiled as he thought of his neighbors' reaction to a similar barrier around Rugby Hall.

"*Finalmente!*" the driver announced with noticeable relief once the gate swung open and they were inside.

Leaning forward and clapping his shoulder, Julie told him he'd done well. "*Fatto bene,*" he said.

"*Grazie, Don Julio,*" he replied with a brief salute.

Unlike the outer defoliated zone, the grounds inside were verdant and carefully tended, with scented shrubs and trees, many heavy with fruit. Surprisingly, there were peacocks, at least a dozen that he counted, roosting on branches or roaming freely, with those beside the gravel drive shrieking aggressively as they passed them. Farther along, there was a cluster of outbuildings which Julie assumed were bunkhouses, and beyond them, perched on a rise overlooking the compound, the sprawling villa with its orange roof tiles gleaming brightly in the sunlight. As they reached the house, an elderly couple in starched uniforms who'd been waiting stiffly in the arched doorway stepped forward.

"*Benvenuto, Don Julio,*" the male servant said bowing as he opened the door.

Happy to have arrived safely, Julie stepped stiffly into the sun and stretched, causing the old man to draw back. "What is it?" he asked. "*Che fai?*"

"It's the gun," the familiar voice called from the shadows. "Makes the staff nervous."

"Paolo!"

"Welcome, my friend," he said coming over and plucking the weapon from Julie's belt, and tossing it onto the rear seat. "You don't need it now."

Julie's smile faded. "What's going on?"

"Whatya mean?"

"What do I mean? That gun. The clown on the train. The arsenal in the car. The reception in the valley. Are we at war?"

"We're always at war." Then, leaning closer, "There's talk people want to disrupt our meeting."

"Disrupt? How?"

"How else? Kill us." And when Julie glanced back at the gun, he said, "Forget it, nobody's going to bother us here."

His suitcase had been transferred to the woman, and now both husband and wife were standing at a discrete distance waiting to follow them inside.

"Who wants to kill us?" he asked.

Gava shrugged. "If I knew that…," Then, "We got enemies we don't know about. Could be anybody. Maybe even our Sicilian cousins," he said nodding at the house, "or those crazy Calabrians. The important thing is to take precautions."

"Like the gun?"

"You had more than the gun. You had escorts since you landed. And that guy you call a clown, he don't miss when he shoots. The gun was extra protection," he said, adding, "We do the best we can."

"You're serious?"

"You know I don't kid about this stuff." He was steering Julie inside, the servants trailing behind. "You saw how easy it was to pop you on the train. We're bigger targets now, so get used to it." Then more cheerfully, "How do you like this layout? Not too many guys own a fucking mountain."

"He *owns* it?"

"Owns, controls, what's the difference. It's his."

"It's some fortress."

"You should know. Where you got the cliff and the water, he got the mountain."

"You forgot the valley."

He laughed. "Those guys down there? There's more you didn't see—in the fields, the woods, all the way up this friggin' mountain. Nobody gets up here without an invitation."

"Not even the police?"

Again he shrugged. "It wouldn't do any good. There's a dozen ways off."

"What's with the peacocks?"

"You like 'em?" he said with a grin. "Your old man had a pair."

"I never knew that!"

"Had to get rid of 'em after you were born. Mean little bastards. There's no getting past 'em without setting 'em off. But they got dogs, too. Mastiffs. Tear you to shreds."

"I didn't see them."

"They come out at night."

They were standing in the foyer, shadowed corridors leading off in three directions, a cantilevered oak staircase angling high above them to the right. The air was cool with a scent of burnt wood, giving the place the feel of a luxurious hunting lodge.

"So you like it?"

"Nice." Then, indicating the intricate mosaic floor, he said, "Looks like the villas in Pompeii."

"It should. It came from there."

"And what about those?" he said pointing to a pair of black iron sconces. "You going to tell me they're from some medieval castle?"

"The real McCoy. What's the point of living in Italy if you can't own a few antiques?" he said, his manner suggesting he had little interest in any of it.

The walls, painted a deep Pompeii red, held an assortment of battle-scarred shields, maces and battleaxes and, above a heavy oak door at the end of one corridor, an enormous double-edged, two-handed sword.

"This stuff belongs in a museum," Julie said as they passed the dining room, where a young housekeeper setting the table glanced up at them.

"It was."

Julie met the girl's eyes and she quickly turned away. "The staff must pick up a lot," he said.

"Not if they know what's good for 'em."

When they reached the door with the sword above it, Gava paused and said, "These Sicilians are a cold bunch." Explaining, "Don't take it personally, it's their way." And when Julie said he wasn't looking for new friends, Gava told him, "I wasn't talking about making friends. These guys are vipers and they're never going to be our friends. You got that?" And when Julie nodded, "We don't have friends in our business, only associates, which is why they're important to us.

"If they're with us when we finish here everybody wins, otherwise it's all been a waste." Then, as if to steel Julie's resolve, he pulled him close and whispered, "What I'm saying is, just remember everything happening in there's because of us. You and me," he said thumping his chest. "This fucking commission came together because *we made it happen.* And whatever deals we walk away with today, it's because of who we are and what we did. These Sicilians are tough—way tougher than the ones back home—but they don't have a fucking clue about the world we're carving out for ourselves."

"I get it," Julie said.

"Good." Then, grasping the knob, he said, "So what're we waiting for? Let's show those bastards the future and what real power's all about."

The room was a good fifty by thirty feet, with a bank of windows facing the surrounding mountains at one end, and across the room, away from the windows, a huge stone fireplace, which is where nine of the most powerful men in Italy were gathered. Their expressions flat, they assessed Julie with cold eyes as he approached. Five looked to be about Gava's age. And like him, they wore stylish slacks and shirts; the older ones preferring the simpler attire of their countrymen.

"*Fratelli*," Gava announced as they neared, "this is Julio Vittorio from America. He alone is responsible for our new wealth, and the one who will put our man in the White House. He comes as an equal and, like all of us, his connection to our circle remains inside these walls. Now, for the proper introductions."

As Julie passed among them he met each man's gaze and handshake with equal intensity.

Later, when it was his time, he told them of the government skims and how they functioned and what each was capable of earning. Without mentioning Goodmann, he also told them of the men he'd placed in strategic government positions and of his plans for them and for Jeffries. It was a lengthy discussion prompting many questions, most of which he willingly addressed. The others, those aimed at seeking specific data, such as Kelly's identity, and how and where the skims were channeled, he avoided.

The hour was late when they finished and, holding to the ancient rule of outlaws—to never spend a night together in one location—they staggered their departures and altered their routes off the mountain, each vanishing quietly into the night.

Julie arrived at his aging relatives' house in Portici before the sun broke over Vesuvius; coffee was made and fresh *cornetti* brought from a nearby bakery. And though both aunt and uncle noticed the gun, neither commented on it.

* * *

Two days later he caught up with Gava in Istanbul, where, together, they brokered new deals with men of equal stature from Eastern Europe, Asia and South America.

CHAPTER TWENTY-SIX (1972-1973)

It was the week after Christmas, and the only significant publicity about the organization over the past year centered mainly on the immensely popular *Godfather* movie and its romantic depiction of the Corleones, along with what Julie considered director Coppola's warped distinction between good and evil killers. To his surprise, even Nikki chose to believe the film's fictitious code of honor and loyalty despite all she knew about the outfit. Together, they'd seen the film three times.

In the real world, meanwhile, Julie was no longer learning of mob executions postmortem. Since Benevento, he and Gava had strategized over those with a potential of generating headlines or creating waves within the organization—as they were about to do with Joseph Lavacci.

"Who is it this time?" Julie asked when Gava suggested some housecleaning.

"Crazy Joey," he said of his long-time friend and ally.

While he never met Lavacci, Julie knew of his bizarre and often excessive behavior. He knew, too, Gava was using the Harlem-based mobster as a convenient counterforce against the other New York bosses, a tactic that worked well when Lavacci didn't exceed his orders or stray too far from his territory, as he was doing lately. In those instances Gava would intervene and cool things down, promising to keep the maverick in check, which he'd do before turning him loose again. "What's he done now?" Julie asked.

"He's pushing the other families."

"Isn't that what you keep him around for?"

Gava shrugged, much as a parent might when discussing an unruly child, leading Julie to ask, "Why not just tell him it's time to retire?"

Gava shook his head. "Never happen. Joey isn't happy unless he's in the middle of things. If I send him to Florida it won't be long before he's shitting in somebody else's yard, and then I'm dragged in where I don't wanna be. No," he said, his mind made up, "retirement won't work with him."

Julie had no reason to defend the gangster, but killing him seemed extreme. "Why not talk to him, let him know how it has to be?"

Again Gava shook his head. "It's my own fault. I let him think he's too important, and now he wants more power than I can give him." And when Julie smiled, he said, "What's so funny?"

"I was thinking we wouldn't be having this discussion if he wasn't greedy, but then he wouldn't be of use to you."

"Yeah. Interesting how things work out."

They were in Yonkers, several stories above the Saw Mill River Parkway, in a modest two-bedroom apartment belonging to the cousin of one of Gava's men, a union mechanic who knew little of the organization or its operations, but enough to take his wife to dinner for the evening without questions when asked. The artificial Christmas wreath wired to the doorknocker had seen more than its share of holidays; likewise the molded plastic Santa and oversized candy cane hanging in the windows blinking into the night. The sofa and armchairs, covered in clear plastic, were pushed together to accommodate an aluminum Christmas tree and folding table fitted with green felt and a detailed Neapolitan crèche scene set within a snowcapped mountain village.

Julie sat across from Gava in one of two armchairs, a low coffee table between them. With little advance notice, the man's wife had set out cold cuts, potato salad, pastries and cookies, along with holiday paper plates and napkins. Sensitive to the inconvenience he'd caused, Gava would later place ten one hundred dollar bills beneath the tree before leaving.

"He's making moves on Colombo's old family," he said between bites. "The dumb shit shows up in Brooklyn with the niggers he recruited from prison and then expects me to back him. There's no way I'm letting a bunch of spooks in, even with Joey in charge. The guy's gone fucking *pazzo!*" he said, spitting crumbs.

"He won't listen?"

Gava nearly choked. "Joey listen? Give him an inch and the sonofabitch'll take Manhattan. He's like a bull in heat. If we don't rein him in now...," His thoughts trailed off as he washed his food down with red wine he'd found in the kitchen. "He's been after Colombo's operations for a long time, but that ain't all. Now I learn he's hustling hot bonds and loan sharking down on Wall

Street where he's got no business. When the guys whose
territory he crashed told him to get out, his coons put
two of them in the hospital. Almost killed them. We
can't let him get away with that," he said, his eye taking
an angry roll. "Not even friendship can save him now.
Our Brooklyn cousins wanna skin him alive, but I said
we'd take care of it." Gulping his wine, he said, "If the
fighting starts again it'll weaken our position with the
Benevento commission. So, Joey has to go, and it has
to be public and by our hands. Later, out of respect to
his brothers, who've been straight with me, we'll send
somebody around to square things."

* * *

The following March, while a late winter snowstorm
pounded the Great Lakes, four Neapolitans commenced
the final leg of their journey from Italy. Entering Buffalo
from Canada, they drove the long distance to the
Fordham section of the Bronx and settled into a furnished
apartment on Belmont Avenue, where they dutifully
waited for Nunzio's phone call. It came ten days later, in
the early morning hours of Friday, April sixth, while wiry
Joey Lavacci celebrated his forty-third birthday at the
Copacabana with his recent bride and several associates.

An hour later, as the eastern sky turned purple
over Manhattan's Little Italy, a dark Plymouth sedan
maneuvered around delivery vans before discharging three
men in trench coats a block from Umberto's Clam House
at Mulberry and Hester Streets, where Lavacci had come
for an early morning meal. From there, the driver parked
near the restaurant and waited. With his headlights off
and engine idling, he sat in the shadows cradling a semi-

automatic while his comrades entered the nearly empty restaurant, two via the front door, the other slipping in through the side entrance.

From their car a half block away, Julie and Reni watched the drama play out.

"This ain't the movies," Gava had cautioned Julie when he said he wanted to witness the execution. "These things get pretty messy, lots of blood and stuff. Plus, they don't always work out exactly how you want 'em to. Bullets can go anywhere. You might even catch one." But Julie held firm, insisting it was time he saw it to its conclusion.

Inside Umberto's, Lavacci was seated at a corner table, his back to the far wall, pushing food in his mouth and paying little attention to those around him. Despite the turmoil he'd created within the organization, he had no reason to believe he was in any danger. He'd surrounded himself with trusted allies, and, more importantly, his relationship with Gava was rock-solid. And if he had misgivings, it wouldn't have mattered. He'd been told by a fellow inmate years earlier he was invincible. The scrawny American Indian and self-proclaimed shaman with an uncanny ability to predict events had said he'd never die in battle, that he'd been endowed with superhuman power that shielded him from his enemies and would enable him to live a long and healthy life. Since then, obsessed with testing the prophecy, he'd walked into the center of any number of frays and always walked away unscathed. Now, looking up and seeing the detached stares of his executioners, he knew before they opened their coats what was about to happen. His face twisting with rage, the seasoned warrior spit out his food and, pushing from the table, went for his gun in a useless bid to defend himself.

In an odd pantomime, accompanied by the scrape of his chair and clink of his fork on the tile floor, his assailants leveled their weapons and fired. The pristine dining room exploded as Lavacci was lifted and slammed against the wall, where somehow he remained upright, gurgling blood and twitching, his hand still groping for the holstered gun.

What occurred next was an added bit of drama intended to signal a new era of mob discipline. With the harsh smell of cordite infusing the air and the others forced to watch, the second man grabbed Lavacci's traumatized wife and quickly put a bullet into her forehead. The message was clear. Henceforth, anyone stepping out of line could expect no less for his family.

Turning, both men sprinted to the street under cover of their partner, who stepped forward and, as a further sign of Gava's contempt for Lavacci's allies, fired several rounds into the two black hoods at the table while sparing Joey's two white soldiers.

Fascinated at how quickly it all went down—by his calculations, not more than a minute from when they'd entered the restaurant—Julie assumed the drama was over when he saw the Neapolitans speed away, but he was mistaken. A moment later, Lavacci came bursting through the plate glass door firing wildly into the night before finally collapsing onto the pavement.

"Gee, I thought I'd get to finish the job," Reni said as they drove away. Then, turning, he asked, "So, how'd you like it?"

An added bonus to easing the tension Lavacci had caused within the organization was the scant news coverage of his death. Pushed off the front pages by White House Counsel John Dean's abrupt dismissal in the escalating Watergate imbroglio, the shooting rated barely a mention in the papers and nothing at all by the television networks. Fortunately for Gava, mob politics couldn't compete with the resignations of Attorney General Kleindienst and Nixon confidants Haldeman and Ehrlichman, and Dean's subsequent revelation that Nixon had been involved with the cover-up a full six months earlier than he'd previously admitted. By July, when presidential assistant Alexander Butterfield inadvertently disclosed that the president had been secretly taping the Oval Office, interest in Watergate had become so intense that had he wanted, Gava likely could've eliminated all his rivals without garnering any media attention.

* * *

It was barely six months later, during his visit to Rugby Hall, when Gava asked Julie about Vice President Agnew's forced resignation as it related to Nixon.

"If it wasn't so serious it'd be funny," Julie replied. "I can't imagine this fool having his kickbacks delivered to his office. The guy's an idiot. But the real issue isn't Agnew and his kickbacks. It's those Oval Office tapes. From what I hear, it's only a matter of time before they bring him down."

"Dumb shit should've destroyed 'em," Gava said.

Julie nodded his agreement. "He's mortally wounded, and everyone knows it but him." And when Gava asked how he thought it would play out, he replied, "He'll have to step down, of course."

Throwing in the towel made little sense to Gava. "That'd be a mistake," he said. "Nobody with that kind of power should let go without a fight."

"But he won't have the power when the House impeaches him."

"You think they got the balls to go through with it?"

"Yep, they got the balls *and* the votes. And if he doesn't resign they'll go after him."

"Then what?" Gava asked, re-lighting his cigar.

"Once he's out that'll be the end of it, and the obstruction charges will evaporate. We don't kick our leaders when they're down. And if he's smart he'll keep a low profile for a few years before attempting to salvage his place in history. Americans have short memories, and at his age he has plenty of time to rehabilitate himself."

Gava shook his head. He was remembering Luciano and Costello and, more recently, Lucchese—all forceful men who tried wielding power after stepping down. All had failed. "You fix things when you got clout," he said, "not after you lose it." After a moment, he asked, "How's all this gonna play against our guy?"

Julie was at the window gazing down at the river, his thoughts far ahead of Gava's. "He's handling himself well," he said of Jeffries. "But how it plays out depends entirely on what Ford does in office. If he disassociates himself from Nixon and Watergate quickly and gets us out of Vietnam with some dignity, he'll stand a good chance of being re-elected."

"Why you so sure he'll run? This could be it for him."

Julie shook his head. "He's got to. He doesn't want to be the only man to have held both offices without being elected to either of them. That isn't a distinction any politician wants. "

Gava was biting into his cigar, his expression suggesting he wasn't pleased. "Our goal was to avoid an incumbent."

"I know," Julie said coming from the window. "And that leads us to another aspect of this mess we haven't discussed, the impact of Watergate on Jeffries."

Gava frowned. "Whadaya mean?"

"Whether Nixon fights or steps down, this scandal has damaged the image of the presidency, and that won't be good for Ford or Jeffries," he said. "The country already has a low voter turnout, the lowest in the free world, and Watergate could easily make it worse."

Gava shrugged. "So what?"

"So, the ones who turn out for this next election are sure to be the angry and the disenchanted, and getting their support won't be easy."

Frowning, he said, "How about you get to the bottom line."

Julie nodded. "I've been thinking Watergate could be the final straw when viewed through the prism of the past twenty years." Then he explained, "Think about it. We ended world war two as the most powerful nation in the world, and with few exceptions it's been downhill since. First," he said, counting off his fingers, "there was Korea. Over a hundred and fifty thousand casualties and we walk away with just a truce, no victory. Then we let the Soviets take the lead in space, first with Sputnik and then that Gagarin guy. Then we make complete asses of ourselves against a two-bit dictator with that botched-up Bay of Pigs invasion. And to make it worse," he said, still counting off, "we allow the Soviets to put nuclear missiles in our front yard. And then what do we do? We let the bastards coerce us into taking our missiles out of Turkey in return for pulling theirs out of Cuba.

"And if all that wasn't bad enough, we do exactly what the French did, and follow them into an unwinnable war in Vietnam. Fifty thousand Americans dead! Meanwhile, we got a civil war here at home with protesters, and rioters torching over a hundred cities. Now, throw in a crooked vice president and this Watergate debacle, and you have to wonder how much more the voters will tolerate."

"What choice do they have?"

"That's my point!" he said. "They're going to look at Ford and Jeffries and conclude if this is the best there is why bother, and then the election becomes a coin toss. We didn't build up Jeffries to be in a coin toss."

Gava considered it. "So what do we do?"

"You're not going to like it."

"Try me."

"We need someone else, an outsider who's not connected with Washington or tainted by the system, someone who'll provide the voters with a real choice."

"And what're we supposed to do with Jeffries?"

"I haven't decided yet."

CHAPTER TWENTY-SEVEN

J ulie had been away from CCC several weeks. Upon returning he immediately sensed a subtle shifting of sand beneath the water, nothing overt, just a gut feeling something wrong was about to surface. As it happened, he didn't have long to wait. He'd been at his desk about an hour when the door suddenly swung open and Brian Moorehead, looking drawn and anxious, barged in unannounced and uninvited. Recalling all had been fine between them when last they spoke, he set his papers aside while Moorehead paused, his hand on the knob and an uncertain expression on his face, as if he were reconsidering his mission. Then, deciding otherwise, he shut the door and marched forward, planting himself before his former desk, his hands balled up by his side.

Julie leaned back. "I guess we'll skip the good morning and welcome back," he said, noting Moorehead's puffy eyes and pasty complexion.

Moorehead blinked. "Morning," he said hoarsely, his thoughts clearly elsewhere.

"Is there a problem?" Julie asked.

"A problem?" he said curling his lip.

"As you can see, I've got a lot of catching up to do," Julie said, gesturing to the work before him. "Let's not play games."

"I'm not playing games. I've been going over our programs."

"Can it wait?"

"No, goddamn it, it can't!" he shouted.

Before he uttered another word Julie was around the desk and on him, grabbing his jacket and shoving him back across the room. "Who the fuck do you think you're talking to!" he said pinning him to the door.

"Don't hit me," he cried twisting his head, when Julie raised his fist.

"Hit you?" he said, their faces inches apart. "I oughta punch your goddamn lights out."

"I…, I'm sorry," he stammered, with what little color he had draining away. "It was a mistake."

"You bet your ass it was a mistake," Julie said lowering his arm, but still holding him there. "I don't give a damn what your problem is, you pull that shit with me again, mister, and you're outta here. You got that?" he said with a final shove, before turning and walking away.

"Yes, I got it," he said. "I apologize. It's just that I haven't had much sleep. Been working hard," he said, smoothing his jacket. Then edging closer, "Mind if I sit down?"

"Do as you like," Julie said. And when he was seated, he asked, "Now what's this about?"

Moorehead approached the chair and eased into it. "Well," he said biting his lip, "as you know I attended the federal acquisitions seminar in New York while you were gone."

"So?"

Moorehead wiped his mouth. "One of the presenters was a fellow by the name of Kelly—Frank Kelly—he's with Social Security Administration, but you already know that," he added, his voice growing stronger. And when Julie didn't respond, he said, "I thought of confronting him afterwards, to ask what's going on, but then decided against it."

"Why?"

"Why what?" he said frowning.

"Why *didn't* you confront him?" Julie said irritably.

"Uh, because I needed time to think," he said, pressing into the chair. "To understand why someone of his stature would jeopardize his position *and ours* by hooking up with us in what's clearly a legal and ethical conflict of interest. And more importantly, to determine what he's really doing here."

"That's no secret. I explained that to you at the time."

"If you mean making the organization more efficient, we both know that's a lie."

"Excuse me?" Julie said, half rising again.

"Sorry," Moorehead said shrinking back. "I mean we both know that was a cover story."

"Really? Then suppose you tell me the real reason."

"Very well," he said, gathering his courage again. "I've determined the man's committing a felony, and we're a part of it."

Julie frowned. "That's a serious accusation."

Moorehead nodded nervously. "I'm aware of that, and I can prove it."

"Go on," Julie said more evenly now.

Squaring his shoulders, he said, "I know about the…, the money transfer." And when Julie didn't deny it, he said more confidently, "I know plenty."

"If you got something to say, come out with it."

"All right," he said, holding Julie's gaze. "Let's start with that ruse about having to clear program alterations and changes with Peters, I mean Kelly, or whatever he prefers to be called."

"I initiated that policy to ensure uniformity," Julie reminded him.

"Pardon my French," he said warily, "but we both know that's bullshit. It's to ensure no one inadvertently alters the changes you and he inserted into our programs." Then, his voice rising, he said, "You've taken this company—*my company!*—and turned it into a…, into a criminal operation."

"You want a glass of water?"

Moorehead shook his head. "I'm fine. Angry, but fine." Continuing, he said, "At first I wanted to believe perhaps I was being overly suspicious about Kelly. That he was simply investing in a business about which he knows a great deal. And I thought whom am I to judge him, particularly in a town where everyone bends the rules. But something about this arrangement didn't ring true—like the name change, and the way he put us off when we offered to help—so I stayed with it, searching and running programs at night and over the weekends. It wasn't easy. Then I spotted an anomaly in one of the programs. It didn't mean much until I traced it backward. That's right," he said squaring his shoulders, "I found it. Found how you're gathering data and altering it and then re-inserting it into the original program. You think you're clever, you and your Mister Kelly. Well you aren't the only ones who can manipulate programs."

"Go on."

"I'm talking about altering data and imbedding the changes into disbursements so they're nearly impossible to detect. Am I getting close?"

"I'm impressed," Julie conceded. "You're much brighter than I thought."

"Thanks," he said, warming to the praise. "I'll say this. What you've done is ingenious. I couldn't have conceived of it in a thousand years. And if I had, I certainly wouldn't have the guts to carry it out." Then, encouraged by Julie's smile, he said, "I haven't uncovered the entire scheme yet. I believe it's much broader. Nor have I identified all the specifics of this one, but I've grasped the concept, and I'm certain in time I can figure out how and where it all comes together."

Julie leaned forward. "Just what did you uncover?"

"To start with, a pattern," he said, "a very distinct pattern." Then, anxious to demonstrate his skills, he detailed his findings, concluding, "By my calculations we're stealing upwards of several million dollars from the government."

"You're not even close," Julie told him. "It's more like several hundred million."

"That's not possible!" he said with a resurgence of anger. "You're trying to make me look foolish."

"It is possible," Julie assured him in an even tone, "and I'm not interested in making a fool of you. You're far too clever for that."

Frowning. "How can that be?! I…, I had no idea."

"That was the plan. We didn't expect anyone would uncover it."

Moorehead shook his head as he struggled to understand. "Incredible."

"It's very big and very profitable."

"How long? Since Kelly…?"

Julie nodded. "More or less. So, who have you told?"

Moorehead blinked. "You think I'm nuts?! No one."

"Don't lie."

"I'm not," he insisted.

"Not even your wife?"

"No, not a soul."

"You're sure?"

"You think I want to go to prison?"

Scratching his chin, Julie said, "So then should I assume the purpose of this meeting is—what shall we call it—a friendly shakedown? That you're here to tell me you want your share?"

"Well, it did cross my mind."

"I'd be surprised if it hadn't."

"You're taking this better than I'd expected," Moorehead told him.

Shrugging, Julie said, "What choice do I have."

"That's what I figured, too."

"So what do you have in mind?"

Moorehead adjusted his glasses. "Let me first say that shakedown isn't a term I feel comfortable with."

"Okay. Call it whatever you like."

"I prefer thinking of it as an extension of our current arrangement. After all," he said, his eyes searching Julie's face, "I do have a personal stake in this company."

Julie appeared to consider the notion. "Yeah, I suppose you do," he conceded, "an original stake."

"Exactly," Moorehead said more eagerly now. "In that sense I see no reason why I can't be a partner like Kelly. Certainly not an equal partner," he stressed. "That wouldn't be fair, considering I am a latecomer in this phase of the operation. And, besides, you two have done the hard part. Yet, an equitable share would be appropriate. Don't you agree?"

After an uncomfortable silence Julie nodded. "Seems reasonable."

"Well," Moorehead said with a quick grin, "that was easy."

"Like I said, I don't suppose I have a choice."

Moorehead clicked his tongue. "As I see it, you really don't." Then clapping his hands, he said, "So how shall we work this?"

"It isn't that simple."

"But, you just said…,"

"I know what I said, but it's not my decision to make."

Moorehead frowned. "Not your decision? I don't understand."

"There are others," Julie told him.

"You mean besides Kelly?" he said, perplexed at the notion of outside partners.

"Surely, you can't think we could pull off something of this magnitude alone?"

301

"Frankly," he said still frowning, "I hadn't considered that part of it, but considering the amount, I guess not." Then cautiously, "Who are they, these others?"

"That isn't something you need to know, is it?"

Moorehead thought a moment. "Probably not. But they aren't likely to object, are they? I mean, it's obvious I'm entitled to a share, right? I can't imagine they wouldn't see that," he said, having already counted himself in. And when Julie didn't reply immediately, he quickly added, "And, besides, it's in everyone's best interest."

Julie couldn't resist. "That sounds like a threat."

"I guess it does."

"Is it?"

Skirting the question, he said, almost pleading, "Look, if they need a reason, tell them that having a backup for Kelly—someone with the same expertise—is good business. They'll understand that."

Julie nodded. "They'd be fools not to. But there's one proviso," he said, coming around the desk, "a very important, ironclad one."

Moorehead narrowed his eyes. "Proviso? What kind of proviso?"

"None of this goes beyond this room. Once you're in, no one must know."

"Oh, geeze," he laughed, "you needn't worry about that. It'll go to my grave with me."

Julie smiled. "They'll be pleased to hear that."

* * *

On a gray Monday morning several weeks later, along a stretch of Maryland Route 301 between Waldorf and La Plata, a motel cleaning crew found Moorehead cold and naked across the bed. According to the police report, nothing among his belongings appeared to be missing, not his gold watch, wedding ring or billfold. And with no signs of a struggle or external bruises or wounds, the officer on the scene made an initial assessment the liquor and cocaine packets found in the room were factors in his death. He also concluded from the woman's panties tangled among the sheets that Moorehead hadn't been alone, a fact later verified by the desk clerk who recalled seeing a very attractive, short-haired young woman when he'd checked in that previous Saturday.

All this was confirmed several weeks later at the county inquest, along with the medical examiner's findings linking Moorehead's heart failure to a lethal combination of drugs and alcohol. Lacking evidence to the contrary, the court ruled the death accidental.

CHAPTER TWENTY-EIGHT (1974, EARLY SPRING)

Spring typically came late in the Poconos, and this year was no different. The days were still cool and the nights brisk, with stretches of snow through the piney woods where the March sun didn't reach. But none of that mattered to those gathered at Mosca's lodge—the New York commission and several upstate and New England bosses. With few exceptions they were an aging group who had grown noticeably wider in the waist over the years, but no less calculating.

Among the problems that drew them there was a spate of recent subpoenas based on thousands of hours of incriminating conversations gleaned from bugs planted in the junkyard trailer of Lucchese family captain Paul Vario, conversations that revealed the organization's control of more than two hundred legitimate businesses throughout the city and points north. Surrounded by high barbwire-topped fences and patrolled by vicious dogs, the trailer had been a convenient meeting place long after the Brooklyn DA had discovered it and infiltrated it.

"So, this kid reporter from Milan heads down to Palermo," Reni said during a break in their discussion, his tone suggesting the tale had a twist to it. "He's filing stories about the high Mafiosi—the lawyers and financiers who control the judges and politicians—and the low Mafiosi who keep everybody else in line with force, plus the usual bullshit about Sicilians paying more for their gas, food and clothing than the rest of the country, which he naturally blames on the Mafia. He writes how there'd be more profits and more jobs if businesses didn't have to pay protection. He even names companies and farms that folded or were taken over because they couldn't meet expenses. No one pays any attention because the stories are being written for the northern politicians, who sent him there and who use them during the elections."

The men listened in quiet amusement, some having heard it before.

Reni went on, "It's winter up north and he's soaking up sun, screwing his brains out and knocking out a couple of stories a week. Since he's not writing anything new nobody bothers him.

"One day he goes too far and names the bosses, figuring it's no big deal since everybody in Palermo knows who they are anyway. What he don't understand is there's a difference between knowing and printing it. The next morning in the espresso bar he's elbowed and somebody whispers, *'Basta!'* The kid spins around, but all he sees is blank faces. Whoever it was is gone or, worse, standing next to him. He gets the message—next time it'll be a knife. That night he's back in Milan. Bing! One word is all it took. You got to hand it to those Sicilians."

Julie smiled and said, "Much wisdom often goes with brevity of speech." And when Reni frowned, he explained, "Sophocles, a Greek playwright about two thousand years ago."

"Makes sense," the Sicilian from Buffalo said. "Wasn't it the Greeks who occupied the island first."

"I bet every Sicilian kid knows that story by heart," Mosca said.

"If not that one, one like it," Reni replied.

"You need a new one," Gava said, "or give it a different ending."

"Yeah, like he disappears," Nunzio volunteered. And with a wink at Julie, "Maybe take him for a boat ride."

"It's like Joe Profaci used to say, Mosca added. "The man who says the least is the most powerful."

Carlo Gambino, the 72-year old Machiavellian Brooklyn boss, and once-likely candidate for the position now held by Gava, cleared his throat, and in a low brittle voice, asked, "Speaking of power, what's happening in Washington?"

"Nixon's finished," Julie told him. "They're ready to start impeachment hearings, likely any day now."

Mosca grinned. "Looks like I win ten grand."

Gambino was no stranger to politicians, having recently dodged deportation by offering two U. S. Senators each twenty-five thousand a year for life. "How sure are you?" he asked.

"Senator Ervin's confident the Senate will try him if he's impeached, and the president knows it. He told me, if Nixon had fessed up in the beginning this whole Watergate business would've been history, and he'd be back in North Carolina fishing instead of sitting there on the Hill frying him."

Gambino seemed unimpressed. "How's this play out for Jeffries?"

"It'll put him up against an incumbent, which, as you know, we wanted to avoid."

"I haven't forgotten," Gambino said. "So the question now is, what're we gonna do about it?"

"We don't have much choice. We need a new man," Julie told him flatly.

"A new man! What're you talkin' about?" said Tommy Eboli, the fiery acting head of the Genovese family, and no friend of either Gambino or Gava. "You wanna dump the guy after all we did for him? It don't make sense."

"If this goes as expected," Julie said, "Nixon'll be out by September, which gives Ford three years in office. It'll be like going against an incumbent."

"But an incumbent who wasn't elected," Gambino reminded them. "And that isn't the same."

"True," Julie conceded, "but it gives Ford time to establish his administration, and get this inflation problem under control. If he does that, we'll have a tough battle on our hands."

Turning to Gava, Gambino asked, "And you support dumping Jeffries?"

"We didn't come this far to lose," Gava replied. "Hear Julie out."

"I'm listening," the short man said.

"Hold on," Eboli interrupted. "I wanna know what's wrong with Jeffries."

"He's tainted," Julie told him.

"Who the hell ain't in that friggin' town!"

"Maybe Julie wants to nominate the pope," Gambino said, drawing a few laughs.

"Actually, I was thinking of Billy Graham," he countered.

"The preacher?" Gambino asked.

"Yeah, and while you're at it," Eboli said, "maybe you should consider whatshisname, that Bishop Sheen guy."

"I wasn't joking," Julie told them.

"Say you're right," Gambino said. "What makes you think Graham's interested?"

"His ego and longstanding belief that he's got a special calling to lead the nation," Julie told him.

Salvatore Ciro, the Providence don, was shaking his head. "All this dough we laid out for Jeffries and now you gonna back a preacher. That's the best you can come up with?"

"No. There's Reggie Sutherland," Julie said.

"Who the hell's he, another preacher?" Eboli said.

"He's the governor of Georgia. Family's big in tobacco and peanuts. He's honest, principled and he'd jump at the chance to lead the country back from this national tragedy. Those are his words, *national tragedy*."

"And that's it?" the man from Rhode Island said.

"There aren't many white knights out there," Julie told them. "L. Patrick Gray would've worked, but he blew it when he destroyed the Watergate documents John Dean gave him."

Gambino's sad face grew sadder. "A preacher, a peanut farmer and an ex-FBI director," he said. "We're in deep shit. Maybe we should go with the pope."

"I admit it doesn't look promising," Julie said. "But if we're going to win we need a credible candidate, someone who can deliver the message that it won't be business as usual if he's elected. I don't believe Jeffries can't do that now, but the right man, an outsider not connected to Washington, can do it."

"And what about Jeffries?" Eboli asked, still not convinced.

"He won't have to step aside."

"You just said he can't win."

"Not the presidency, but he's still a player. He just can't be number one."

"I'd like to see you convince him of that," Ciro said.

"That's the easy part," Julie said.

"When do we start?" Gambino asked.

"If everybody's on board, we start immediately."

Chapter Twenty-nine (1974)

"We're ready," Jeffries confided with uncommon solemnity.

Neither the announcement nor his sullen mood surprised Julie, who understood long before Jeffries that the tide of public opinion had shifted back to Nixon, who was now perceived by many as the underdog in this fight, and that lynching him would detract from the Democrats rising popularity.

"Damn him and his uncompromising stance," Jeffries grumbled. "The bastard had every opportunity, now he's going down and I'll have his blood all over me. In the end, instead of being the dragon-slayer I'll be that SOB who kicked the president when he was down."

"You sure there are enough votes to impeach?" Julie asked.

He nodded sourly. "They have to go along if he refuses to resign," he said of his Republican colleagues. "The evidence is too compelling." He was standing behind his desk gazing toward the White House, his hands balled up behind him. "Both the majority and minority leaders are delivering the ultimatum to him as we speak." Then, turning, he said, "There's another aspect to this thing, one you won't hear in public." After settling in his chair, he said, "We're in trouble. The barbarians are at the gate and this constitutional standoff could be a boon for them."

Julie had heard all this before. "You mean the radicals?" he said, referring to the loose network of feminists, Black Panthers, and other dissidents, like the American Peace Movement.

"Yeah," he said glumly, "that's exactly who I mean. We can't afford anymore polarization, which is what'll happen if that obstinate son-of-a-Quaker hangs on," he said, thrusting his chin toward the White House. "The more divided we are, the stronger those pinko bastards become. They could pull it off—a third party—and you know what that means."

Julie certainly did. Factionalism and gridlock in the people's House worked well for the mob. "You don't really consider them a threat," he said.

Jeffries looked across the desk, his expression serious. "You bet your ass I do. And, while they won't admit it publicly, so do many others in this town."

"So you'll do whatever's necessary to keep the bastards out, including flushing the president down the toilet if that's what it takes."

"What choice do we have?"

Julie smiled at the irony.

* * *

Meanwhile, more interested in saving himself than the two-party system, the president sent word back to the Hill that he was digging in for the long fight regardless of how much blood was spilled. But his plans were cut short in late July when the Supreme Court unanimously upheld Judge John Sirica's order that he release the White House tapes. Suddenly, to everyone's relief, the bitter dispute was over. Two weeks later Nixon capitulated and the headlines confirmed what official Washington already knew. *Watergate Forces Nixon to Resign, Ford is President. The New York Post* said it more succinctly, *Ford In, Nixon Out!*

Long before images of a defiant Nixon boarding his helicopter for the first leg of his journey back to San Clemente flashed around the world, Julie had decided on Ford's opponent. All that remained was to alert Jeffries, which he did the following month while they strode the footpaths around Rugby Hall.

"I'm not going to mince words on this, Bob," he said. "There's been a change in plans. Our people believe you're no longer a viable candidate."

Jeffries stopped and turned. "What're you talking about?"

"It's been decided. They want someone else, someone electable."

It took a moment to grasp the message. "Me, unelectable? You're joking!"

"No, I'm not."

"That doesn't make sense."

"That's how it is," he said without apology.

They were by the wall, the river running silently seaward below, a cool breeze riffling the trees.

Jeffries' face grew red. "That's it?!" he shouted. "That's the message?" And when Julie nodded, he said, "Where the hell've they been, on the moon? The sonofabitch wasn't impeached. No blood's been spilled. Watergate is history. Even the fucking commie radicals are out of the picture. I'm golden and they're telling me I'm *unelectable!*"

"It's more than that," Julie said. "It's this anti-Washington mood. The polls show you're too much of an insider, and that's enough to sway them."

"That's absurd. I've seen the polls and they're a passing thing. They're meaningless, just a snapshot. They don't count, and they certainly won't be relevant come election time. Ford's the one who should be worried. The fool should never have pardoned Nixon. It'll be his undoing," he said of the previous week's pronouncement. "It was political suicide, the dumbest thing he could've done. It smacks of cronyism, which is what the voters'll remember."

But Julie held firm. "They've made up their minds. You're a liability."

"They're nuts! With my backing I'm a shoo-in."

"That's the point. You no longer have their backing. They can't chance losing this one. They've waited too long."

"That's precisely my point. They won't lose, not if they stick with me."

"It's too late."

His voice cracking, Jeffries said, "They can't do this, not when I'm this close." And when Julie didn't yield, he declared, "I'm not quitting, not after all I've done. It's my race to win."

"Listen, my friend, they don't like it anymore than you. They've spent a bundle getting you this far, not to mention the chits they've called in along the way. Believe me, it wasn't a hasty decision, but it's final."

"It's my life they're playing with."

"They're not *playing,* and this isn't a game, Bob."

Again he shook his head. "Look," he said, more urgently now, "they know I busted my ass getting here. I've punched all the tickets and then some. Whoever came up with this crackpot idea…, If I can talk to them I'll turn them around. Tell me who."

Julie almost felt sorry for him. Placing a hand on his shoulder, he said, "This doesn't mean you're out. You'll still be on the ticket."

With the sun low on the horizon the river looked especially peaceful. It was a familiar scene that rarely failed to lure Julie from his fortress, but now it went largely unnoticed.

Jeffries jerked backward. "The vice presidency?! They can't be serious!"

"You're an important player, very important. Your presence on the ticket will make a difference."

"Then I should stay on as number one."

"It's too late for that."

Sneering, he said, "What was it Truman said about the job? It isn't worth a pitcher of warm spit."

"Actually, it was Garner, FDR's first vice president. And it's no longer the same position it was then. Times have changed. Look what it did for Nixon and Humphrey, both got the nomination."

But Jeffries wasn't listening. Squaring his shoulders, he said, "What if I refuse? I've got the name and the party solidly behind me."

Julie shook his head. "Don't start believing your own press releases."

"Yeah, well I'm no longer the nobody they pitched earlier," he argued. "I'd be a damn fool to drop to second place now. Ford's going to lose and I'm the man to beat him."

"Not without their backing," Julie reminded him.

"We had a deal, and I'm sticking to my end. I want the presidency, and I will *not* step aside and allow someone else to claim what's rightfully mine." Then jabbing Julie's chest, he said, "Go tell the assholes that hatched this cockamamie scheme that Bob Jeffries is going all the way, and if they're smart they'll stick with me. Otherwise, it's sayonara muchachos."

"That won't be necessary," Julie said, brushing his hand aside.

"What do you mean?"

"You just did."

"Did what?"

"Told the asshole."

"Uh?"

"It was my decision."

"You?" he said, his eyes narrowing.

"Who do you think brought you this far?"

"I'm not getting any of this."

"You get it, all right. You choose not to admit it."

Jeffries stared at his friend. "Admit what? That you've been of enormous help? Of course you have. I certainly wouldn't deny that. But this entire campaign...,"

"Look, I'll spell it out for you," Julie said. "I brought you to this point. Me. I chose you. I got the backing you needed when you needed it. And now I'm telling you it's over."

Jeffries bristled. "You're a friend, but don't insult me."

"You really don't get it. Since you like quoting Truman I'll put it another way. The buck stops here. There's no one else for you to convince."

Jeffries stood silent, his face twisted. "Let me get this straight. The money, the endorsements, the editorials, all that was *your* doing?" And when Julie nodded, "How's that possible?"

"How do you think?"

It took a moment. Then, shooting glances around the grounds, he stepped back and shook his head. "No. I don't believe it."

"Believe it," Julie said.

Dropping his voice, he said, "Your union connections, the quick cash when we needed it. It came from…, Jesus, you're in with them."

"Does that bother you?"

"It's not possible. I've known you too long."

"We're not all Al Capones. Nor are we the hoods Kefauver dragged before his committee twenty years ago. It's a different operation."

"Get serious!"

"I'm dead serious."

"What about the extortion, the gambling, the prostitution, the drugs—and the *killings*?! I suppose that's in the past, too."

Julie shrugged. "Hardly anyone gets killed nowadays."

"Tell that to Jimmy Hoffa. This can't be happening to me," he said looking away.

"Put that aside for the moment. The important thing is I can and will get you the presidency when it's time,

317

but that time isn't now. Now is the time for you to be flexible."

He snorted. "Don't you mean compliant?"

"Let's keep this civil."

"Civil?!" he said edging backward. "Ferchristsake, you're tied to the Mafia, and now I learn you've got me involved as well." Julie grabbed him and he paled. "Please, don't kill me!" he said, raising his hands.

"Don't be stupid," Julie said, pulling him away from the low wall. "That's the last thing I want." Then, steering him to the bench, he said, "Let's get a few things straight. First, forget all that bullshit in the papers and the movies. There is no Mafia here in America, certainly nothing like they portray it. That isn't how it works, not even close. Next, and this is very important, this is the last time you say anything that links me to the organization or anything related to it. And finally, for you and your family's protection, this conversation *must* stay between us." And when Jeffries began to object, he silenced him. "Now you listen to me. Tell no one what I've told you, not your wife, your girlfriends, not a soul. Is that clear?"

Jeffries sat heavily, and for a moment it appeared he was about to cry. Shaking his head, he looked up and said, "What've you gotten me into?"

"Nothing you can't handle."

"I don't understand any of this."

"Don't try. The only thing you need to remember is that you want the presidency and we will deliver it for you. That, my friend, is a promise."

"But you just said I can't be the candidate."

"That's right, but I didn't say you wouldn't be president."

"What the hell's that supposed to mean?"

"It means trust me."

"But I'll never get another shot at it."

"Do as I say and it's yours," Julie assured him.

Smiling weakly, he said, "You left off the *'or else'.*"

Julie didn't reply. He didn't have to.

Driving home, Jeffries broke out of his silence after crossing the South River, telling his wife of the unexpected change in plans.

"What do you mean you're shifting to the number two spot?!" she screamed, something Laura Jeffries rarely did.

Summing up what Julie had said, he explained how his backers had become overly cautious about his candidacy. And when she disputed the notion he cut her off, saying that all were in agreement the timing wasn't right for him, and there was nothing he could do about it. She remained unconvinced but he didn't care, since none of it made sense to him, either.

She'd always supported him, and now that he seemed so close she felt this decision was foolish, and told him so. His silence as they drove confused her.

But Jeffries wasn't thinking about her. His eyes locked on the road ahead, he was gripping the wheel and struggling with a range of conflicting emotions. Having left home that evening a powerful senator, he was now returning emasculated. And if that didn't destroy his ego, he had to contend with the agonizing realization that he had not been responsible for his political fortune, as he he'd thought. And perhaps most troubling, was the gnawing fear he was now beholden to ruthless mobsters. Yet, despite all that, the little boy in him was perversely excited at being in league with such powerful men. He was wondering if Julie had personally killed anyone when she brought him back, asking who might head the ticket.

"I don't know and I don't think they do either. He'll likely be someone not connected with Washington." He saw the disappointment in her face and wanted to say, "Don't worry, I'll still be president, they promised me." But that would've raised more questions than he was capable of answering.

* * *

It wasn't long afterward, while at the Cosmos Club, that he learned who his running mate would be.

"Holy Jesus!" he blurted, drawing stares from around the lounge. Then, lowering his voice, he said, "I never would've picked him, not in a million years. You sure you know what you're doing?"

"Don't worry," Julie assured him, "he's your ticket to the White House."

Jeffries gulped his drink and immediately signaled for another. "But Reggie Sutherland?" he said, shaking his head. "Just when you think you've seen it all. BAM! And along comes Mister Nobody." The notion of relinquishing his place to a naïf like Sutherland was humiliating, and he quickly said so.

"Who heard of you a few years ago?" Julie reminded him.

"That was different," he countered, but his manner suggested he knew it wasn't.

The waiter delivered a double bourbon and quickly retreated. After a long swallow, he wondered aloud, "Does anyone really control his own destiny in this town?"

"Hard to tell." Then weary of Jeffries' protests, Julie said, "Look, I agree you should be heading the ticket, it was our plan from the start, but it isn't going to happen. What's meant to be is Reggie Sutherland."

Jeffries swished the ice in his glass before draining it. "So what do you want me to do?" he asked, unable to conceal his disappointment.

"That's the spirit," Julie said with a smile. "It's critical Sutherland believes you're making this sacrifice for the good of the country, and the only way he'll believe it is to hear it from you."

"Hear what?"

"That America needs someone with his leadership skills and moral convictions, someone untainted by the process, someone who can step in and pull the country back together again."

Jeffries rolled his eyes. "What a load of crap."

"He won't think so."

"So, in addition to relinquishing my place on the ticket," he moaned, "I have to recruit the sonofabitch and then convince him to run. I'm beginning to feel like Alice in fucking Wonderland."

"I knew you'd see the humor in it."

He heaved a sigh. "Notice I'm not laughing, but if that's what you want."

"That's exactly what we want."

Jeffries shook his head. "Here's to me, one helluva patriot," he said, raising his glass. Seeing it empty, he mumbled, "It figures."

CHAPTER THIRTY (1976)

"I guess that pretty much confirms what the exit polls have been telling us all day," the well-coiffed newsman announced with unmasked satisfaction to his co-anchor.

Both were seated beneath a banner proclaiming, *CBS Election Central*, and in smaller script below, *America '76*. In the studio behind them a bank of shirt-sleeved workers with headphones were busily recording and posting incoming returns in what clearly had been a one-horse race.

"Yes, Dan, it's turning out just as we've been predicting. I guess you could say it's all over but the shouting now. Early reports from the West, where polls closed just over an hour ago, are confirming victory for Governor Sutherland and Senator Jeffries."

"Just a moment, Roger," his colleague interrupted while leaning into his earphone. "We need to cut to Atlanta for an update."

A moment later viewers were inside a raucous ballroom festooned with campaign signs, banners, streamers and hundreds of red, white and blue balloons. In the background, a jazz combo in candy-striped blazers and straw hats was performing for a crowd of revelers sporting *Reggie for President* campaign buttons and hats.

As the camera panned to the waiting newsman, the crowd began chanting, "Reggie! Reggie! Reggie!" in an orchestrated attempt to coax the unofficial winner down from his fifth floor suite, and show America this was the place to be.

"As you can see, Dan," the overwhelmed correspondent shouted into his mike, "there's an army of jubilant folks in Atlanta tonight. The sweet aroma of victory, pervasive all day, is overpowering. And," he said, acknowledging the animated man beside him waving to well-wishers, "no doubt a welcome reprieve from one who's crisscrossed America with the candidate. Standing with me is Bobby Lee Scoggins, the man who everyone, regardless of party affiliation, agrees did a magnificent job of managing the governor's campaign from that first day, when he surprised us by throwing his hat into the ring. Bobby Lee," he said, "you've been predicting a solid win for months. What do you say now to the naysayers who doubted Reggie Sutherland, an outsider, could pull this off?"

The wiry man swiped his forehead with a handkerchief. "Well, Peter…" he drawled, and suddenly he was yanked out of camera range, but not from the newsman's iron grip, and for a brief moment viewers were treated to Scoggins' flailing elbow as the determined correspondent worked against unseen forces to recapture his quarry.

"As you can see, Dan, we've got a lively crowd down here," the newsman said, hauling Scoggins back into view.

"Y'all gonna hafta 'scuse us," Scoggins sang in his familiar homespun accent, while smoothing his jacket and straightening his trademark red bowtie. "We're kinda exuberant down here as you might expect." In the next instant his smile faded and he was the seasoned campaigner again. "As y'all've heard me say bafo, there was a contingent, mostly folks up there in *Washington*," he said, pronouncing the word with practiced disdain, "who thought the guvenah couldn't reach the people, but we knew different. We knew once the people examined his record of service and heard where Guvenah Sutherland stood on the issues, they'd want him in the White House. Evra poll goin' back to bafo New Hampshire verified he was puffectly in tune with Americah. The people jus' hadda hear his message, is all."

"So, you don't think Ford and Rockefeller ever had a chance?" came the rehearsed response.

"Nevah," Scoggins replied confidently. "Reggie Sutherland is a man of the people," he said, echoing the carefully crafted Madison Avenue catch phrase designed to distance the candidate from tainted Washington insiders.

"And the people have indeed spoken," the newsman informed his audience as the camera zoomed in for a headshot that excluded Scoggins. "Thank you, Bobby Lee. This is Peter Attenboro, reporting from Sutherland headquarters in Atlanta, where we expect to hear from Governor Sutherland shortly. Back to you, Dan."

"Thank you, Peter," said the man in New York. "Now, before shifting to our correspondent at the White House, let's recap the events that brought us to this historic juncture," he said somberly. "This hasn't been a particularly bright period in Gerald Ford's long public career. On the whole, this president—the only president not elected to the office—has had a tough time of it. Having been chosen to replace the disgraced Spiro Agnew, he stepped into the Oval Office only after its occupant was himself forced to resign rather than face impeachment.

"And, while Gerald Ford has an unblemished public record, his attempt at healing the nation by pardoning former President Nixon may have been his undoing. Despite strong denials to the contrary, there were persistent rumors throughout his tenure of a sweetheart deal. Thereafter, his agenda—as noble as it was—was dogged by the shadow of Watergate and the nagging specter of Richard Nixon lurking in the background."

Gava spat at the screen. "Yeah, along with you and your scumbag friends stoking the fire in case anyone forgot. Who the fuck's he think he's kidding?" he said to no one in particular. And to Reni as he entered the room, "What's the time?"

"Why're you getting all worked up? You know they're all commies. Besides, they helped push our man in," Nunzio reminded him.

"I hate 'em just the same." Then with a wide grin, "They'd shit if they knew the real story."

"Better they don't," Nunzio said.

"You're right." Then shifting in his chair he asked, "What's the time?"

"Quarter to," Reni said. "We oughta get going."

"Okay," Gava said in a tired voice, suggesting he'd prefer the others went on without him. But he'd promised, and so he rose and struggled into his coat. "Getting too old for this," he mumbled as they stepped into the frigid night.

It was after midnight when they entered Jack's and walked unnoticed past the few late-night patrons to the rear table beyond the *Section Closed* sign. Excepting Reni, they were a group of paunchy old men who no longer dressed stylishly, but rather for comfort and warmth, and who'd agreed to gather there at Julie's insistence for, as he'd said, old times' sake.

As they waited, Gava grumbled about sitting around a cold diner, and only brightened when Julie came through the door, brushing past the cashier and grill man, both strangers to him.

"Good job," Reni said, rising and clasping his friend's hand as the others voiced their approval.

Julie looked around at those who'd engineered tonight's victory; the only one missing was Gigi Mosca, dead three months now of stomach cancer. In his place was Tony Volpe, known to some as *The Fox* or *Tony Fox*, and every bit as astute as his predecessor.

This was Julie's first trip to the Bronx on organization business in several months. He'd even skipped Mosca's funeral, a small affair intended to eschew unwanted public scrutiny. Tonight, he'd come directly from the Manhattan townhouse of an NBC vice president, where he'd dined with two of Sutherland's advisors and a handful of media friends, departing only after the NBC White House correspondent phoned to say Ford had conceded the election and would make a formal announcement the following morning.

Now seated across from Gava, he waited for the waitress to set his coffee down.

"This is how it'll go," he said when she'd gone, passing across a folded sheet of paper. "Jeffries'll see to it."

While Gava studied the list of titles and corresponding names, Nunzio looked over and said, "It's like ordering at the Chinks, one from column A and one from column B."

With few exceptions, all Gava knew of the men listed to fill the posts was that Julie had selected them. "How soon?" he demanded impatiently, a trait that had surfaced with regularity in the months following Mosca's death.

"Right after our boy's sworn in," Julie told him. "These'll be among the first nominees submitted. As president of the Senate, Jeffries will grease their confirmation hearings."

Expressing yet another recent eccentricity, Gava asked not for the first time, "You sure these mokes are reliable?"

"They're solid," Julie said. And when Gava raised an eyebrow, "These are my people, Paolo. There'll be no negotiating," he said, aware of the man's increasing need of assurances. "They do what we want or they're out."

"They goddamn fucking better. We can't afford screw-ups."

"You'll see," Julie vowed, "things'll move smoothly once they're in place."

"And what about this hayseed Sutherland?" Volpe asked, knowing the question was on Gava's mind.

"Don't worry about him. He'll be too busy trying to be president, a job for which he isn't qualified. Jeffries is our man."

"Even after he's number one? You know once these guys get what they want they forget about us."

"Even then," Julie assured them.

"You did good," Gava finally conceded, shoving the paper in his pocket. And though he smiled, there was no masking his uneasiness.

Pleased with themselves, each man slipped a twenty beneath his saucer before departing.

Soon after dropping Gava at home, Reni was at Ferry Point Park, beside the massive concrete abutment supporting the Whitestone Bridge, the steady hum of traffic above him. He sat in the shadows with the window partially open, looking out on Manhattan's distant skyline, the glow from his cigarette the only sign of his presence. After a while, he saw the headlights of an approaching car bounce across the rutted road and then complete the broad arc around the ball field before heading toward him.

"Waiting long?" Julie asked when he'd come alongside and rolled down his window.

"Uh-uh," he said, dropping his cigarette between the cars. "You talk with Volpe?"

Julie nodded. "He's satisfied. What about Paolo, he have anything more to say before you tucked him in?"

"He don't talk much after these late meetings. He's more interested in hitting the sack."

"He isn't looking too well."

"Yeah, this thing with Mosca's changed him."

"Are you hearing anything from the others?" Julie asked of the other bosses.

Reni shook his head. "It's business as usual with them, at least for now."

"I worry how much longer that'll last, particularly after Gambino's death last month."

"Carlo was old and sick," Reni reminded him. "That was no surprise."

"Still, we can't afford any power moves now," Julie said.

"Volpe won't let it happen."

"Bringing him in was a good idea."

"It didn't go over too good with your uncle. He figures it should've been him."

"Yeah, so he's been telling me. Meanwhile, it's critical that you and Volpe keep the old man on a short leash."

"You ask me, it's time he retired. He won't be worth shit in six months."

"Six months is all we need, maybe less if things go as planned. If you two can give me that we're home free."

Reni nodded.

"If he gets worse…," Julie began.

"You'll know before anyone."

CHAPTER THIRTY-ONE (1977-78)

When the official count was tallied, it was determined that sixty-one percent of Americans eligible to vote had cast their ballots, a much higher proportion than those voting in the Nixon-Humphrey race. Additionally, Sutherland's landslide win increased his party's majority in the Senate to twelve, where his nominations, as Julie'd promised, sailed through the confirmation process. As one of the early submissions, Frank Kelly wasted little time upon being sworn in as Social Security Commissioner in placing an indefinite hold on his predecessor's plans to upgrade the organization's computer systems, thereby ensuring the annual skim—now in excess of eight hundred million dollars—would remain intact and undetected.

But not all Julie's nominees were as accommodating as Kelly. Some, like Harold Hatters, now Deputy Assistant Secretary of Defense for Acquisitions and Logistics, needed prodding.

"We're not prepared to make a commitment," he told Julie as they sat in his expansive Pentagon office overlooking the Potomac River. His abruptness intending to close off further discussion of which aerospace firms would be chosen to develop separate prototypes of a new line of jet fighters for the Navy and Air Force, a project that originated with the previous administration and had now entered the selection stage. "We're withholding all decisions until we've evaluated the services' analyses. As you know," he stressed, from across his wide desk, "we can't get ahead of ourselves in the process, particularly one of this magnitude."

"I understand fully, Hank, but there are exceptions," Julie said, ignoring the rebuff. "Unlike their competitors, who have contracts well into the next decade, Grumman and Lockheed need this work to sustain their production lines. Without it they stand a chance of folding."

What he didn't mention was the link between the companies' financial difficulties and the mob-controlled union contracts that had boosted production costs and made competing in the bidding process difficult. Nor did he reveal the kickbacks that would accompany these new contracts, payments that would continue as long as the planes were flying.

There was a soft knock at the door and a Marine aide peered in. "Pardon me, sir. The test and evaluation team is standing by in the conference room."

"Thank you, major," Hatters replied. "Be right there." And when they were alone again, he explained, "We can't eliminate the other firms from the process. These aren't small contracts. We're talking billions of dollars and thousands of man-years. No," he said gathering a sheaf of blue folders stamped *TOP SECRET*, "we must wait and see how it plays out. Now, if you'll excuse me," he said rising and wedging the package beneath his arm. And when Julie remained seated, he said, "Look, my friend, we have an obligation to weigh the recommendations of the services flying those aircraft. And, as you might expect," he added, glancing at his watch, "they may have other preferences."

"Harry, we both know a third of what comes through this office is congressional-mandated pork. And as far as adhering to the services' wishes, they didn't get a voice when McNamara rammed the F-111 down their throats," he said of the multi-use medium-range strategic bomber, reconnaissance, and tactical strike plane.

"This is a new administration," Hatters reminded him. "You're mistaken if you think it's business as usual."

Julie was tiring of the game. He knew the Navy had already eliminated Grumman from the competition, and also which way the Air Force was leaning. He folded his arms and studied the photos behind Hatters' desk. The faces were different, but the poses were the same in every office along the coveted outer E-ring. These happened to be of Hatters in a variety of command ball caps and flight suits grinning alongside admirals and generals at outposts around the globe.

"I have people waiting," Hatters said.

"Let's cut the bullshit. The Navy already told you they want Martin-Marietta, and the Air Force will announce in another week, and it won't be Lockheed."

"I don't know where you're getting your information, but…,"

"Listen, Harry. It's simple. The services don't get a vote on this one."

"You're stepping over the line," Hatters warned, his face reddening. "The decision will be made in good time and *without outside interference*. Now I really must go," he said crossing the room.

"The country can't lose these high tech jobs, Harry, not while the Soviets are playing hardball."

"Save the lecture," Hatters said, eyeing his watch again. "We're dealing with the Soviets just fine."

"Goddamnit," Julie said pounding the arm of his chair, "these contracts *must* go to Grumman and Lockheed."

Hatters let out a long breath. "I don't know how many different ways I can say this, but *I* am the chief procurement officer in this building, and *I* will make that decision at the appropriate time. And this isn't the time. Now please leave before this gets ugly."

Julie shook his head. "I thought you understood."

"Understood what? That you can waltz in here and tell me how to do my job, and I'd simply roll over? This isn't the Hill, my friend. We don't jump on this side of the Potomac the way they do over there." Then, taking a calming breath, he said, "Look, I've been more than fair allowing you to insert your opinion into the process. That isn't something many folks get to do. But that's as far as it goes. Now you need to go back to your people and tell them you've delivered their message and it's out of your hands."

"I meant, I thought you understood you're in this job because of me."

His eyes bulging, Hatters moved toward the door. "That does it! This meeting's over! Finished!"

But Julie didn't move. "Better take a look at this before you storm out," Julie said, taking a business card from his jacket and tossing it on the desk.

Hatters froze. "I don't believe this."

"I'm not going until we settle this."

"What kind of game are you playing?"

Julie didn't respond. Instead, he held Hatters' gaze until the man wavered.

"I've got a full agenda. We'll discuss this later."

"Don't be foolish," Julie warned.

There was a long silence after which Hatters let his hand slip from the doorknob. "Okay. Have it your way," he said, returning to his desk. "Whatever it takes to end this idiocy." Without touching it, he looked down at the engraved card and read the single phone number. There was no name or address, just the recognizable federal government prefix. Arching an eyebrow, he asked, "What is this?"

"Dial it. Don't ask your secretary to do it, and use your private line," Julie instructed, indicating the credenza behind the desk. "You don't want your aide listening in on this one."

"Why the hell should I?"

"You're one stubborn bastard," Julie said, shaking his head. "Because it's going to save your job."

Hatters' frown suggested none of this made sense. Still, he edged back around his desk, set the folders down and reluctantly eased into his chair. Then, pulling the card toward him, he picked it up and, holding it by the edges, studied the number while shooting glances across the desk.

"Go on," Julie said, and watched him lift the phone. From where he was sitting, he could hear the ring and the familiar voice on the other end, and saw Hatters go pale.

He'd bypassed the White House switchboard and reached the vice president in the Old Executive Office Building.

His voice faltering, he said, "This is Assistant Secretary of Defense Harold Hatters calling, sir."

"Damn it all," Jeffries bellowed, "I know who it is, and why you're calling. How many folks do you think have this number?"

Perched on the edge of his chair, Hatters cleared his throat and said, "Sir, I've tried explaining to Mr. Vittorio that we must consider the services' preferences before making a determination on these contracts, but he refuses to...,"

"Don't be an ass! The decision's already been made as was explained to you."

"But, sir, we can't...,"

"Damn it, Hatters! It's in the national interest. What we can't do is lose those jobs. Can you understand that?!" Then, without providing him a chance to reply, he said, "Because if you can't, I'm prepared to ask the president to accept your resignation, which, as you very well know, I hold on file along with every other appointee. Am I making myself clear?"

Hatters' shoulders were slack and his throat dry. "Yes, sir. It will be as you wish." He was asking, "Is there anything more, Mr. Vice President?" when Jeffries hung up, leaving him wondering if his career had suddenly derailed. "You certainly know how to make a point," he said after carefully replacing the receiver.

Julie wasn't amused. "When can we expect the announcement?"

Hatters thought a moment. "Five, six weeks acceptable?"

"That'll be fine," Julie said, reaching over and retrieving the card. "Let's try working together. We have at least three years ahead of us." He left without saying goodbye.

* * *

Julie's phone call to Scott Remmington, his former schoolmate, came in early spring, a year after the death of Remmington's wife and youngest child, both victims of a pileup along a foggy stretch of the New England Thruway. Until Julie's call, he'd been dealing with his loss by channeling his energy into the family law practice. Not surprisingly, the summons to come to Washington was a welcome diversion.

"We need someone with your qualifications down here, "Julie said, when inviting his friend to head the Budget Review Division in the Office of Management and Budget.

Now, sitting in Jeffries' high-ceilinged office, the two men listened as the vice president shared his thoughts with them about the appointment.

"This is a unique opportunity to make significant contributions to the nation," he said from behind his ornate desk, the west wing of the White House framed in the window behind him. To many Washingtonians, including Julie, Jeffries projected more of a presidential aura than Sutherland, who insisted on clinging to the contrived down-home image that had served him so well throughout the campaign.

"OMB's credibility has suffered over the years," he told them. "First, when Nixon foolishly allowed Watergate to distract him, thus enabling the Director to overstep his authority and insert himself in policies in which he had absolutely no business. And later, under Ford, when the operation got so politicized it came to be known as the *Office of Meddling and Bumbling,*" he said, eliciting the anticipated smiles. "We want to change all that," he said, "which is where you'll come in."

"How so?" Remmington asked.

"As you know, the president is publicly committed to expanding entitlements and bolstering our sagging social programs, in effect, picking up where Johnson left off." Then, leaning forward, he confided, "But to make it work, OMB needs to take the lead."

"I'd wondered how he intended paying for those programs," Remmington said.

"Simple. By trimming the fat and with zero-based budgeting."

"Will Congress sit still for that?"

Jeffries grinned. "They will. And then they'll do what they always do—blame the cuts on us. It's all bullshit."

Remmington looked at Julie, who shrugged.

"So that we aren't accused of being unfair," Jeffries continued, "we'll naturally have to do some trimming here in Washington as well."

"Naturally," Remmington agreed.

What Jeffries didn't bother mentioning were the forced early retirements Remmington would be implementing as part of the plan, retirements that would push nearly a thousand senior FBI agents off the payroll and which, along with Sutherland's campaign pledge to pursue white-collar criminals, would effectively de-rail a number of the department's organized crime programs.

* * *

Julie's attention wasn't focused entirely on the new administration. To his growing frustration, he was being drawn with disturbing frequency back to New York, where Gava's recurring dark periods were threatening to become a serious liability. By summer, his bizarre behavior, first exhibited the previous November, had become worrisome. Among other things, he was openly confiding to those around him that he was in regular communication with dead former associates and rivals, including Baratta, Gambino and Colombo, all of whom, he claimed, assured him he could avoid the dreaded cancer by not relinquishing the reins of power.

Fearing rivals in the other families would learn of Gava's deteriorating condition, Julie determined it was time for him to go, but in a manner that didn't destabilize the organization, as past changes had. Accordingly, working through the Camorra chieftain, he sought and received the blessing of the Benevento Commission. The details and timing of Gava's removal, they informed him, were left to him. First, though, he had to resolve the troubling issue of his father's murder.

And while the subject of his father's death wasn't banned between Julie and his mother, neither was it discussed. Simply, with each grieving separately over the years, there had been little point in raising the issue—until now.

It was a painful meeting, during which they sat in his father's study, still furnished as it was twenty years earlier, and where the only sound was the rattle of windows from a late night storm. And though alone, they spoke in whispers, and when tears came, as he knew they would, they too were muted. In all, it was an exhausting discussion

339

of uncovered secrets and ensuing arguments and counter-arguments of what must be done about rectifying them. Not surprisingly, she offered less harsh measures than he proposed. And though he usually deferred to her on other matters, on this one he remained firm. Thus, it was late when she finally yielded and, with nothing more to be said, he took her arm and gently led her upstairs.

Upon reaching the landing, she raised her eyes and asked again, "You're absolutely certain?"

"I am," he said embracing her, "and equally sure of what I must do."

She nodded and shuffled away. And as he watched her, he felt no satisfaction in having prevailed.

It had been an arduous night, and when he slipped into his room, he eased the door shut and leaned heavily against it.

"Well," Nikki whispered in the dark, "how'd she take it?"

He didn't respond. Instead, he peeled off his clothes, leaving them where they fell, and walked softly to her. "She understands," he said, sliding in beside her.

She heard the pain and touched his arm. "It's the best you could hope for."

"I suppose," he sighed.

"When?"

"Soon. Next week," he said pressing into the pillow.

She drew the covers around him and, leaning over, kissed his face. Once his breathing grew steady she too fell asleep.

That was Thanksgiving, and they returned to Rugby Hall the following day, but not before he took Nunzio aside. "We have to talk," he told his uncle.

"No problem."

"Under the circumstances it's best we do it away from Paolo and the others."

Nunzio grinned and nodded his understanding. "Good idea."

* * *

Julie awoke before the alarm sounded and immediately dialed the Coast Guard weather recording. The message had changed little from the preceding night. A small craft warning was still in effect as a precaution against the approaching storm, now predicted to reach the northern Chesapeake region that afternoon.

Together, he and Nikki ate a hasty breakfast, and soon he was underway for Baltimore beneath a gunmetal sky and the smell of rain in the air. He'd made the journey often, but always in fair weather and usually in two hours. Today, he allowed himself three. The powerful diesel engine purred as he rounded Hackett Point and moved into the choppier shipping channel, where a rising stern wind enabled him to reach the Inner Harbor forty minutes before he was to meet his uncle.

For the most part, the pending storm and cooler-than-usual weather kept the tourists away. And of the few boats in port, all were tightly shuttered. With so much open pier space, he moored by the boardwalk, across from the playing field fronting the distinctive red brick McCormick Spice factory, and waited. Nunzio would be along shortly. When the yellow cab arrived he sounded his horn, drawing a quick wave from his uncle, who bent into the wind and darted across the field, his topcoat ballooning around him.

Years of easy living coupled with a lifetime of smoking had him panting when he climbed aboard. "Jesus," he gasped, "you couldn't have picked a lousier day."

"Just a little breeze," Julie replied. "Nothing to worry about."

But Nunzio remained skeptical, particularly after they cleared the harbor and encountered the wind. "You sure about this?" he said eyeing the swells.

"Relax. It's a passing storm."

"Maybe we should turn around," he said as he hammered a pack of Camels against his palm. "Wait it out."

"We're not going back," Julie told him. "But we can duck in there till it passes if it makes you feel better," he said, pointing to the rusting Dundalk Shipyard.

"I don't care," his uncle replied with false bravado, cigarette smoke clouding around his head. "Do what you want."

Julie shrugged. "Probably not a bad idea," he said, and altered course.

It was nearly one o'clock when they anchored in the lee of the old dry dock; its ghostly cranes idled after a decade of decline in the industry.

"You hungry?" he asked.

"I could eat."

"Good," he said, leading him aft, where he set out a pair of deck chairs and the cooler of sandwiches Nikki had packed earlier.

As they ate, they spoke of Gava's increasingly strange behavior and the urgency of having him step down, and, most importantly to Nunzio, his own expectations once the change was implemented.

Rather than abating, as Julie had promised, the wind grew stronger, sending waves into the shallow inlet.

"You're going to be a good boss," Nunzio told him, pleased with Julie's timetable for moving Paolo aside, and the promotion it meant for him.

"I like to think I come by it from my father," he said as he cleared the table.

The mention of Julie's father drew a smile. "Your old man, now there was a stand-up guy, one of the best," he said, cradling a beer bottle in his lap. "A real *mensch*, like the Jews say."

"You really think so?"

"Absolutely. Wouldn't say it if I didn't."

Julie was standing by a cabinet, the drawer open and his hand inside gripping the gun he'd placed there earlier. Keeping it concealed, he turned and asked, "Then why'd you kill him?"

Nunzio's head snapped up. "Whattaya talking about?!"

Julie felt the boat straining against the anchor and he knew they'd have to leave soon or risk being blown ashore, but he couldn't stop now. "Cut the crap. I know it was you. What I can't understand is why you'd kill him, your own sister's husband."

There was a tense silence while Nunzio looked away, his gaze wandering to the bleak shoreline. Then running his hand across his mouth, he looked back, and said, "You've been around long enough to understand when I tell you it was strictly business, nothing personal."

"I find that difficult to believe," Julie said, waiting to see if Nunzio would go for his gun.

"It couldn't be helped, I swear."

"I'm listening," Julie said.

Nunzio took a breath. "He was expanding his operation out to the Island around the same time as the Brooklyn crews. The Sicilians told him to back off. They said Long Island was an extension of Brooklyn and they weren't sharing it with some Neapolitan from the Bronx. Not only did they want him to stop, they wanted what he'd already built up—his meat and produce businesses, vending machines, the new garbage routes—all of it. He told them to fuck off, said they had their chance and lost it. You know," Nunzio said with a touch of bitterness, "he could be thickheaded sometimes, your old man." And when Julie didn't reply, he continued. "He vowed not to give an inch. As a capo, he could take it to the commission, which is what he did—for all the good it did. The Sicilians naturally backed their own, but they also gave him a way to save face. They told him he could keep what he had, but he couldn't expand.

"Of course it was a setup. He knew if he agreed they'd squeeze him out later. So he told Gava he couldn't accept the offer. Said he was entitled to better. Gava agreed, and told them it was a bad decision and they should reconsider, but the bastards refused. After that the only option was war, which Gava figured they wanted so they could make a move on the Bronx, too."

The boat was swinging close to shore, but Nunzio seemed not to notice. Continuing, he said, "That's when they snatched me up and brought me to Brooklyn and knocked me around a little. Thought they'd scare me, but I knew what they were up to. The next day they took me to the big man, who tells me what with Congress and the feds investigating us, the last thing anybody wants is a war. He says the Island always was and always will be Brooklyn territory, and the offer to your father is more than generous. And, since the commission already decided, it's now a matter of honor. In other words, they'll fight if they have to, which meant it's us against all of 'em.

"I took the message back, and *still* your father wouldn't budge. He was ready to drag everybody into it, including Gava, who only just took over, and under who we were all making out better than before. Naturally nobody wanted to give that up. Don't get me wrong," he stressed. "Gava would've gone the distance for your father. That's how it was between them, always supporting each other, but now he had the family to worry about."

Julie released the gun, but left the drawer open, resting his hand on the counter above it.

"Believe me when I say your father's mind was made up. He refused to listen, not to me, not to Gava, not to nobody. So far as he was concerned, he'd invested a bundle opening that territory and no *Siciliani* were going to take it from him, not without a fight. We told him to forget about it, to chalk it up to the cost of doing business. Besides, we were moving upstate and into Connecticut, where the population was exploding. We told him screw the Island, that he could do ten times better up there, but he wouldn't listen. He said what good was being a capo if they could fuck him over whenever they liked.

"That's when Gava said it was up to me to turn him around or...,"

"...or he's dead," Julie interjected, ready to grab the gun. "Because, as you say, it was business."

"No, it wasn't like that," Nunzio argued. "I swear, I tried talking to him, we all did, but the sonofabitch wouldn't go along. Said he wasn't rolling over. That he'd talked it over with Gava, who didn't agree a hundred percent, but was willing to back him."

"Which you knew to be a lie," Julie pointed out.

"He was trying to keep the dialogue going."

"Sounds more like he was trying to save his own ass."

Nunzio reached out. "You weren't there!"

"So you killed him."

"I HAD NO FUCKING CHOICE!" he shouted over the wind, his facial muscles tightening. "We're married to this organization. It's all we got, and that means we must do what's best for it no matter what. You took the oath. You know that."

They were dragging the anchor now, and drifting toward the rocks. Julie closed the drawer. "I'm glad you leveled with me."

"There was no other way," he said in a tired voice.

"Yeah, I see that now."

"I knew you'd understand. You forgive me then?"

Julie shook his head. "I can't do that." Adding when Nunzio frowned, "Forgiveness only comes from the man you killed. You need to ask him when you see him. But I do understand that you had no choice."

"I swear, I loved him like a brother," Nunzio affirmed. "Trust me, if there was another way I'da done it. But, as you know, we live under different rules."

"I wish I could've talked to him. I might've changed his mind."

"Believe me, kid, there was nothing you could say that we didn't."

He heaved a sigh. "But at least I would've tried."

"Don't blame yourself."

"You know," Julie said, shaking his head, "I've been carrying around this hate since that day, and when I finally learned the truth I wanted to kill you."

"I don't blame you," he said coming out of his chair and placing a hand on Julie's shoulder. "I'da felt the same. But it's over, and now you gotta put it behind you, like I did—like we all did—or it'll poison you," he said clapping his shoulder. "We got lots of good days ahead of us."

"I guess you're right," Julie said. Then gauging the distance to shore, "But first we need to get out of here."

Going forward, he started the engine and immediately began winching the line in while easing toward the anchor.

"I need some help," he said when they were above the anchor. "Climb out on the bow and guide the anchor into place while I keep us from being blown ashore. Be careful," he cautioned, "the deck's slippery."

"I knew we shoulda stayed in port," his uncle said before stepping outside. Twice he lost his footing on the narrow walkway but kept his balance.

"This weather sucks," he said when he returned, running his hand through his hair. "Whatya say we head back?"

"Quit worrying, this baby's made for much rougher weather than this. Besides, Nikki's got a nice meal planned."

Heading south, Julie returned to the shipping channel, where they rode in silence. After a while he pointed ahead, and said, "See that on the horizon, it's the Bay Bridge."

"What about it?" Nunzio said from the chair beside him.

"We'll be home in no time once we reach it." He'd barely spoken when the rain came, a nearly vertical sheet of water. "Damn, I thought we'd beat it," he said.

"I can't see a fuckin' thing!" Nunzio complained.

"It'll pass," Julie assured him. "Meanwhile, keep an eye out." Then flipping on the running lights, he said, "Probably should've done that sooner."

Nunzio was chain-lighting a cigarette when Julie turned, and said, "Hear that?"

"Hear what?!"

"Sounds like a ship's horn. There it is again."

Nunzio cocked his head, the cigarette dangling from his lips. "All I hear's the rain. How close you figure it is?"

"Can't tell. Keep a sharp lookout," he said sounding the horn at intervals.

"Whataya talkin' about? I can't see shit!"

"Relax. We can out-maneuver these old buckets—that is, if we see `em. Though it helps if they can see us," he said peering ahead.

"Maybe we oughta move closer to shore," Nunzio suggested.

"We're okay here," Julie replied. After several minutes he said, "Better check the running lights."

"The hell you talking about?"

"Make sure they're on."

"Didn't you turn `em on?"

Julie nodded. "But that doesn't mean anything in this weather."

Nunzio shot him an angry look. "I thought you said this tub was made for this weather."

"I'm not going to argue about it," Julie snapped as they dropped into a trough. "Either check the lights or take the goddamn wheel and I'll do it."

"*I'll* fucking check `em," his uncle said, stabbing out his cigarette. "Where the hell are they?"

"Where do you think? On the mast," he said pointing up.

"All right, calm down already. Just watch where the hell we're going." He opened the door and took a hit of spray. "Jesus!" he yelled, jumping back.

"Ferchrissake, it's only water."

Nunzio gave him an icy look. Then, yanking up his collar, "Where'd you say they were?"

"Straight up!" And as his uncle stepped out, he called, "Step away so you can see past the overhang, you won't melt—and hold on to the railing!"

Shielding his eyes, Nunzio yelled, "It's a goddamn typhoon out here!" Then, arching against the railing, he leaned back and looked up. "No lights! No fucking lights! Hit the switch again."

But instead of hitting the switch, Julie spun the wheel, much as he'd done with Charlie Matches twenty years earlier, and watched as the railing he'd loosened earlier broke away under his uncle's weight.

"J-U-L-I-E!!!" Nunzio shouted, and then he was gone.

As he'd also done with Charlie, he held the wheel over until the boat came around and he saw Nunzio up ahead working to stay afloat. Rescuing him would've been simple; just keep him in the lee of the boat, and come along side and pull him out. But that wasn't the plan. Holding the wheel steady, he pressed the throttle and kept it there.

"You dirty bastard!" he shouted into the wind, and in the next instant the bow shuddered as if he'd struck a log.

When he came around again, Nunzio was on the crest of a wave floating in a halo of blood, and then he was gone. Intending to deliver a final blow, he repeated the maneuver, but his uncle had disappeared. After circling the area without results, he radioed the Coast Guard and reported a man overboard. Twenty minutes later, while passing beneath the Bay Bridge, he radioed again saying low fuel was forcing him to break off his search.

* * *

Understandably, Nunzio's death came as a blow to Gava, who, seeing it as yet another sign of his own mortality, refused to attend the memorial Mass at St. Theresa's. While Julie and his family gathered at the church that morning, Reni stepped into the kitchen and, unlocking the rear door, quietly admitted two darkly clad men.

"In there," he told the Neapolitans, directing them to the living room, before turning and leaving.

They found the aging mobster dozing in his easy chair before the darkened television, his liver-spotted hands folded on his lap, a wool Army blanket draped across his legs.

"Wake up, Don Paolo," one of them said standing over him. And when he didn't respond, he reached down and shook him roughly. "I said wake up, Don Paolo!"

Gava's eyes fluttered. *"Che cosa?* What's happening?" he muttered in the dim winter light.

"Don Paolo, it's important that you wake up. Are you awake?" the man asked in his native tongue.

Gava blinked, his good eye struggling to focus, the other rolling in its socket like a large marble. *"Chi `e?* Who are you?" he said looking up at them. And when he tried to rise, the second man pressed him down again.

"Do you know what this is, Don Paolo?" the first one asked, opening a gloved fist to reveal a glossy black stone, no larger than a pigeon egg.

Gava looked at the object and rubbed his salty whiskers. "Who are you?" he said, his voice rising. Then, shouting past them, "Reni, where are you?!"

But the men remained calm. *"E un niger lapillus,* Don Paolo," the Neapolitan said in Latin as he'd been instructed, giving Gava his first clue of who they were and what their mission was.

His eyes widened as he recognized the symbol used by the ancient Romans in their trials to signify a guilty verdict, it was similar to the one he'd used on victims years earlier. "Why do you show me this?" he demanded.

"We are soldiers from Napoli, Don Paolo, sent by Don Julio to avenge his father."

His face twisting in anger, he said, "I don't give a fuck who sent you. I am the boss."

"You were the boss."

"The hell, you say." And again, he called out, "Reni!"

"You are finished, old man."

"Now listen to me."

"We don't get paid to listen, Don Paolo. You better than anyone know that."

"Goddamnit, I give the orders! Stop now if you want to live."

He was stalling and they knew it. Grasping Gava's jaw, the second man jerked his head back, twisting his mouth open.

"This is your fate," the first one said, pressing the stone into his mouth, the other clamping it shut.

Gava's chest heaved and his veins pulsed as he struggled to breathe. And though he lacked the strength of his youth, he did his best to resist, twisting and kicking.

"Julius Caesar was merciful," the first soldier said. "He didn't allow those he crucified to suffer. Also Don Julio," he said, flashing a dagger and plunging the blade into Gava's chest—once, twice, three times.

They held him until the life drained from him, and then they hauled him away in a trashcan.

* * *

Two high-velocity sniper bullets struck President Sutherland precisely at eleven A.M., Monday, Valentine's Day, while he was working the greeting line prior to dedicating a new public housing project in Chicago—one above the right eye, the other squarely through the chest. As noted by the evening news reports, the grisly shooting occurred not far from where seven members of Bugs Moran's gang had been massacred in a power struggle with the notorious Al Capone exactly forty-nine years earlier. It was a chilling bit of irony that didn't elude Bob Jeffries.

CHAPTER THIRTY-TWO (DECEMBER, 1977)

Julie gazed at the homes across the Severn, marveling at how close they appeared. Those trimmed with Christmas lights, like the VanDoren's—no longer theirs now that Miriam had passed on and he'd moved into a Pensacola retirement home—seemed to be floating on the river.

He stood there for a while enjoying the scene before stepping to the long mirror and adjusting his tie and cummerbund. Satisfied, he reached into his pocket and, withdrawing his father's ring, slipped it on with a finality that spelled the end of an era. In tribute to the dead man, he'd vowed to wear it again on the day he entered the White House. He hadn't worn it since Gava had presented him with one crafted like his own, insisting Julie wear it instead of his father's as a symbol of their special bond. Having accepted the gift with dignity, it remained on his hand until the day of his mentor's death, when, leaving the church after Nunzio's memorial service, he tossed it unceremoniously into a nearby sewer.

"What do you think?" he asked Nikki without turning around.

"How long have you known I've been watching?" she replied from the shadows.

He smiled through the mirror. "Since you came in."

"Can't surprise you," she said.

"That's how I stay alive."

Coming over, she took his hand, the one with the ring, and said, "I sense profound contentment tonight."

He looked at her. "It took a while."

"Are you happy?"

His smile faded. "What would make me happy is if they'd never killed him."

Later, as they drove into Washington, Nikki broke the silence. "Still thinking about your father?"

He shook his head. "I was thinking now that we control the hill, how do we get down."

"The hill?"

"Did you ever play king of the hill when you were a child?"

She laughed. "Sure."

"Remember what happens when you finally get to be king?

"There's a pack of kids ready to knock you off."

"Exactly," he said. "And getting knocked off can be fierce."

"Then perhaps it's time to quit," she said, her smile fading. "Let someone else take the hits."

He shook his head. "It's tempting, but I can't walk away."

"You can do whatever you want," she said. "You're the king."

"What I mean is I enjoy being king. It's like someone said about power. 'Power corrupts. Absolute power is wonderful.' Besides, quitting isn't an option just yet."

"What do you mean?"

"My father once told me, 'If you dance with a bear, you don't stop dancing until the bear lets go.'"

The implication was clear and she shuddered. "I don't want you to end up like your father." When he looked over, she said, "How do we get down from this hill?"

"I'm working on it," he said. "I'll let you know when I figure it out."

* * *

The president's guests were preparing to depart when Jeffries drifted over to Julie and said with a nod toward the adjoining room, "Please hang back a moment, will you? I won't be long." And then he was gone.

"What was that about?" Nikki asked when she reached him.

"He wants to talk."

"Making a run up the hill?"

He smiled. "He's about due, don't you think?"

The holiday dinner had been for White House staffers and their spouses, including a contingent of Sutherland loyalists whom Jeffries had retained out of kindness. Like Julie and Nikki, it was their first social gathering with the president since he'd moved into the office ten months earlier.

"You know," she confided, "he's much more presidential than Sutherland."

"Yeah, he's a natural," Julie replied, aware of the secret service agent lingering nearby. "The country's lucky to have him."

Leaning into him, she whispered, "He's lucky to have us."

"Something tells me he may not share that thought."

Several minutes later, Jeffries and his wife swept into the small room. He thanked the agent for his help that evening, and asked that he close the door on his way out.

"I'm glad that's over," he said when they were alone. "That Sutherland bunch can be tiresome." Then with a brighter face, he turned to Nikki. "We're delighted you could join us tonight."

"It's an honor. Thank you for including us."

"Have you seen the national Christmas tree?" he asked, gesturing to the window and the ellipse beyond. "It's quite spectacular." And when she said she hadn't, he turned to his wife and asked, "Laura, would you take Nikki upstairs where she'll have a better view? We'll be along shortly."

The instant they left, he said, "I apologize for not getting with you sooner, but, as you know, it's been a helluva roller coaster ride these past several months."

Julie nodded. "The important thing is you're here now."

"Right," he said with a crooked smile. Then, with a knowing nod, he said, "No sense lingering on the past when we have the future to deal with. Don't you agree?"

"Absolutely."

"Good," he said, rubbing his hands together, "because tonight we have something special to celebrate, my friend."

"Really? Then why send the wives out?"

"We'll include them in good time," Jeffries assured him. "Right now," he said stepping to the portable bar, "what I have to say is between us." Then holding up a decanter, he asked, "Brandy okay?"

"No champagne?" Julie teased.

"You're right, that would be more appropriate. I can send for a bottle if you prefer."

"I don't know what we're celebrating yet, Mr. President?"

"Ha, you sly devil," he said pouring out two glasses, "you won't get it out of me that easily. And let's drop the formality, we're way beyond that."

"I prefer it," Julie said, thinking of Nixon and his penchant for taping conversations.

"Don't be silly," Jeffries said, handing him a heavy crystal snifter. "You can trust me."

Julie smiled. Nikki was the only person he trusted. "So, other than Christmas what are we celebrating?"

Jeffries pretended to consider the question. Then, grinning broadly, he said, "Oh, what the hell! No sense dragging it out. I've decided it's time you received some well-deserved recognition."

Julie shook his head. "I'm afraid you're mistaken, Mr. President."

"No, no, there's no mistake."

"I'm not comfortable with this conversation," he said setting his glass down.

357

"Don't be so quick," Jeffries said. "I'm simply reciprocating for all you've done."

"All I've done?"

"You know," he said.

Again, Julie demurred. "No more than anyone else."

"Nonsense. You've done for me, and now it's my turn to do for you. You know, a little *quid pro quo*."

"I know all about quid pro quo," Julie said stiffly. "And I repeat. I haven't done anything, certainly nothing to warrant special recognition."

"Now don't be hasty. Just hear me out, okay?" he said, returning to the bar.

Julie shrugged. "It's your party."

"Yes it is," he said refilling his glass and holding it to the light.

Julie wanted to say, "Get on with it. I know what you're up to." Instead, he stood silent allowing Jeffries to prolong the moment.

When he finally came from around the bar, he said, "With your permission I intend placing your name in nomination for the post of Ambassador to Italy. Will you allow me that small token of gratitude?" he asked proudly. And then frowning when Julie failed to respond, he asked, "What's wrong? Aren't you pleased? I can just see it. You making your entrance at the presidential palace in Rome, and some major-domo announcing, '*His Excellency, the Honorable Julius Vittorio, United States Ambassador!*' or however they do it. Doesn't that grab you?"

Julie crossed the room and, gripping Jeffries' arm, leaned into him and whispered, "Nice try, but that wasn't part of the deal."

"But you've earned it. You're going to be our number one man in Italy, the country of your ancestors."

"What do you mean, earned it?"

The question drew a puzzled expression. "You know," he said with an awkward smile. "Must I spell it out?"

They were inches apart, the president trying to pull free and Julie not letting him.

"No need to."

"Well, then?"

Julie shook his head. "As your late predecessor might say, Mr. President, 'That dog won't hunt.'"

The unexpected reference to the slain president caused Jeffries to blink nervously. "I…, I don't understand. I thought you'd be pleased. This is a tremendous honor." Then, his face brightening, he said, "Oh, Jesus! It's the hearings. You're concerned about the hearings, aren't you? Well you needn't be. I've already discussed the matter with the Majority Leader and the Foreign Relations Committee Chairman—informally, of course—and you'll sail through the confirmation process."

Again, the offer was met with silence.

"If not the hearings, what then? What am I missing?" he asked, his confidence waning.

"I'll tell you what you're missing," Julie said tightening his grasp. "Get that fucking idea out of your head."

"What idea?"

"You're incredibly stupid, or you think I am."

"But, I thought you'd be pleased," Jeffries insisted, a thin line of perspiration forming on his upper lip.

"Pleased that you're dumping me?"

"*Dumping you?!* What do you mean?"

"In case you forgot, we're partners in this thing."

"I haven't forgotten anything," he said lowering his voice. "But I thought this was something you'd want."

"I'll tell you what you thought. You thought you could ship me off, be rid of me. And I find that deeply insulting."

"That's absurd. The notion never crossed my mind, I swear. Nor did I mean to offend you. I was simply trying to do the right thing."

"You want to do the right thing?"

"Yes, of course."

"Then stick to our agreement."

"It never it occurred to me not to."

"It better not, because if it does, those Secret Service agents aren't going to protect you," he said releasing him.

Jeffries paled. He still held images of Sutherland lying crumpled on the pavement, along with the knowledge his killers hadn't been caught and likely never would be. "I was only trying to…,"

"Enough!" Julie said. "We both know what you were trying to do. I'm not going anywhere, understand?"

The President nodded as he smoothed his jacket. "Yes."

"Good. Now, shall we join the ladies?"

* * *

"So what did he have to say?" Nikki asked when they'd turned out of the White House and onto Pennsylvania Avenue.

Julie shook his head. "The dumb shit tried to cut us out."

"The game never ends, does it?"

Julie looked over and smiled. "Not as long as we control the hill."

* * *

Later that spring, Goodmann's phone rang shortly after midnight. "Hullo," he mumbled into it.

"This Goodmann?" the caller asked.

"Who is this?" he groused in the glow of his alarm clock.

"It doesn't matter."

"Who the hell is this?" he snarled, irritated at the rush of cold air when his wife rolled away with the covers.

"Someone you need to talk to."

The comment and the caller's tone reminded him of similar calls years earlier. Suspecting he already knew the answer he sat up and asked, "What can I do for you?"

"It's what I can do for you."

"I'm listening," he said, swinging his feet to the floor.

"There's a lot happening you need to know about."

"Go on, please."

The end.

ACKNOWLEDGEMENTS

I began writing this novel many years ago. It was my first attempt at serious writing, and like most novices who proudly complete their first manuscript, I foolishly believed no more was required of me. Through the kind efforts of many talented friends and acquaintances I soon realized that most writing is re-writing. And thus I entered an on-again, off-again cycle that took this book into the new century. So, to those good folks, as well as those who encouraged me to persevere, I extend my sincere gratitude. Sadly, some have left this world before I could formally thank them. Still, recognition is merited, and so I include their names among those who provided invaluable assistance and insight into crafting a feasible and credible story of an otherwise impenetrable and complicated world.

Thanks to Petrina Aubol and the Tri-State Writers Group, Lou Cherico, Bill Creswell, Al Eastman, Arthur Hamparian, George Manno and the Northern Virginia Writers Group, Frank Miller, Tony Palazzo, Mary Rizzo, Joe Riccio, Gay Talese, David Tomlinson, Rona Westra, and finally, those who wish to remain anonymous. And special thanks to my wife Barbara, whose constant

George Vercessi

support and sound judgment kept me focused and, most importantly, productive.

And to Ed Jaffee and Bernie Katz, whose proofreading skills proved invaluable, I owe you one.

About the Author

George Vercessi is a retired U.S. Navy captain residing in Northern Virginia with his wife, Barbara. His next novel, *Iceman*, centers on Jerzy Shore, the star Naval Criminal Investigative Service cold case sleuth and Feng Shui disciple, who unexpectedly walks into a high-stakes game of political intrigue engineered by top Pentagon brass intent on winning at all costs.